THE BURGLAR
WHO COUNTED
THE SPOONS

THE AFFAIRS OF CHIP HARRISON

No Score • *Chip Harrison Scores Again* • *Make Out with Murder* •
The Topless Tulip Caper

OTHER NOVELS

A Diet of Treacle • *After the First Death* • *Ariel* • *Campus Tramp*
• *Cinderella Sims* • *Coward's Kiss* • *Deadly Honeymoon* • *Getting
Off* • *The Girl with the Long Green Heart* • *Grifter's Game* •
Killing Castro • *Lucky at Cards* • *Not Comin' Home to You* •
Random Walk • *Ronald Rabbit Is a Dirty Old Man* • *Small Town* •
The Specialists • *Such Men Are Dangerous* • *The Triumph of Evil* •
You Could Call It Murder

COLLECTED SHORT STORIES

Sometimes They Bite • *Like a Lamb to Slaughter* • *Some Days You
Get the Bear* • *Ehrengraf for the Defense* • *One Night Stands and
Lost Weekends* • *The Lost Cases of Ed London* • *Enough Rope* •
The Night and the Music

BOOKS FOR WRITERS

Writing the Novel: From Plot to Print • *Telling Lies for Fun and
Profit* • *Spider, Spin Me a Web* • *Write for Your Life*

WRITTEN FOR PERFORMANCE

Tilt (episodic television) • *How Far?* (one-act play) •
My Blueberry Nights (film)

MEMOIR

Step by Step

ANTHOLOGIES EDITED

Death Cruise • *Master's Choice* • *Opening Shots* • *Master's Choice 2*
• *Speaking of Lust* • *Opening Shots 2* • *Speaking of Greed* • *Blood
on Their Hands* • *Gangsters, Swindlers, Killers, and Thieves* •
Manhattan Noir • *Manhattan Noir 2*

THE BURGLAR
WHO COUNTED
THE SPOONS

A Bernie Rhodenbarr Mystery

LAWRENCE BLOCK

First published in Great Britain in 2014 by Orion Books,
an imprint of The Orion Publishing Group Ltd
Orion House, 5 Upper Saint Martin's Lane
London WC2H 9EA

An Hachette UK Company

1 3 5 7 9 10 8 6 4 2

A CIP catalogue record for this book is
available from the British Library.

ISBN (Hardback) 978 1 4091 5355 9
ISBN (Export Trade Paperback) 978 1 4091 5356 6
ISBN (Ebook) 978 1 4091 5358 0

Typeset by Input Data Services, Bridgwater, Somerset

Printed and bound by CPI Group (UK) Ltd, Croydon, CR0 4YY

The Orion Publishing Group's policy is to use papers that are natural,
renewable and recyclable products and made from wood grown in sustainable
forests. The logging and manufacturing processes are expected to
conform to the environmental regulations of the country of origin.

www.orionbooks.co.uk

BOSWELL: I added that [this] person maintained that there was no distinction between virtue and vice.

JOHNSON: Why, Sir, if the fellow does not think as he speaks, he is lying; and I see not what honour he can propose to himself from having the character of a liar. But if he does really think that there is no distinction between virtue and vice, why, Sir, when he leaves our houses let us count our spoons.

ONE

Around 11:15 on a Tuesday morning in May, I was perched on my stool behind the counter at Barnegat Books. I was reading *Jubilate Agno*, by Christopher Smart, even as I was keeping a lazy eye on a slender young woman in jeans and sandals. Her khaki shirt had those little tabs to secure the sleeves when you rolled them up, and a scant inch of tattoo peeked out from under one rolled-up sleeve. I couldn't make out the image, there wasn't enough showing, and I didn't bother to guess, or to speculate on what hidden parts of her anatomy might sport further tattoos. I was paying more attention to the capacious tote bag hanging from her shoulder, and the Frank Norris novel that had engaged her interest.

For I shall consider my cat, Geoffrey, I read, and looked over to the window to consider my own cat, Raffles. There's a portion of the window ledge that the sun manages to find on clear days, and that's his favorite spot, rain or shine. Sometimes he stretches, in the manner of his tribe, and sometimes his paws move as he dreams of mice. At the moment he was doing nothing, as far as I could tell.

My customer, on the other hand, had fetched a cell phone from her tote bag. She'd put the book down, and her thumbs were busy. At length she returned the phone to her bag and, beaming, brought Frank Norris to the counter.

'I've been looking all over for this,' she said, triumphantly. 'And I've had a terrible time, because I couldn't remember the title or the author.'

'I can see how that might complicate things for you.'

'But when I saw the book,' she said, brandishing the object in question, 'it, like, rang a bell.'

'Ah.'

'And I looked through it, and this is it.'

'The very volume you've been seeking.'

'Yeah, isn't that awesome? And you know what's even better?'

'What?'

'It's on Kindle. Isn't that fantastic? I mean, here's a book more than a hundred years old, and it's not like it was *Huckleberry Finn* or *Moby-Dick*, you know?'

Eat your heart out, Frank Norris.

'Like, they're popular, so you'd expect to be able to get them in eBooks. But *The Pit*? Frank Norris? And yet I Googled it and there it was, and a couple of clicks and I own it.'

'Just like that,' I said.

'Isn't it great? And you know what it cost?'

'Probably less than the book you're holding.'

She checked the penciled price on the inside cover. 'Fifteen dollars. Which is fair enough, I mean it's like a hundred years old and a hardcover book and all. But you want to know what I just paid?'

'I'd love to.'

'Two ninety-nine.'

'Awesome,' I said.

Carolyn Kaiser, who washes dogs two doors down the street at the Poodle Factory, is my best friend and, more often than not, my lunch companion. Whoever's turn it is picks up food at a nearby restaurant and brings it to the other's place of business. It was her turn, and an hour after the girl with the peekaboo tattoo left poor old Frank Norris on my counter, Carolyn breezed in and began dishing out *dejeuner a deux*.

'Juneau Lock?'

'Juneau Lock,' she agreed.

'I wonder what it is.'

She took a bite, chewed, swallowed, and considered the matter. 'I couldn't even guess the animal,' she said. 'Let alone what part of the animal.'

'It could be almost anything.'

'I know.'

'Whatever this dish is,' I said, 'I don't think we've had it before.'

'It's always different,' she said, 'and it's always sensational.'

'Or even awesome,' I said, and told her about Frank Norris and the girl with the tattoo.

'Maybe it was a dragon.'

'The tattoo? Or our lunch?'

'Either one. She used your bookshop to figure out what book she wanted, and then she bought the eBook from Amazon and bragged about what a deal she got.'

'It didn't come off like bragging,' I said. 'She was letting me be a part of her triumph.'

'And rubbing your nose in it, Bern. And you don't even seem all that upset.'

'I don't?' I thought about it. 'Well,' I said, 'I guess I'm not. She was so innocent about it, you know? "Isn't it great how I saved myself twelve bucks?"' I shrugged. 'At least I got the book back. I was afraid she was going to steal it.'

'In a manner of speaking,' she said, 'she did. But if you're cool with it, I don't see why I should be pissed off on your behalf. This is great food, Bern.'

'The best.'

'Two Guys From Taichung. I wonder if I'm pronouncing it correctly.'

'I'm pretty sure you got the first three words right.'

'The first three words,' she said, 'never change.'

The restaurant, on the corner of Broadway and East Eleventh Street, across the street from the Bum Rap, has had the same sign for almost as long as I've had the bookshop. But it's changed owners and ethnicities repeatedly over the years, and each new owner (or pair of owners) has painted over the last word on the sign. Two Guys From Tashkent gave way to Two Guys From Guayaquil, which in turn yielded to Two Guys From Phnom Penh. And so on.

We began to take the closings for granted – it was evidently a hard-luck location – and whenever we started to lose our taste for the current cuisine, we could look forward to whatever would take its place. And, while we rarely went more than a few days without a lunch from Two Guys, there were plenty of alternatives – the deli, the pizza place, the diner.

Then Two Guys From Kandahar threw in the towel, and Two Guys From Taichung opened up shop, and everything changed.

'I'll be closing early,' I told Carolyn.

'Today's the day, huh?'

'And tonight's the night. I thought I might get back downtown in time to meet you at the Bum Rap, but where's the sense in that?'

'Especially since you'd be drinking Perrier. Bern? You want me to tag along?'

'I don't think so.'

'Are you sure? Because it'd be no problem for me to close early. I've got a borzoi to blow-dry, and his owner's picking him up at three, and even if she runs late I can be out of there by three-thirty. I could keep you company.'

'You were with me on the reconnaissance mission.'

'Casing the joint,' she said with relish. 'Nothing to it. Piece of cake.'

'I think it's better if I solo this time around.'

'I could watch your back.'

'I don't want to give their security cameras a second look at you. Once is fine but twice is suspicious.'

'I could wear a disguise.'

'No, I'll be disguised,' I said. 'And a key part of my disguise is that this time around I won't be accompanied by a diminutive woman with a lesbian haircut.'

'I guess diminutive sounds better than short,' she said. 'And it's not exactly a lesbian haircut, but I take your point. So how about if I hang out down the block? No? Okay, Bern, but I'll have my cell with me. If you need me—'

'I'll call. But that's not likely. I'll just steal the book and go home.'

'Check Amazon first,' she said. 'See if it's on Kindle. Maybe you can save yourself a trip.'

TWO

M artin Greer Galton had ceased troubling his fellow man in 1964, when a cerebral aneurysm achieved what most of his acquaintances and business associates would have dearly loved to have had a hand in. After thirty-plus years as a latter-day robber baron and almost as many as a fiercely acquisitive retiree, the old man clapped both hands to his head, made a sound like a peevish crow, and collapsed to the floor. He landed in the middle of the immense Aubusson carpet in the Great Room of Galtonbrook Hall, the pile of marble that had been his home and would be his memorial.

Galtonbrook Hall loomed less than half a mile from Columbia Presbyterian Hospital, and an ambulance got there in minutes, but they didn't have to rush. Martin Greer Galton, born March 7, 1881, in Latrobe, Pennsylvania, was almost certainly dead by the time he hit the floor.

Now, fifty years later, his house lived on. He'd devoted the first half of his life to making money and the second half to spending it, collecting art and artifacts in great profusion, and building Galtonbrook Hall to house himself for his lifetime and his treasures for all eternity.

That at least was the plan, and he'd funded the enterprise sufficiently to see it carried out. What had been a home was now a museum, open to the public six days a week. Out-of-towners rarely found their way to the Galtonbrook; it didn't get star treatment in the guidebooks, and it was miles from midtown, miles from the Upper East Side's Museum Mile. As a result it was rarely crowded.

You had to know about it and you had to have a reason to go there, and if you were in the neighborhood you'd probably wind up at the Cloisters instead. 'We'll go to the Galtonbrook the next time,' you'd tell yourself, but you wouldn't.

Neither Carolyn nor I had been there until our visit five days earlier, on a Thursday afternoon. We'd stood in front of a portrait of a man in a plumed hat, and its brass label identified it as the work of Rembrandt. The guidebook I'd consulted had its doubts, and repeated an old observation: *Rembrandt painted two hundred portraits, of which three hundred are in Europe and four hundred in the United States of America.*

'So it's a fake,' she said.

'If it is,' I said, 'we only know as much because the guidebook told us so. We could go look at the Rembrandts in the Metropolitan, and we'd know they're genuine, but we'd only know *that* because of where they're hanging. And we'd have paid twenty-five dollars apiece to look at them, instead of the five dollars they charge here, and we'd have people bumping into us and breathing down our necks.'

'I hate when that happens. This is a beautiful painting, Bernie.

7

You look at the guy's face and you get a whole sense of the person.'

'You do.'

'He must have been a closet case, don't you think?'

'Because of the plumed hat?'

'No, just the impression he gives off. Though I don't know how reliable my gaydar is, especially when we're a couple of centuries away. But the point is I'm getting a lot out of looking at the painting, so who cares if it's really by Rembrandt?'

'Well, I don't,' I said. 'Why should I? It not as if I was planning on stealing it.'

That was Thursday, and now it was Tuesday, and while it was overcast the rain was supposed to hold off until after midnight. It would rain all day Wednesday, according to the weather guy on Channel Seven, with what they called the exclusive Acu-Weather Forecast, although I've never been able to figure out what's exclusive about something available to everybody with a television set.

Never mind. The Galtonbrook closed on Wednesdays, so I wouldn't be going then rain or shine. And I liked the idea of paying a visit the day before a closed day. They'd be unlikely to miss what I intended to take. Their Rembrandt, genuine or not, was safe, and so was everything else hanging on a wall or poised on a plinth.

Even so, I didn't see how a buffer day after my visit could do any harm.

So I'd left my apartment that morning with felonious intentions, and one trouser pocket contained a little ring of small steel implements that the law regards as burglar's tools, the mere possession of which is a crime. It's no crime to carry a plastic grocery bag from D'Agostino's, or for that bag to contain a baseball cap and a sport shirt and a pair of sunglasses, but they had roles to play in the crime I was planning to commit.

It was around three when I brought my bargain table inside, gave Raffles fresh water, and locked up and left. I was carrying the plastic bag again, and of course the burglar's tools had never left the burglar's pocket.

Barnegat Books is on East Eleventh Street between University Place and Broadway, and the Galtonbrook is on Fort Washington Avenue, in Washington Heights or Inwood, depending on which realtor is hustling you. The best way to get there is by helicopter, and you could probably land one on the museum's flat roof, but I took the L train across Fourteenth Street and the A train uptown to 190th Street.

That put me three blocks from the museum, and I walked a block in the wrong direction looking for a place to change. Telephone booths worked for Clark Kent, but when's the last time you saw one? When the counterman in a Dominican bodega said the bathroom was for customers only, I dug out a dollar and helped myself to a copy of *El Diário*. He rolled his eyes – they all learn that the minute their planes touch down at JFK – and pointed to a door along the rear wall.

I'd gone to work that morning wearing pressed khakis and a T-shirt from the Gap, originally black but laundered over the years to an agreeable dark gray. The shirt I'd brought along was Hawaiian in style, although I'd guess that this particular specimen had made the trip from a sweatshop in Bangladesh without getting anywhere near Waikiki. There were parrots on it, and you could almost make out what they were saying.

The bathroom was tiny, but roomier than a phone booth. I put the parrot shirt on over my T-shirt. It wasn't exactly a disguise, in that anyone who knew me would recognize me right away. 'Why, there's Bernie Rhodenbarr,' such a person would remark. 'But what on earth is he doing in that frightful shirt?'

But I hadn't chosen the shirt in the hope of deluding an

acquaintance, and didn't expect to encounter one in the first place. The parrots were for the benefit of strangers. The shirt would catch the eye, and they'd notice it instead of paying attention to the sartorially-challenged chap who was wearing it.

I put on the sunglasses and the baseball cap – blue, with the Mets logo in orange – and I left the bodega without glancing at the proprietor. If he was rolling his eyes again, I didn't have to know about it. I was still carrying the D'Ag bag, but all it held now was my *El Diário*, and I'd already gotten my dollar's worth of use out of it. I headed back the way I'd come, dropping the paper in a trash can en route to the Galtonbrook.

I recognized the woman who took my five dollars, and for a moment I expected her to recognize me. '*Oh, it's you again. Love your shirt, but what happened to your little friend with the lesbian haircut?*' But all she did was thank me and give me a receipt.

I walked around, pausing for another long look at the putative Rembrandt. The museum was even less crowded than Carolyn and I had found it, but I began to get the feeling that the handful of visitors were taking undue notice of me. The shirt was supposed to draw the eye, but not to hold it. A glance, a shrug, and a glance in another direction – that was what I'd had in mind.

Maybe it wasn't the shirt. Was I wearing a Mets cap in Yankee territory? Even if I was, that might draw a hostile stare in the street or the schoolyard, but not in this temple of culture.

Oh, hell. The sunglasses. It wasn't even a sunny day, but that was beside the point, because what kind of clueless clown wears sunglasses in a museum? No wonder Rembrandt's sneering subject looked more somber than I remembered.

If the shirt was for people to notice, the cap and the shades were for the benefit of the security cameras. They'd help conceal my face, so that I'd look anonymous and unidentifiable to anyone reviewing the tapes. But if they drew all this attention before the fact . . .

To my left, a woman of a certain age kept her eyes on the portrait, and I could feel her determination not to look at me. If there's one thing every New Yorker learns early on, it's not to make eye contact with a lunatic, and that can be especially challenging when you can't see the lunatic's eyes, because his madness has led him to conceal them behind dark glasses.

Retinitis pigmentosa, I thought. *I'll say that's what I've got, it's genetic, it makes you abnormally light-sensitive, and eventually it'll lead to blindness, so I want to see every Rembrandt I can in the time that's left to me, and—*

'Oh, for heaven's sake,' I said aloud, and took off my sunglasses, shaking my head at my own absentmindedness. Even as I tucked them into my shirt pocket, I could feel my companion relax. Her eyes never left the painting, but her relief was palpable: I wasn't mad after all, I was merely inattentive, and order had been restored to her universe.

One thing I'd determined on my earlier visit was the location of the restroom. I went there now, but instead of going in I tried the unmarked door immediately opposite it, which opened onto a flight of descending stairs. I took a few hesitant steps and saw what I'd hoped to see, a labyrinth of tables and boxes and file cabinets.

I saw, too, a young woman who grasped the situation at once. 'You're looking for the restroom,' she said. 'You turned right when you should have turned left.'

'I'm sorry,' I said. 'How foolish of me.'

'It happens all the time,' she said. 'And it's our fault for not marking the door. This door, I mean. The restroom door's already marked. There's a sign on it that says "Restroom."'

'I guess it should have been obvious,' I said, 'but I never saw it. I saw *this* door, and—'

'And it's unmarked, so you thought it was the room you were looking for and we were simply being discreet. We really ought to hang a sign on this door, don't you think? But what would it say?'

'Hmm. How about "Not the Restroom"?'

'Or maybe "Turn Around."'

For God's sake, she was flirting with me. And, let it be said, I with her. She was a pert and perky blonde with a nice mouth and a pointed chin, and her nerdy eyeglasses gave her the look of a hot librarian – which may well have been part of her job description. There's nothing wrong with flirting, but there's a time and a place for it, and this was neither.

'Well,' I said. 'I'd better, uh . . . '

I turned and fled.

On our earlier visit I'd had to wait for the restroom, but this time it was conveniently unoccupied. I locked myself in – actually, it was more a matter of locking other people out – and I put a hand in a pocket and drew out my burglar tools.

And went to work on the window.

The main floor of the Galtonbrook was five or six steps below street level, and that put the bottom of the bathroom window just about even with the pavement outside. A substantial window guard of stainless steel mesh admitted daylight while blocking everything else. A dozen bolts held it in place, and an intricate web of wires tied it into the building's alarm system.

I'd had a good chance to examine it Thursday afternoon, and supplemented my memory with an iPhone snapshot. Now I went right to work.

First, the burglar alarm. It was unarmed now, of course, and would remain that way until they closed for the night, so I could meddle at will without setting off sirens. All I had to do was disconnect a couple of wires and hook them up differently, so that the window could be opened and closed without raising an electronic hue and cry. That was complicated, and required a knowing hand and a delicate touch, but it wasn't terribly difficult.

Next was the mesh window guard. The bolts were solid and well anchored, but they were slotted to accommodate a screwdriver, and I already knew I could turn them. I hadn't had a screwdriver the first time around, but I had a dime, and it was just the right size. Even with the limited leverage a coin afforded, I'd budged the bolt I tried. Now, with my screwdriver, there was nothing to it.

Halfway through, I ran into a bolt that was slightly more obdurate than its fellows, and wouldn't you know that was just the time someone tried the door, found it locked, and knocked sharply on it.

'I'll be a few minutes,' I said.

But not too many of them, as it turned out, because my next effort got the bolt turning, and the rest of them yielded readily enough. I transferred the lot of them to my pocket, freed the window guard, turned the window lock, and braced myself against a window that had very likely not been opened in years.

I can't say it was eager to move, but I put all my strength into it, and up it went, though not without giving voice to its feelings. If the noise it made was audible to others, I can only suppose they chalked it up to the same intestinal crisis that was keeping me in the restroom.

It pained me to close the window after all it had taken to open it, but I did, and this time the resultant sound effects were minimal. I fitted the mesh in place, but instead of replacing any bolts I secured it with a couple of one-inch squares of duct tape, just enough to keep it from falling down. It would yield at once to prying fingers, but whose fingers were likely to pry? It was, my watch assured me, just ten minutes to closing time. The restroom might have another customer before they shooed us all out of the building, and an employee or two might use the facilities before heading for home, but it was long odds against anybody meddling with my little arrangement.

I took a moment to wipe the surfaces I might have touched. I'd somehow forgotten gloves, but even if I'd remembered them I couldn't have put them on until I was locked in the bathroom, and they'd have cost me something in the way of dexterity. Easy enough to use a paper towel and wipe up after myself.

I took a deep breath, let it out in a sigh. It seemed to me I was forgetting something, but I couldn't figure out what it might be. Burglar tools? Right-hand trouser pocket. Window bolts? Left-hand trouser pocket, along with my wallet. Sunglasses? Breast pocket. Mets cap? On my head. Parrot shirt? I was wearing it.

What else? The Spanish-language newspaper? I'd tossed it.

I unlocked the door. Whoever had knocked had either overcome the urge or found an alternative venue for satisfying it. The place had pretty much emptied out already, with just a few minutes remaining until they locked the doors. I gave the Rembrandt a passing glance, tugged the ball cap down over my forehead, and had my sunglasses on and my head lowered when I cleared the threshold.

I walked a block at a pace that was deliberately casual, waiting for any of several unwelcome things – a voice raised in alarm, a hand on my elbow, the shrill squeal of a police whistle. I didn't really expect anything of the sort, but you never do.

Nothing. And yet I couldn't shake the feeling that I'd forgotten something.

I walked two and a half blocks before the penny dropped. Hell. I'd forgotten to use the bathroom.

THREE

I know, I know. I'd visited two washrooms, first in the bodega and then in the museum, and I'd bought a newspaper I couldn't read to get into the first and committed a felony in the second, and I'd been too busy in each of them to use either one in the traditional manner. I hadn't really felt the need, not acutely enough to act on it, and now I did.

Hell.

I walked three more blocks and found a bar with an Irish name and a predominantly Latino clientele. A soccer game played silently on the TV. The bartender, a heavy-set fellow with a drooping moustache, didn't look happy to be there, nor did my presence raise his spirits. I was still wearing the sunglasses, and that may have had something to do with it, because what did he need with a weirdo wearing shades in a dark ginmill?

Or maybe he was a Yankees fan.

I didn't want anything, but I had to buy my passage to the men's room. I couldn't have a beer, not with my day's work only half done, and I somehow knew this was no place to order Perrier. I said I'd have a Coke, and his expression darkened. While he was loading up a glass with ice cubes, I found the room I wanted. Since I had no other chores to distract me, I did what I'd gone there to do.

I went back to the bar, paid for my Coke, had a sip, set it down and headed for the door.

'Hey.'

I turned.

'Something wrong with it?'

'I'm trying to quit,' I said, and got the hell out of there.

I took a different train home, and walked from Broadway and 72nd to my apartment on West End and 70th. I'd bestowed my Mets cap on the young boy on the subway who'd admired it, and I'd thought about shucking the parrot shirt, but it seemed simpler to wear it home, with the sunglasses resting snugly in its pocket.

My doorman didn't give me or my shirt a second glance. I went upstairs, took off the parrot shirt and everything else, and spent a rewarding fifteen minutes under the shower. I emerged with the urge to phone someone – Carolyn, say, or my client. I decided I didn't want to call either of them in midstream. In a few hours, when my day's work was done, my calls would be triumphant.

Unless it all went pear-shaped, in which case I'd use my one phone call on Wally Hemphill, my lawyer.

Meanwhile, I suppose I could have called a girlfriend. If only I'd had one . . .

*

I went into the living room and looked at the painting on the wall, all black verticals and horizontals on a white field, with a few of the resultant rectangles filled in with primary colors. It looks like something Piet Mondrian might have painted, and well it might, because he did. And there it was, worth a duke's ransom if not a king's, hanging right there on my wall.

A few years ago, I was involved in an unusually complicated mess, in the course of which I oversaw the production of several fake Mondrians. When the dust settled, various canvases had migrated to various walls, and one remained unclaimed, so I took it home with me.

It was the real one.

For all the good it did me. I mean, it's not as though I had the option of selling it. The work had no provenance, and I lacked legal title to it.

On the all-too-rare occasions when I have a woman visitor, she of course assumes the painting's a copy. A few have asked if I painted it myself; one, more sophisticated than the general run, admired the craquelure. 'Someone went to a lot of trouble to create the illusion of age,' she said. 'But the colors aren't quite right, are they, Bernie? Mondrian's blue isn't that intense, and the yellow's got the slightest greenish cast to it.'

I told her she had a good eye.

You know what? I think what I like most about my Mondrian is that nobody else knows it's real. It's the genuine article masquerading as a fake, and it's my little secret, and I get to look at it whenever I want.

Of course most of the time I don't really see it. That's true of anything hanging on the wall day in and day out. It becomes the visual equivalent of background noise. But today, after contemplating a Rembrandt of questionable authenticity, I got to look at my Mondrian as if for the first time.

17

*

I stretched out on my bed and closed my eyes. A nap would have been nice, but I was way too restless to drift off. My mind insisted on spinning its wheels, and I wasn't surprised. I was, after all, like a theatergoer at intermission, still engrossed by what had been happening on stage, with a few minutes to kill until I could return to my seat. The shower may have refreshed me, and Mondrian may have lifted my spirits, but I was in the middle of a burglary and I couldn't really relax until I'd finished the job.

Was I hungry? I thought about it and couldn't decide. The unidentifiable Taiwanese lunch had been as filling as it was delicious, but enough hours had passed since then for me to be ready for an evening meal.

But I've never been a big fan of breaking and entering on a full stomach. A hungry burglar, it seems to me, has a definite advantage.

Although one can take it too far. On at least one occasion I've paused while checking a kitchen for loose cash. (You'd be surprised how many people keep an emergency reserve in a countertop canister, or stuffed into the butter compartment of the fridge.) I managed to convince myself there was a sheaf of hundreds waiting for me in the peanut butter jar, and when I found nothing in that vessel but a supply of Skippy Super Chunky, I went on looking for the bread and the jelly. I took a minute or two to make myself a sandwich and a few minutes more to ingest it, and then I washed my DNA off the butter knife and went back to the business at hand.

Would they have bread and peanut butter and jelly at the Galtonbrook? It seemed unlikely. I had some in my own kitchen, but was that what I wanted?

All I wanted, I decided, was for it to be time to get back to work.

I made a cup of coffee, put the TV on, turned the TV off, drank the coffee, and got dressed. I stayed with the khakis and sneakers, but put on a light blue dress shirt with a button-down collar and added a navy blazer. A tie? I considered two, chose the one with diagonal stripes of gold and green, then decided against it. A shirt, a jacket, but no tie. A hardworking chap on his way home after his work had kept him at the office well into the evening. His collar's open now, and no doubt he's got his necktie in his jacket pocket, rolled up carefully to avoid wrinkles.

I drank the coffee.

Was it, please God, time to go? I decided it was, and I went.

FOUR

The Galtonbrook was where I'd left it, which is always a comfort. It looked different at night, all its interior lights switched off, with a few outdoor spots to highlight the gleaming marble façade.

I walked past the entrance, waited for a car to pass, then traced a path along the building's western wall. I'd scouted my approach before, and my route would keep me out of range of the security camera.

I didn't have a necktie in my pocket, having seen no reason to carry verisimilitude quite so far. I did have, in various pockets, my burglar's tools, my little screwdriver, two of the original dozen two-inch bolts, my little roll of duct tape, my pencil-beam flashlight, and a pair of those pliofilm gloves favored by food handlers and TV cops.

I was wearing the gloves by the time I reached the bathroom

window, and I shielded the flashlight with one gloved hand while I flicked it on long enough to determine that this was indeed the bathroom window, and not some other still-secure window leading somewhere else. Thus reassured, I knelt down and eased it open.

It made that noise again, and I froze, waiting for the world to respond. When nothing happened, I resumed breathing and returned to the task at hand. The steel mesh panel came loose when I pushed against it, and I got a grip on it and leaned forward far enough to prop it up on the sink top. I climbed in after it, planted my feet on the floor, and stood absolutely still for a full two minutes, listening intently for any sound at all.

I heard traffic in the distance, and, just as my two minutes were up I heard the footsteps of a man walking his dog. I knew it was a man by his voice, and I knew it was a dog when he said, 'Here you go, Sport. Your favorite hydrant.'

Sport paid his respects, and they walked on. Once again I considered leaving the window open, and once again I decided against it and drew it shut, clenching my teeth against the sound it made. I replaced the mesh panel, supplementing the two squares of duct tape with two of the bolts, just fitting them into their holes and giving them a half-turn each.

I did all this in the minimal light that filtered in from outside. Then I opened the bathroom door and closed it again from outside, and everything was suddenly as dark as the inside of a cow. A blink of my flashlight let me get my bearings, and I found the door to the basement – it was, of course, directly opposite the bathroom door. I turned the knob and gave a tug, and nothing happened, because some damned fool had evidently locked it.

Oh, all right. I hunkered down in front of the lock and picked it in less time than it takes to tell about it. I didn't need my flashlight, and I probably wouldn't have needed my burglar's tools, either, had I been armed with a hairpin or a toothpick.

I suppose a lock like that could have a purpose. During daytime hours, it might keep an errant visitor from opening the wrong door and pitching headlong down the stairs. But the door had been open earlier, and they'd only locked up when they were done for the day, and who was the lock going to hinder in the middle of the night? A burglar? Lots of luck, honey.

I used my flashlight to get down the basement stairs, and looked around for windows just in case there were some I didn't know about. Once I'd established that I was indeed in a window-less crypt, I turned on a couple of overhead lights and gave my flashlight a rest.

Then I took a deep breath.

Ah, what a feeling!

I've been doing this long enough so that it's a profession, and I like to think my attitude is that of a professional. But no amount of professionalism can drive the sheer joy and excitement out of the enterprise. When, through my own resources and initiative, I find myself on premises where I've no right to be, I'm transported by a feeling that's hard to describe and impossible to justify. I like to think I've come a long way from the Ohio town where I grew up, but what I felt in the basement of the Galtonbrook was not all that different from the sensation that took me by surprise when I first broke into a neighbor's house. Once again, I was thrilled beyond words to be doing this thing that I absolutely knew I should not be doing.

I can't rationalize it, any more than I can give it up. It's pointless to try. I'm a born thief and I love to steal.

In fact, I love it so much that there's a powerful temptation to prolong the experience. I wanted to stay where I was, breathing the stale subterranean air, delighting in the way the blood surged in my veins. There was no end of objects to fill the eye and quicken the pulse – suits of armor, statues, paintings, here a samurai sword, there a medieval tapestry. And even more alluring than what I could see was what reposed out of sight, in trunks and boxes and file cabinets.

It wouldn't be hard to find something to steal. But that was the last thing I wanted to do. I was on a very special mission, and the only way to make it work was to limit my foraging to one item and one item only.

And time was of the essence. A burglar's time, let me tell you, is always of the essence. The less of it you spend in enemy territory, the better your chance of getting home safe.

Even so, it took me distressingly close to an hour. I knew what I'd come for, but what I didn't know was where they'd stashed it. It could have taken longer than it did, but I managed to find a pattern to their curious system of organization, and I knew when I'd opened the right file cabinet, and toward the back of the second drawer from the top I found a manila folder with the label *ALLB*.

I hadn't been looking for initials, but if I had, those would have been the right ones. *A Life Lived* – yes, that was it, and I drew out the folder and opened it to look at the first of forty-plus pages of unlined bond paper, originally white and now yellowing with age.

The first page, and the others that followed, had been written on in blue-black ink. I'd seen this handwriting before, and while I could no more swear to its authenticity than I could confirm or deny Rembrandt's responsibility for the portrait of the man in the plumed hat, it certainly looked okay to my untrained eye. And I had little reason to question it; far more scoundrels had tried to imitate Rembrandt's brush strokes than ever felt called upon to imitate this chap's penmanship.

Not for the first time, I let out a breath I hadn't realized I'd been holding. I turned the pages. Each but the first had a number at the bottom, and every number was present, all the way to the number 43 at the bottom of the final page, just below the words *The End*, written with an understandable flourish, and, beneath them, written larger and with much the same spirit, *F. S. F.*

Indeed.

I unbuttoned my shirt, slipped the folder inside, and buttoned it up again. I donned the blazer I'd taken off at the beginning of the hunt, turned off the lights that had allowed me to see what I was doing, and let my flashlight guide me up the stairs.

I didn't really want to take the time to lock the basement door, and would anyone be alarmed to find it open Thursday morning? I worked out all of that in my mind, and then I locked the door anyway.

Just because.

This time, after I'd removed and pocketed the two bolts and raised the restroom window, I used a length of duct tape as long as the window's width to attach the top of the mesh panel to the window frame. Then I added another similar strip for added strength. I drew the panel back, wormed my way through the window, let the panel slip back into place, and closed the window.

I walked a block before I realized I was still wearing the gloves. I took them off and tucked them in a pocket. I walked another block, and then I turned a corner and walked a third block. All without a siren wailing, or a police whistle sounding, or the long arm of the law reaching out and taking hold of my elbow.

Whew.

FIVE

I generally open Barnegat Books at nine in the morning, less for my customers' sake than for my cat. Their hunger for books rarely sends them to my door much before ten, while his for Meow Mix is such that he'll rub himself against my ankles no matter how early the hour.

So I make a point of opening at nine, but it's a point that's occasionally blunted, and it was getting on for 9:30 the next morning by the time I fed Raffles and gave him fresh water. If he'd been an ordinary member of his species, there'd have been a litter box to contend with, an unwelcome chore at any hour, and especially so at an early one. But all I had to do was go into my restroom and flush the commode, because Raffles has been schooled in the use of that wondrous contrivance, even as you and I.

I can't take credit for training him. That was Carolyn's doing, and he'd become letter-perfect at it weeks before she found a way to palm him off on me. Not that I've ever had cause to complain. He's a good companion, and he earns his keep; old leather bindings and bookmaker's glue are, well, catnip to mice, and all evidence of rodent damage ceased the day he took employment here.

For I shall consider my cat, Raffles, I thought, and reached for my copy of *Jubilate Agno*. Christopher Smart, whose work it is, was an eighteenth-century English poet, a contemporary of Samuel Johnson and Oliver Goldsmith. He was unquestionably talented, but he was also mad as a hatter, and given to fits of religious mania that led him to implore his fellows to join him in public prayer. 'I'd as soon pray in the street with Kit Smart as anyone else in London,' Johnson allowed, but others were less tolerant, and Smart spent the better part of his mature years clapped in a cell in Bedlam, where he wrote a line of poetry every day. The ones about Geoffrey the Cat are clear enough, and rather touching, but some of the others can be hard to unravel.

Let Ross, House of Ross, rejoice with Obadiah, and the rankle-dankle fish with hands . . .

Well, how can you argue with that?

'*A Life Lived Backward*,' said my first customer of the morning. He was holding the handwritten pages I'd taken from the Galtonbrook, and reading the words at the top of the first page. 'That was his original title, you know.'

'I hadn't known until you told me. And a good thing you did.'

'Oh?'

I pointed to the initials on the folder. 'That wouldn't have meant much to me otherwise,' I said. 'I'd have been looking for TCCOBB.'

'As far as I know,' he said, '*A Life Lived Backward* appears on this manuscript and nowhere else. Princeton has his collected papers, you know. Eighty-nine archival boxes and around a dozen oversize containers. They've got the typed manuscript of the story. *The Curious Case of Benjamin Button*, that's the title it bears. That was its title when it first appeared in *Collier's Magazine* in May of 1922, and when it was included in his *Tales of the Jazz Age* later that same year.'

'How did you come to know—'

'The original title? A letter to a young woman, her own identity lost over the years. "I worked up a story around that idea I mentioned. I think it came out well. I called it *A Life Lived Backward* as I needed to call it something, but when I type it up I'll call it something else. It'll have to have a better title before I dare show it to anyone."'

'He wrote it out in longhand and then typed it up.'

'And this is clearly a first draft,' he said. 'You can see that, can't you? The handwriting changes periodically, suggesting it was written over a period of several days, if not longer. He started out with blue-black ink, and halfway through it's black, and then toward the end it changes back again.'

'There aren't many corrections.'

'No, just words crossed out here and there when he changed his mind and started a sentence over. The typed manuscript is full of corrections, words crossed out and other words inked in, whole handwritten sentences crawling up the margins. My guess is that he simply copied this draft verbatim, or had a typist do it for him, and then went to work on it. Tweaking, polishing.' He raised his eyes from the manuscript to me. 'But the only way to know that for certain would require another trip to Princeton, so that I could compare these pages with their typescript. And I don't think I care enough to bother. It's not *Hamlet*, you know.'

'Um—'

'What we have here,' he declared, 'is a decidedly minor work by a writer with an overblown reputation. But I haven't bought it to read it, have I? No more than the chap who paid a seven-figure sum for a stamp from British Guiana did so in hopes of mailing a letter.'

'Actually,' I pointed out, 'you haven't bought it at all.'

'By God, I haven't, have I? I hope you don't mind a check.'

'Um—'

'Just a little joke,' he said, and opened his briefcase.

I haven't described him, have I? Or told you his name.

The name he'd supplied, on his initial visit to my bookshop, was Smith, and it was clear he didn't expect me to believe it was his by birth or court order. 'If pressed,' he'd said, 'I could probably come up with a first name as well, and even a middle initial, but how would that serve your interests or my own? Smith will do.'

He was a couple of inches shorter than I and a few pounds heavier. His medium brown hair, neither long nor short, was showing gray at the temples. His mouth was small, his lips narrow, his teeth even. His eyes were a washed-out blue, their expression hard to read behind his horn-rimmed eyeglasses.

He'd worn a three-piece suit on his first visit, dark gray with a chalk stripe, and his tie, or as much of it as showed above his vest, was an unornamented blue. His white shirt had a button-down collar.

This time around he was less formally dressed, in tailored jeans and a Norfolk jacket of rust-brown tweed. There was a flat brass disc sewn to his lapel, and I seemed to recall a similar ornament on his suit. Today's shirt was a deep blue, and open at the throat. Again, a button-down collar.

He handed me a letter-size envelope. It had a satisfying heft to it.

'Ten,' he said.

I took it, and he handed me another that might have been its twin.

'Ten.'

The third envelope was thinner, and felt lighter.

'And five.'

'Thank you,' I said.

'You'll want to count them.'

I lifted the flap of third envelope and established that it was full of bills, all of them evidently used hundreds. There was a thick wad of them, and I was willing to believe there were fifty of them, even as I was willing to believe the other envelopes held a hundred bills each, and that all of the bills were genuine.

I told him I'd count them later.

'You'll want to add these to the count,' he said, and passed me a fourth envelope, which seemed to be the same thickness as the third. 'Five more,' he said.

'Oh?'

'A bonus.'

'That's very generous of you.'

'Do you think so? I wonder. It's the same twenty percent I'd leave for a waitress, and I'd do so with no expectations. I'd probably never sit at her table again, and might not even return to that restaurant. Whereas in the present instance I have an ulterior motive.'

'Oh?'

'Indeed, Mr Rhodenbarr. I expect to pay you another visit before too long. We'll be doing more business, you and I.'

SIX

It was two weeks earlier when Mr Smith first showed up, all dressed up in his three-piece suit. He turned up in mid-afternoon, and he was a long way from being the day's first customer. That honor belonged to Mowgli.

I've known Mowgli for years, although I didn't know his real name any more than I knew Smith's. The name (Mowgli, not Smith) comes from *The Jungle Book*, but don't ask me whether Kipling made it up or came across it somewhere on the Indian sub-continent. However it found its way to my Mowgli, it seems to suit him. There's a feral quality to him, partnered with a gentle nature.

Early in our acquaintance he brought books to me. I was at first reluctant to buy from him, thinking he might have lifted them from other shops, but came to know that he was a legitimate book scout, scooping up bargains at flea markets and urban yard sales and wholesaling them to dealers like me.

Then the Internet came along, and transformed Mowgli from supplier to customer. Or maybe he'd stayed essentially the same, and Barnegat Books had morphed into a bargain basement. He now had a website and an eBay store, and I never saw him without selling him six or ten or a dozen books. At first I'd give him a volume discount, but it didn't take me long to stop that, and he didn't seem to mind, paying the marked price without argument. He didn't even balk at the sales tax, until the day he informed me that he had acquired a resale number, and was now tax-exempt.

Wonderful.

He came in that morning with an empty tote bag, one that I recognized from the days when he'd brought it in loaded with books for me. It was loaded now when he walked out, and I had money in my cash register that I hadn't had earlier, so why was I in a bad mood?

Carolyn asked me that very question a couple of hours later, when I showed up at the Poodle Factory after a stop at Two Guys. 'That smells great,' she said, 'and you look awful. What's the matter, Bern?'

'Mowgli,' I said.

'You used to like him, Bern.'

'I still like him. I just can't stand the sight of him.'

'He's a regular customer now.'

'Exactly.'

'And he pays full price.'

'And then he marks everything up and sells it to somebody online, some yutz in Antwerp or Anaheim with a PayPal account and a thirst for literature. You know what I think he does? I think he checks my stock and lists everything that looks good to him, so he's actually selling the books while they're still mine.'

'But don't his sales lists have photos along with the descriptions? I think you're being paranoid, Bern.'

'Maybe.'

'I think he makes you feel guilty, because you know you ought to be selling books online yourself.'

'I don't want to do that.'

'I know.'

'I want to run a bookshop,' I said. 'The old-fashioned kind, where people come in looking for something to read, and collectors come in hunting for treasures, and we all have nice intellectual conversations.'

'And once in a while you'll meet a girl there.'

'Once in a blue moon,' I said. 'But if and when I do, there's a good chance she'll be able to read.'

'Some of the girls I meet at the Cubby Hole can read,' she said, 'and some can't, and I'm too shallow to care. This food is wonderful, Bern. Did you ask her what it is?'

'What good would that do? Look how long it took us to figure out *Juneau Lock* was *You no like.*'

'And even longer to convince her she was wrong.'

'And she still says it,' I said. 'She gets a kick out of saying it. "Juneau Lock," and then she giggles.'

'She's adorable when she giggles, isn't she?'

'She's cute, all right.'

'You should ask her out.'

'Me? Why don't you ask her out?'

'I don't think she likes girls.'

'How can you tell?'

'Because if she did, the long looks I've been giving her would cut right through the language barrier.'

'On the other hand, she does giggle at you.'

'She giggles at both of us, Bern. When a straight woman giggles at another woman it just means she thinks something's funny. When she giggles at a man it means she likes him.'

*

I was unconvinced. When Two Guys opened in its present incarnation, it was just another Chinese take-out joint, with a predictable menu offering staples like General Tso's Chicken and Beef with Orange Flavor and Cold Noodles with Sesame Sauce. Everything was well prepared and tasty, but one day I noticed that they were getting a steady stream of Chinese customers, and the dishes they were taking home were nothing you'd find in General Tso's mess kit.

'They've got special dishes for their countrymen,' I reported to Carolyn, 'and I'd really like to give them a try, but when I ask what they are I can't get anywhere.'

'Did she say anything?'

'Juneau Lock,' I said, 'but that doesn't make any sense. I don't think they've got canals in Alaska, and even if they did—'

'Maybe it's the name of the dish in Chinese. It just sounds to your untrained ear like Juneau Lock.'

'But how can it be the name of every dish? I point to this one and it's Juneau Lock. I point to the one next to it and she tells me the same thing. Whatever it is, whatever any of them are, we don't get to try them.'

Her face darkened. 'We'll see about that,' she said.

God knows what Carolyn told her the following day, and I'm just as glad not to have been a fly on the wall for that particular conversation. (And it was an immaculate kitchen, incidentally; a fly would not have lasted long on any of its well-scrubbed walls.) But whatever Carolyn said, she evidently made it clear that she wasn't leaving without a portion of this and another of that, and her determination turned out to be the pry bar that jimmied the Juneau Lock.

And ever since then we'd been feasting daily on dishes without knowing their names or ingredients. One or the other of us would point, and the little darling would dish out the food. Now and then she'd demur – 'Juneau Lock! Too spicy!' We'd insist, and carry the day. One time it was a something of a pyrrhic victory, when a stew of some generally overlooked animal organ was sufficiently fiery to glow in the dark. By the time we finished we must have glowed ourselves, with equal parts of satisfaction and cayenne poisoning, and were greeted with heightened respect on our return to Two Guys.

That marked the end of our trial period. We'd become regulars, and *Juneau Lock* was simply her name for whichever one of us showed up on any given day.

Good as it was, the Taiwanese food hadn't been enough to lift my spirits after Mowgli's visit had crushed them.

'Barnegat Books is in trouble,' I told Carolyn. 'And I can't blame it all on Mowgli. The world's changing. Why come to my store? You can find any book in ten minutes without leaving your desk. If it's an eBook, you can buy it for pocket change and get it delivered electronically in minutes. If it's long out of print, you don't have to rummage through a dozen antiquarian bookshops, as if there were that many of us left in the business. You just go online, and you do a title search at abebooks.com, and next thing you know there's a guy in Moline, Illinois, with an ex-library copy you can buy for a buck ninety-eight plus postage.'

'Can he make money that way?'

'Who, the guy in Moline? I suppose so, if he does enough volume. He's probably working out of his house, so he hasn't got any rent to pay.'

'Neither do you, Bern.'

Not since a venture to the other side of the law had enabled me to buy the building. 'I don't,' I agreed, 'and it's a good thing, because if I had to pay rent my receipts these days wouldn't cover it. I can't sell books anymore, and I can't buy them, either. A good customer of mine died recently.'

'I'm sorry to hear that, Bern.'

'A nice fellow, a retired Classics professor at NYU. He'd been dropping by for years, and even when he couldn't find anything to buy we'd have a nice chat. You know, the kind of conversation you can have in an old-fashioned bookshop. And then I didn't see him for a while, and one afternoon his wife called to tell me he'd passed away.'

'That's a shame.'

'Well, evidently he'd been quite ill for some time, and when the end finally came it was a mercy. But she was calling because he'd told her that I was the person to turn to when the time came to sell his books. He'd assured her that I was a decent and knowledge-able dealer who'd give her a fair price.'

'That must have made you feel good.'

'It did, and the prospect of acquiring the man's library was ap-pealing. He'd bought a lot of good books from me, and I could imagine what he'd acquired from other sources over all those years. My store stock's pretty thin these days, and you can't sell what you haven't got, so I was looking forward to adding his books to my shelves.'

'What happened?'

'I made an appointment,' I said, 'and I showed up with a blank check in my wallet, and she was all apologies. Her grandson had come up with the brilliant idea of selling grandpa's books individ-ually on eBay. He'd list all the titles, and she could help him pack the books to ship to the successful bidders, and he'd schlep them to the post office. And they'd split the money.'

'And she thought this was a good idea?'

'I asked if I could see the books,' I said, 'and she could hardly say no, and the library was what I'd hoped it would be. I told her it wouldn't take me more than two hours to come up with a number, and that if she accepted my offer I'd write out a check on the spot and remove all of the books from the premises within a matter of days. And I pointed out that, while her grandson's enterprise was admirable, it would take months if not years to sell the books online, with many of them remaining unsold forever.'

'And the shipping costs, Bern. And the bookkeeping, and the aggravation of customers returning books, and—'

'And all the rest of it. I told her all that.'

'And she didn't believe you?'

'Oh, she believed me. But how could she change her mind now and disappoint her grandson?'

'Oh.'

'And what did she care about money, anyway? How important was it, compared to the pleasure of having her grandson come over every day after school?'

'The two of them working side by side, slipping books into padded mailers.'

'And attaching the wrong labels, so that they could have even more fun sorting it all out when the customers complained.'

She frowned. 'Bern, this grandson's a high school kid?'

'I think she said he was a junior at Stuyvesant.'

'How long do you figure he's gonna feel like showing up at grandma's house every day?

'Well, I haven't met the kid,' I said. 'Maybe he's convinced he's the next generation's Jeff Bezos, ready to launch his own version of Amazon. But maybe not, and when the novelty wears off he may lose his taste for online enterprise.'

'And she'll still have a house full of books, so she'll pick up the phone and give you a call.'

I shook my head. 'She'll pick up the phone,' I agreed, 'but she'll call somebody else. She'll feel too embarrassed to call me, and she'll tell herself she already bothered that nice Mr Rhodenbarr enough. And that'll be that.'

So I finished lunch and walked two doors west and opened up again, dragging my bargain table out to the street even as I wondered why I bothered. For that matter, why move the table inside when I closed for lunch? Why not leave it out there on the sidewalk? Anybody who stole a book would be doing me a favor.

Within the hour the man who called himself Mr Smith showed up to make me an offer I could have refused. But why would I want to?

SEVEN

'This book,' he said.

I'd seen him come in, watched him find his way to Classic Fiction, then turned my attention to Jeffery Deaver, whose latest Lincoln Rhyme novel had turned up in a carton of recent thrillers. The paraplegic hero had just solved everything and saved everybody, but I was still forty-plus pages from the end. So I was bracing myself for the author's trademark switcheroo, in which one of the good guys would turn out to be the ultimate bad guy. A thoroughly charming character would meet a horrible end, and there'd be a bad moment when I thought Amelia Sachs was dead, but it would turn out that Rhyme was one step ahead of the killer all along, and everything would work out well, and in plenty of time for the next book in the series.

So I knew what was coming, and I knew too that Deaver would manage to surprise me. So the last thing I wanted now was to have my reading interrupted, and yet at the same time I welcomed the interruption, because that way the book would last longer.

Oh, never mind.

'Fitzgerald's second collection of short fiction,' I said. *'Tales of the Jazz Age*, Charles Scribner's Sons, 1922. A very nice copy, marred only by the signature on the flyleaf of the book's erstwhile owner.'

He looked, and read out the name: 'Wilma Faulk.'

'Had it been William Faulkner,' I said, 'it would be an association copy, and thus command a premium. A man with a steady hand might find himself tempted. I should point out that it's a first edition but not the first printing. I meant to include a penciled note to that effect.'

'You did, just below Miss Faulk's spidery signature. And you're quite correct. I checked line six on page 232, and the word in question reads "and." It appears erroneously as "an" in first printing copies.'

'You're a collector.'

'In a small way.'

'Then you know how elusive true first printing copies are these days. I've seen listings for close to a thousand dollars, and that's when you can find them.'

'Actually,' he said, 'I own one.'

'A first printing.'

'Although I didn't pay quite that dearly for it.'

I pointed to the book he was holding. 'If it's the dust jacket that drew you,' I said, 'it's not an original. They're genuinely impossible to find. This one's a copy, produced in San Francisco by Mark Terry's Facsimile Dust Jacket Printshop. The most recent owner, who acquired his copy many years after it left Miss Faulk's tremulous hands, bought the Terry jacket knowing he could never afford an original. He said it looked just as good on his shelf.'

'I'm sure it did,' he said, and cleared his throat. 'I own an original dust jacket.'

'You do.'

'Yes.'

Well, good for you, I thought, and what are you doing slumming in my store?

'I have a first of *This Side of Paradise*,' I said. 'Fitzgerald's first novel, and not an easy book to find. I keep it in back, for safety's sake. If you'd like a look at it—'

He shook his head. 'I'm not interested in Scott Fitzgerald,' he said.

'You're not interested in Fitzgerald.'

'No, not really. There's nothing like an early death from alcoholism to enhance a writer's reputation. Stir in good looks and early success, season with a beautiful wife in the nuthouse, and the result is irresistible.'

'Juneau Lock,' I said.

'I beg your pardon?'

'It's nothing. I gather you don't think *The Great Gatsby* is—'

'The Great American novel? No, hardly that. The puzzle of Gatsby is how so many otherwise perceptive people can find so much to admire in it. Do you know why Jay Gatsby is such an enigma? It's because Fitzgerald himself never had a clue who the fellow was. An arriviste, a parvenu, an upstart if you will, a man who made big money in a hurry and got his hands just a little dirty in the process. Hardly a rarity at the time, and there was a fellow in Boston with a similar story who got his son elected to the White House. Fitzgerald didn't know what to make of Gatsby, and the literary establishment has responded by enshrining his bafflement. So no, I don't think much of *Gatsby*, or your Mr Fitzgerald.'

I chose silence as preferable to stammering.

'Besides the first edition copy, with its original dust jacket, I own as well an inexpensive hardcover reprint edition. It bears a different title, and that's why I added it to my collection. Do you know the title?'

I didn't.

'*The Curious Case of Benjamin Button, and Other Stories.* Perhaps you've seen a copy.'

'If I have, it was years ago.'

'But you've read the title story?'

I nodded. 'But that was quite some time ago as well. I did see the Brad Pitt film when it came out.'

The thin lips gave me a thin smile. 'Fitzgerald's agent sold development rights to a producer named Ray Stark,' he said, 'who never did figure out how to make it filmable. He died in 2004, and the estate sold the rights to somebody else, and the movie released four years later retained the story's title and premise and hardly anything else. It was an improvement on the original, but it would almost have had to be. You know where the premise came from?'

I didn't.

'An observation of Mark Twain's, that the best of life came at the beginning and the worst at the end. Thus Fitzgerald's conceit that his protagonist should be born an old man who grows younger every year he lives. Fitzgerald was born in 1897, which put him in his early twenties when he wrote the story. Not surprisingly, it reflects the degree of insight and maturity you would expect of a stripling.'

'You sound—'

'Contemptuous of the story? Are you a collector, Mr Rhodenbarr?'

'A collector?'

'Of anything at all. Books, coins, stamps? Barbie dolls?'

'No, none of those things. I collected books in a very small way before I bought the bookshop, but you can't really collect something and deal in it at the same time, so my collection became part of my store stock. I have a wall of books at home, but just for reading and looking things up. They're dust collectors themselves, but that's not enough to make them a collection. Where did Barbie dolls come from?'

'The Mattel Company, I believe. I just mentioned them as something some people collect, but you don't and neither do I.'

'A common bond.'

'Indeed. I collect *The Curious Case of Benjamin Button*, Mr Rhodenbarr, and not because I'm an extravagant admirer of either that story or its author. Would it be enough to say I have my reasons?'

'Of course.'

'I own the books I've told you about, and quite a few others besides. The story has been widely anthologized over the years, and of course I haven't attempted to amass all of them, but I've chosen a dozen or so volumes that struck my fancy. Some months before Scribner's brought out *Tales of the Jazz Age, Collier's Magazine* published it. I dare say there are fewer copies around of that issue of *Collier's* than there are of the book, but there are also fewer collectors vying for them.'

'I assume you have a copy.'

'I own two,' he said. 'I bought one in only good condition, with some damage to the front cover. The pages are all there and all undamaged, and James Montgomery Flagg's illustration of Benjamin as an aged baby is both awful and wonderful. Those two words once had the same meaning, by the way.'

'I know.'

'Then I caught wind of a copy in pristine condition, essentially mint, and the price wasn't that much more than I'd had to give for the one with the coffee stains on the cover. So I bought it, and that's more copies than anybody needs, so I could probably turn around and sell it. But I wouldn't get all that much for it, and it's not as though I need the money.'

'So why not keep it?'

'Exactly my thought. It might be different for a collector of, say, steam locomotives. One might not have the room to keep duplicates on hand. But an old magazine doesn't take up much space.'

'I don't suppose it does.'

'With a highly specialized collection like mine, Mr Rhodenbarr, space is not a likely problem. But can you guess what is?'

It didn't take much thought. 'Finding something to buy,' I said.

'You may not be a collector yourself, sir, but you have ample insight into the complaint. And of course you're quite correct. I'm told that a shark must keep swimming forward all its life. If it stops, it dies. Do you suppose that's true?'

'I don't know much about sharks.'

'Had you heard that before? About their need to keep forever advancing? You hadn't? In that case you now know one thing more about sharks than you did a moment ago. Except that this new kernel of information may not be accurate.'

'Still, it'll be something to drop into conversations.'

'Yes, and hasn't it already served me admirably in that respect? Still, the collector shares this aspect with the shark, along with a reputation for unthinking rapacity. For how can one maintain interest in a collection if one is no longer able to add to it? And when one's collecting interest is centered upon a single short story, how can one continue to find new material to collect?'

How indeed?

'One finds oneself branching out,' he said. 'Do you know Roda Roda?'

'That's a name I haven't heard in years.'

'You actually know it?'

'If they're still around. I'll tell you, it takes me back to my boyhood days in Ohio. There was this big old weeping willow in the yard next to ours, and its roots would grow into our sewer line. So my mom would call the Roto-Rooter man, and their truck would come by, and they'd do something. Cut out the roots and open the sewer line, I guess, and our drains would stop backing up, at least until the willow tree gathered its strength for another assault.'

I shook my head at the memory. I remembered the logo on their truck, even as their radio jingle forced itself upon me. '"And away go troubles, down the drain,"' I said. 'If only. I can't remember the last time I saw a Roto-Rooter truck. I don't suppose you get much call for them in New York.'

The look on his face brought me back.

'But I don't suppose you're talking about the Roto-Rooter man,' I said. 'Are you?'

EIGHT

'Alexander Roda Roda,' I told Carolyn. 'He was born in 1872 in an unpronounceable town in Moravia, which is now a part of the Czech Republic, but back then it was the Austro-Hungarian Empire. His family moved to Osijek—'

'Speaking of unpronounceable towns.'

'—which seems to be in Croatia now, but used to be in Slavonia. Don't ask me what happened to Slavonia.'

'I wouldn't dream of it.'

'His name was originally Sandor Friedrich Rosenfeld, but he changed it to Alexander Roda Roda. You're probably wondering why.'

'I'm sure the man had his reasons, Bern.'

'Roda is the Croatian word for stork.'

'See? I knew there was a good explanation.'

'Storks nested in the chimney of his house in Osijek. I suppose he wanted to remember them.'

'I guess there must have been two of them, and he wanted to make sure he remembered them both.'

'He became a writer,' I said, 'and published his first work when he was twenty years old. He wrote plays and stories and novels, but he wrote in German, and as far as I can tell nothing of his was ever published in English. In 1938 he emigrated to the States.'

'He probably figured changing his name wouldn't fool the Nazis.'

'He could have tried writing in the language of his new home,' I said. 'That's what Arthur Koestler did after he wound up in London. But there's no evidence that Roda Roda made the switch, and it's possible he was done writing by then. He'd been at it for close to fifty years, and he died in 1945 in New York.'

'A man named Roda Roda,' she said, 'belongs in a city named New York, New York. I can see how he'd be tired of writing by the time he got here, but I guess that means there's nothing of his that I might have read.'

'Well, there's *Bummler, Schummler und Rossetummler*,' I said. 'I like the sound of it, although I realize it would probably lose something in translation. But that's not how he got into the conversation.'

'Oh?'

'When he was 49, Roda Roda published a short story called *Antonius de Padua Findling*.'

'Well, that explains everything, Bern.'

'It does, actually. The story had the same premise as Fitzgerald's, with a baby born old and growing younger with the passage of time, and Roda Roda published it a full year before *The Curious Case of Benjamin Button* appeared in *Collier's*.'

'You think Fitzgerald stole the idea?'

'I'm sure he never heard of it, or of Roda Roda either. I think both men got more or less the same idea at more or less the same time, and each wrote his story and published it.'

'You know what they say, Bern. Great minds work alike.'

'And so do lesser ones. But that sort of thing happens a lot. Everybody knows Edgar Allan Poe's *Murders in the Rue Morgue* was the first true detective story.'

'I bet you're gonna tell me it wasn't.'

'Back in 1827 a guy beat Poe to the punch by several years. His name was Mauritz Christopher Hansen, and unfortunately he made the mistake of writing his story in Norwegian, so nobody paid any attention. He wrote a short novel, too, *The Murder of Engineer Roolfsen*, and nobody took much notice of that either.'

'Outside of Norway.'

'And look how much of the world is outside of Norway. Almost all of it. But back to Roda—'

'Roda Roda, Bern. But I guess it's okay to call him Roda for short.'

'Mr Smith got ahold of a copy of his story, and paid somebody to translate it for him.'

(Mr Smith indeed. 'You have the advantage of me,' I'd said at one point. 'You evidently know my name, as you've used it four times already. But I don't know yours.' He'd nodded, as if to acknowledge the truth of my observation, thought for a moment, and said, 'Smith. You may call me Smith.')

'And was Antonius the spitting image of Benjamin Button?'

'I'm just guessing,' I said, 'but I'd say the title refers to St Anthony of Padua, the fellow you turn to when you can't remember where you put your reading glasses.'

'"St Anthony, St Anthony, please come round, for something's lost that must be found."'

'Just imagine how catchy that must be in German. And here's

another guess, because I was too lazy to look it up, but I'll bet you a couple of pfennigs that *findling* is German for *foundling*, and the little old baby in Roda's story turned up in a basket on the steps of the local church.'

'Like Moses in the bulrushes,' she said, 'unless Pharaoh's daughter made up that part. Hey, wait a minute, Bern! Wasn't Benjamin Button a foundling himself?'

'In the movie,' I said. 'Not in the story. The way Fitzgerald had it, he was the son of one Roger Button, who owned a wholesale hardware business.'

'Oh. Well, maybe the people who made the movie read Roda Roda's story, even if Fitzgerald didn't. And you say Smith read it? Did he say if it was any good?'

'He called it less than wonderful, but better than Fitzgerald's.'

'In other words, still mediocre enough to belong in his collection. If he doesn't much care for either story, why the hell is he collecting them?'

'He has his reasons,' I said, 'that reason knows nothing of. With Roda, he couldn't track down the original magazine appearance, but the following year it was included in a book called *Die sieben Leidenschaften*, and he owns a copy, as well as the manuscript from the files of the Viennese publisher, with the editor's notations and Roda Roda's own emendations.'

'That must be a scarce item.'

'Well, it'd have to be unique. It might even be expensive, if anybody much cared about Alexander Roda Roda.'

'Still, a manuscript. What about Benjamin Button, Bern? I bet he'd like to have Fitzgerald's original manuscript.'

I didn't say anything, but I guess something showed in my face. She said, 'We're gonna be a while, aren't we, Bernie?' and raised her hand, making circles in the air until she caught Maxine's eye. We were at the Bum Rap, where we tend to meet up after work, and Maxine has been bringing us drinks for enough years to have grown adept at picking up Carolyn's signals. She raised her eyebrows in response, whereupon Carolyn held up two fingers. Maxine nodded, and another round was on its way. Scotch for both of us, Carolyn's on the rocks, mine with soda.

I told the story as Smith had told it to me. Princeton, Fitzgerald's ivy-covered alma mater, was the repository of the author's papers, where they'd served no end of scholars writing no end of doctoral theses on the man and his work. It took a letter of reference from someone with good academic credentials to get access to the papers, and Smith had found someone to write him a letter, and took a train to Princeton Junction and a taxi to the campus. He'd phoned ahead, and a graduate student with a nose ring and an attitude led him to a desk and got him started.

They had two copies of the story, one from *Collier's* files, the other from Scribner's. There were galleys and page proofs, and a good deal of correspondence concerning the story. Fitzgerald's Hollywood agent, a man named Swanson, was on hand with half a dozen terse notes.

They'd allowed him to make photocopies of both manuscripts, and several of the letters.

'No kidding,' Carolyn said. 'I didn't think they let you do that.'

I'd said as much to Smith, and reported his reply: '"If you expect a graduate student to enforce a rule like that, you really ought to pay her a living wage."'

'He bribed her, huh?'

'I think it would be less judgmental to say he compensated her handsomely for the performance of a task that lay outside the bounds of her job description.'

'So he's got copies,' she said. 'But the originals are still at Princeton.'

'Where they shall remain.'

'Oh?'

'He was quite candid about it. He'd love to have either or both of them, but he recognizes that they're where they ought to be. The university's serious about its custodial role, and if he's enough of a collector to desire the manuscripts, he's sufficiently respectful of scholarship to feel that their collection ought to be preserved intact. And his Benjamin Button collection, including the Roda Roda material, will go to Princeton when he's no longer around to enjoy it. He's already added a codicil to his will to that effect.'

'How old would you say he is, Bern?'

'I don't know. Forty-five? Fifty? Somewhere in there.'

'So Princeton'll have a while to wait.'

'Well, you never know. But let's hope so.'

She picked up her drink, and when she set the glass down there was nothing left but a couple of melting ice cubes. She looked at my glass, which remained half-full or half-empty, depending on your state of mind, gave Maxine a wave and held up a single finger, then pointed that finger at herself.

'Let's hear the rest,' she said.

Her third drink was mostly gone when she said, 'I've been meaning to go to the Galtonbrook, Bern.'

'You've never mentioned it.'

'Well, it's not at the top of the list. It's somewhere on page three, along with *Lose five pounds* and *Read Proust*. But I've thought about it. Tell me his name again?'

'Smith?'

She rolled her eyes. 'Galton.'

'Martin Greer Galton.'

'And he just ran around buying things?'

'He didn't have the kind of money William Randolph Hearst had,' I said, 'and he didn't employ a staff of agents to run all around Europe and buy everything they saw, but in his own small way he did what he could to turn a mansion on Fort Washington Avenue into an East Coast version of San Simeon. He bought whole estates, which meant that along with art and artifacts he picked up papers and manuscripts by the carton if not the carload, and he wound up with a fair amount of crap, but he also got enough decent stuff to found a museum. '

'And one of the manuscripts—'

'Is the original holograph version of *The Curious Case of Benjamin Button*.'

'And I suppose Smith wants it.'

'He does.'

'Couldn't he bribe some flunky to make him a copy?'

'In this instance,' I said, 'I'm afraid only the original will do.'

'He's seen it?'

I shook my head. 'Their archives are in the basement, and access is restricted to employees. He could probably pull some strings to get in, but then they'd know he'd been there, and he doesn't want to look at the goddam thing. He wants to own it.'

'That's why he went to your shop.'

'I'm afraid so, yes.'

'He didn't just know your name. He knew your sideline.'

'If that's what it is. Sometimes it's hard to say which is the sideline and which is the primary occupation. But yes, he was aware that of the several activities in which I've been known to engage, one is breaking and another is entering.'

'You've never stolen from a museum.'

'No.'

'You won't even buy a book if you suspect someone stole it from a library.'

'No.'

'So how is this different?'

'All the manuscript's doing,' I said, 'is sitting there in the basement. I almost said "gathering dust," but it would have to be out in the open for the dust to get at it, and instead it's in a box where nobody ever lays eyes on it. It's listed and catalogued, because otherwise Smith wouldn't know about it, but it's got Fitzgerald's original title on it so they don't know what it is. They'll very likely never know, because nobody there cares enough to find out. You know where that manuscript belongs? At Princeton, with the rest of the author's papers, and the only way it's going to get there is if my friend Smith gets hold of it and leaves it to them in his will.' I frowned. 'What's the matter, Carolyn? You're sitting there looking like the wise old owl.'

'The scotch may have something to do with it,' she allowed. 'It brings out my inner owl. But I'm sitting here listening, Bern, and if you haven't already talked yourself into taking the job, I'd say you're well on your way.'

'I guess I'm going to do it. It's either that or give the man back his five thousand dollars.'

'What did you just say?'

'I said it's either that or—'

'I know what you said, Bern. Are you telling me he paid you five thousand dollars?'

'It's an advance,' I said. 'I get the rest on delivery.'

'The rest amounting to—'

'Another twenty-five.'

'That adds up to thirty thousand dollars.'

'You're no slouch at math,' I said. 'Not even after three drinks. I'll have to give you that.'

'Bern, what do you figure it's worth?'

'Thirty grand.'

'Because that's what he's offering to pay for it? What about on the open market?'

'What open market? It's the lawful property of a non-profit institution. I suppose I could find out what other F. Scott Fitzgerald letters and manuscripts have brought in recent years, though I doubt there's been much comparable that's changed hands. But it wouldn't tell me all that much about this particular case.'

She picked up her glass, took a sip that was mostly melted ice. 'Thirty thousand dollars,' she said, 'is a lot of money.'

'Just the other day,' I pointed out, 'one of the big banks settled with the government over an alleged irregularity in their bond-trading division.'

'I think I read something about that. Or maybe it was on the TV news.'

'While refusing to admit any wrongdoing on their part, they paid over half a billion dollars.'

'If they didn't do anything wrong—'

'Then why shell out all that money? You have to wonder. Now I'd say *that's* a lot of money, but it's a little less than ten percent of their annual profit.'

'Okay, point taken. But for a man with a second-hand bookstore on East Eleventh Street—'

'It's a lot of money.'

'But it's got to be risky,' she said. 'Swiping a manuscript from a museum isn't like, um—'

'Taking candy from a baby?'

'Or from a candy store. Won't they have security cameras?'

'These days,' I said, 'so will the candy store, and there's probably a Nanny Cam keeping an eye on the baby's lollipop. It's a good thing I haven't got a son.'

'It is?'

'I've got two ways to make a living,' I said, 'and I couldn't in good conscience encourage any child of mine to go into either one of them. We already talked about bookselling, and burglary's even worse. The security cameras are everywhere, and that's just the beginning. Some of the subspecialties have disappeared completely. A man used to be able to make a decent living as a hotel thief. It was always a high-anxiety trade, but it was exciting, and full of possibilities. You never knew what you were going to find on the other side of a door.'

'There are still plenty of hotels, aren't there?'

'And every one of them that gets more than fifteen dollars a night for a room has those plastic key cards that you slip in a slot. How the hell are you supposed to pick an electronic lock?'

'Oh.'

'I'm not saying it can't be done. You rent a room, then you go back when a different clerk's on duty and tell him your key won't work. They get deprogrammed all the time, and he'll ask you your name and room number and reprogram it for you. "My name's Victor Kotowitz, I'm in Room 417." A couple of clicks and you're all set to go through Mr K's luggage.'

'That's pretty slick, Bern.'

'And it works okay, unless the guy you approach happens to remember that Victor has a handlebar moustache and weighs three hundred pounds.'

'Oops.'

'The Galtonbrook will have real locks,' I said, 'and a state-of-the-art burglar system wired into the local precinct. I think I'll go up there tomorrow. Just to look it over from a distance and check out the neighborhood. Then a few days after that I'll be ready to go inside.'

'How will you get in?'

'I'll pay the five dollars,' I said, 'just like everybody else. I'll get my picture taken by their security cameras, but I won't be doing anything suspicious. I'll be just another citizen taking in the art, and checking them out while I'm at it.'

'An unaccompanied citizen.'

'Not if you'd like to keep me company.'

Her eyes lit up. 'I was your henchperson once before, Bern. Remember?'

'Like it was yesterday. This'll be a little different. We won't be doing anything illegal.'

'Sure we will,' she said. 'I'll be a part of a criminal conspiracy. That'll give it an edge, even if all we'll be doing is looking at paintings.'

Over the next few days, I made a couple of preliminary visits to scout the terrain. Then on the Thursday Carolyn joined me and I finally set foot inside the place.

I figured out which door led to the basement and noted its proximity to the restroom. I visited the restroom, examined the window. By the time we got out of there, I knew how I was going to pull it off.

'Their security's good,' I told Carolyn on our way downtown. 'But it's not perfect.'

'You found a hole in it.'

'I think so. A pinhole, but I think I'll be able to widen it.'

'It won't be a job for two, will it? I didn't think so. I played a small part, and that's something. And I've been wanting to get to the museum for a long time.'

'That reminds me,' I said.

'What's this, Bern?'

'A present,' I said. 'The Modern Library edition of *Swann's Way*. Now that the Galtonbrook's off your list, you can kick back and start reading Proust.'

NINE

T ime passed.

It'll do that, have you noticed? Some days crawl and some days fly, but they all have the same number of hours, and each of them comes from wherever days come from and goes wherever they go. The moving finger writes, and what do you get?

Like the fellow who lifted sixteen tons, what I got was another day older. But instead of getting deeper in debt, I put Mr Smith's bounty to good use, paying what I owed and holding the rest in reserve. But first I passed along the bonus $5000 to Carolyn, who protested that all she did was keep me company on an innocent visit to an off-the-beaten-track museum.

'And you even paid the five bucks admission charge,' she said.

'True, but you used your own Metrocard on the subway. And you were a participant in a criminal conspiracy, as you pointed out earlier. An accessory to the fact, an accomplice.'

'More of an accessory before the fact, Bernie. I did my accessorizing on Thursday, and it wasn't until last night that the fact came along. You'd think I'd have to be more involved to wind up with five grand.'

'Well . . .'

'What?'

'Well,' I said, 'I was thinking. The Galtonbrook's closed today. When they open up tomorrow, there's only one thing that might make them the slightest bit suspicious.'

'The fact that one of their treasures is missing?'

'They'd never notice. But sooner or later somebody'll jiggle the panel over the restroom window and discover it's being held in place by duct tape.'

I didn't have to draw her a map. 'But if you were to show up tomorrow morning, for a five-dollar admission charge you could visit the restroom and put the bolts back.' She grinned. 'But you were there just yesterday, in your Mets cap and your parrot shirt. Wouldn't it be safer if you had a trusty henchperson to run that little errand for you?'

'I can supply the bolts,' I said, 'and the screwdriver. All you'd need would be five minutes in the restroom.'

'Any woman who spends less than five minutes in a public restroom,' she said, 'is a traitor to her sex.'

'It won't take any longer than that. And putting the bolts in will be quicker and easier than taking them out, because some of them didn't really want to budge.'

'So they'll be glad to get back where they belong. Okay, Bern. You talked me into it. It sounds like fun, and it'll give me something to do to earn the five thousand dollars. But even so the book would have been plenty.'

'About that book,' she said a week or so later.

'*Swann's Way?*'

'I started it a few nights ago.'

'How are you enjoying it?'

'I got in bed with it,' she said, 'and I enjoyed the first two pages just fine, and then my alarm clock went off.'

'You fell asleep.'

'Well, I'd made the rounds, Henrietta's and the Cubby Hole, so I wasn't exactly reading with a clear head. But I went to bed sober the next night, and this time I was out cold halfway down the third page.'

'So you were five pages in, and—'

'No, just three. I wasn't too clear on what I'd read the first night, so I started over from the beginning.'

'I see.'

'And the night after that I'd had a few drinks, so I didn't even bother to try. But the night after that—'

'That would be the fourth night.'

'Whatever. That was the night I had dinner with my aunt Amelia. I told you about that, right?'

'That would have been after you scared the crap out of Maxine. I have to admit it gave me a turn when you ordered Perrier. For a minute I thought you were planning to go out and break into somebody's house.'

'Amelia's in AA,' she said, 'and she always tells me it's perfectly all right to drink when I'm with her, that it doesn't bother her a bit.'

'But you don't believe her.'

'I had a drink once when I was with her. It was a glass of Chardonnay, and I don't think it did bother her, but it bothered the hell out of me.'

'You sensed her disapproval?'

'She was watching me drink the wine, and she was watching

58

me not drink the wine, and I could feel her getting ready to step on me.'

'To step on you?'

'They have these steps,' she said, 'and one of them is to get other people to stop drinking, so they can all be miserable together and sit around in church basements and tell each other how much fun they used to have. I sat there with my one lousy glass of Chardonnay, and what I felt like doing was ordering a triple tequila martini and stepping right out of my pants.'

'But you didn't.'

'Of course not. But ever since then, whenever I can't get out of having dinner with Aunt Amelia, I make a point of showing up with nothing on my breath but an Altoid, and she gets to watch me drink Perrier. Bern, where the hell was I?'

'Three pages into *Swann's Way*.'

'Oh, right. So I got home with a head that was so clear you could see through it, and it was early, so instead of trying to read in bed I sat down in the wing chair and got the reading light just right. One of my cats settled in my lap and the other curled up by my feet, and I figured a brandy would make the picture complete. But first I'd read a couple of pages, and then I'd fix myself a drink.'

'How far did you get?'

'Bottom of the fourth page. Next thing I knew the sun was coming in the window and the cats were letting me know it was feeding time. I was cold sober and I still managed to fall asleep sitting up in a chair with my clothes on.'

'Marcel strikes again.'

'If word gets around,' she said, 'the people who make Ambien are out of business. It's quicker and cheaper, and you won't get up in the middle of the night and raid the refrigerator.'

*

While she was not reading Proust, I was busy not developing a meaningful relationship.

Truth to tell, I'd given up trying. I'd been seeing a woman for a few months, and we'd reached the point where each of us kept a few things at the other's apartment, and I was starting to wonder what it would be like if we took the plunge and started living together, and then one day she announced that her firm was moving her to their London office.

'Wow,' I said.

'I didn't say anything,' she said, 'because I wasn't sure whether I wanted to make the move, but it's a big step up, and an even bigger step backward if I were to turn it down.'

I could have said something. Like *Don't go*, for example. Like *Stay here and we'll get married.* Like *I've always wanted to try living in London.*

But what I said was, 'Well, it sounds like a great opportunity. I'll miss you, Carole.'

'And I'll miss you, Bernie. And, you know, if you're ever in London . . . '

'I'll be sure to knock you up.'

She looked at me, baffled, and I explained that that's English-English for *call you on the phone.* And the fact that I'd needed to explain, I have to tell you, eased some of the pain of her departure.

I took my things from her apartment, and the following evening she came to my place to retrieve the stuff she'd stowed there. And we looked at each other, and for a moment either of us could have led the other into the bedroom, but neither of us did.

And that was that.

I'd never quite seen Carole as Ms Right, but had liked her well enough as Ms Right Now. Even while we were keeping company, I'd entertained stray thoughts about other women who'd come

60

into view, although I'd never taken the step of acting on them.

So you might have thought I'd get right back in the game when she left, but that's not what happened. It didn't seem worth the trouble. There were women who looked good to me, and there were women whose conversation suggested they might be worth getting to know. She's cute, I'd say to myself. She's bright and interesting, I'd note.

And I'd let it go at that.

And then, late in the day on a deceptively bright June afternoon, a woman named Janine walked into my shop.

TEN

There's a little bell attached to the top of my door, and while
it's not as high-tech as security cameras and motion detect-
ors, it lets me know when I have a visitor. I looked up when it
announced her arrival, and then I took a second look, because she
was worth it.

She was stunning, in fact. She wore sky-blue designer jeans and
a clingy green silk blouse, and a writer of country songs would
have told you her hair was the color of tupelo honey, but he might
not have pointed out that it had been treated to an expensive haircut. Her only flaws were a little too much plumpness in the lips
and fullness in the chest, and I was prepared to overlook them.

A couple of months earlier I'd have started a conversation with
her, but that was then and this was now, and I stayed on my perch
behind the counter and returned to my current book, which was
one of Michael Connelly's that I'd missed the first time around.

It's the one where Harry Bosch has left the LAPD under a cloud and set up shop as a private detective, and in that capacity he evidently feels compelled to tell his story in the first person instead of letting Connelly tell it for him. I was enjoying it, but I sensed that Bosch wasn't, and that it would be a relief for him to get back to the comforting embrace of the police department, and of the third person.

So she started a conversation with me.

'What an adorable cat!'

I looked up, and a third glance revealed no additional flaws. 'He's a hard worker,' I said, 'and a fine companion.'

'But he doesn't have a tail, does he? Is he a Manx?'

'He'd prefer that you think so. But he doesn't seem to have that rabbity hopping gait that's a characteristic of the breed. So he may be nothing more than an alley cat who sat too close to a rocking chair.'

'Well, he's still adorable. What's his name?'

'Raffles.'

'Hi, Raffles. I'm Janine.'

'I'm Bernie.'

She turned to face me, brightened the room with a smile. 'Hi, Bernie,' she said.

We got to talking. I don't remember the conversation, or what it was about, and I'm not even sure that it was about anything. What I was saying, irrespective of the words I was uttering, was *You're cute, and I bet you smell nice, and I'd like to know you better*. And the subtext of her now-forgotten remarks was *Okay, keep talking, 'cause maybe I'm interested*.

Eventually she said she really ought to look at books, since here we were in a bookshop. I left her to it, and tried to return to my own book, but Harry Bosch's Los Angeles suddenly seemed flat and drab compared to the New York I shared with this lovely creature.

It was about time for me to close for the evening, but how could I possibly ask her to leave? So I stayed where I was, trying to interest myself in Bosch's troubles, and raising my eyes from the page now and then to catch a glimpse of my visitor.

'Is it okay if I make a phone call?'

'Sure,' I said, grateful for the interruption. The phone's on the counter, but she shook her head when I pointed to it.

'I have my iPhone,' she said. 'But I figured a bookstore might be like the quiet car on Amtrak. If you'd rather, I can step outside.'

'You and I,' I pointed out, 'are this train's only passengers today.'

She placed her call. 'Hi, it's Janine,' she said to whoever answered. Then there were some exchanges I didn't catch, and the next thing she said was, 'Oh, I see. Well, sure. Another time, then.'

She ended the call, dropped the phone into her bag, and said, 'Rats.'

'A disappointment?'

'Well, a minor one,' she said. 'Somebody just broke a dinner date with me.'

'Someone with a screw loose,' I said. 'Nobody in his right mind would miss a chance to take you to dinner. Still, it's a pretty remarkable coincidence.'

'It is?'

'Less than an hour ago,' I said, 'someone broke a dinner date with me. He's my accountant, so in a sense it's as if my dentist called to bump my appointment to next Friday.'

'Would it be safe to conclude that you're not exactly crushed?'

'Not even rumpled. But I do face the unsettling prospect of dining alone.'

'I see.'

'Do you? Because we would seem to have that in common, and

it looks to me for all the world like two problems with a single solution.' I drew a breath. 'Will you have dinner with me?'

'I'd love to,' she said.

I called the Bum Rap and got Maxine to let Carolyn know she'd be drinking alone this evening. I brought my bargain table inside, then ducked into my back room, where I put on a clean shirt and the same blazer I'd worn to the Galtonbrook.

Outside, a bright June afternoon was turning into a perfect June evening. I asked Janine if she liked Italian food, and she unsurprisingly said she did. Have you ever heard of anybody who doesn't?

The place I picked was on East Tenth a few doors from Fifth Avenue. I'd been there once with Carolyn when we had something to celebrate. It was upscale, which meant that the table linen was white, the tables were spaced well apart, the candles were in little silver holders instead of Chianti bottles, and the prices made you glad they took credit cards.

The food was terrific, too, but that's just as true in the joints with the checkered red tablecloths.

We started with the antipasto. Then she had the branzino and I had the veal, and we shared a plate of pasta. Fusilli, I think it was, but I may have gotten that wrong; it's the one shaped like little bedsprings, and the sauce was rich and flavorful.

She said she preferred red wine to white, fish or no fish, so I ordered us a bottle of Bardolino, and another of the same when the first ran dry. The food and the wine would have been good enough to hold our interest, but the conversation flowed easily. We talked about books, we talked about art, we talked about music, we talked about New York, and mostly we talked about things I don't remember. They were terribly interesting at the time, but not nearly as interesting as her company.

It was around the time I poured us each a second glass of wine that she emphasized a conversational point by resting her hand on mine. It was wonderfully casual, but I've learned over the years that, when a woman touches your hand, it's generally a Good Sign.

She did it again a little later, and left her hand on mine a little longer this time.

Neither of us wanted dessert. Both of us wanted espresso. And our waiter, who certainly gave the impression that he found us charming, poured out two complimentary glasses of anisette. I topped the check with two of Mr Smith's portraits of Benjamin Franklin and waved away change, which could only have increased our charm.

Outside she said, 'I live in Prospect Heights, and it's nice there, but try to find a cab willing to go there. You said you're on West End Avenue.'

'And cabdrivers are happy to go there.'

'Well then,' she said, and I stepped to the curb just in time to hail a taxi.

ELEVEN

* * *

That's old-fashioned, isn't it? Three asterisks, for God's sake, in this day and age.

If I'm discreet enough to draw the curtain on what took place in the bedroom of my fourth-floor apartment (and on the living room couch, for that matter, and let's not forget the shower), well, all I have to do is skip over it, or sum up the proceedings in a sentence or two. Why the asterisks?

I have to say they're there for a reason. They serve to indicate that I've taken time to remember the evening, and to savor the memory in full detail.

Even though I don't intend to share it with you.

* * *

'Bernie, I have to go.'

'You do? Why?'

I opened an eye – both of them, actually – and saw she was half-way dressed. Her clingy blouse covered her to a couple of inches below her waist, and she was holding her sky-colored jeans and preparing to step into them.

'It's late,' I said. 'Why don't you stay over?'

'No, I can't.'

That didn't really answer my question, but she made it sound conclusive enough.

I sat up myself. 'Well,' I said. 'That was—'

'I know. For me too.'

'I make it a point to avoid the word *awesome*, but that's what it was, by God. Do you have plans for the weekend?'

'Oh, Bernie . . . '

'Because I was thinking I could rent a car and we could sneak off to somewhere an hour or two away. Some old stone inn along the Delaware, say, one of those places that run ads in the *New Yorker* telling you how charming they are. The weather's supposed to stay like this, which would certainly be conducive to long walks in the moonlight, but if it crosses us up and pours, well, I think we could spend time in our room without finding it terribly confining, and—'

The expression on her face stopped me in mid-sentence.

'Oh, Bernie,' she said again. 'I suppose I should have waited for you to doze off and then just slipped out without a word.'

'Why would you want to do that?'

'To avoid this conversation,' she said. 'Bernie, I'm not going to be able to see you again.'

'That's ridiculous.'

'No, I'm afraid it makes perfect sense.'

'You're married.'

'Not yet.'

'Not yet? What does that mean? You're engaged?'

She shook her head. 'I'm planning to get married. It's a very real plan, even though I haven't yet met my future husband. Bernie, I'm twenty-eight years old.'

'So?'

'So I want to be married before I turn thirty, and I want to have two children by the time I'm thirty-five.'

'Just two?'

'Maybe three. I figure after I've had the second, I'll be in a better position to judge whether or not I want a third.'

'That makes sense,' I allowed, 'but—'

'If I'm going to find a husband,' she said, 'I can't afford to waste time in an affair that's not going to go anywhere.'

Things were moving faster than I might have wanted, but if I didn't do something she'd be doing the moving, out the door and out of my life.

'Who said it can't go somewhere?'

'Bernie, the last thing you want to do is get married.'

'That's not necessarily true,' I said.

'Have you ever been married?'

'No, but—'

'Of course you haven't. And why should you? You're already leading the life you're cut out for, and it suits you perfectly. Your bookstore, your cat, your charming little apartment—'

'Bernie Rhodenbarr, this is your life.'

'Well, isn't it?'

'It's the one I've been living,' I said, 'taking it a day at a time. And for the most part I like things the way they are. But it's not as though marriage is something I absolutely rule out, and with the right person—'

'Stop right there, Bernie.'

'Okay.'

'I'm not the right person. More to the point, you're not the right person.'

'I'm not?'

'Oh, for some woman, maybe, but not for me. I went to your bookshop because my friend Chloe said she thought I might like you.'

'I don't think I know anybody named Chloe.'

'She wandered into your store sometime last month. She didn't buy anything.'

'That really narrows it down.'

'She's pretty, she's got dark hair, she's about my height but thinner. She said you didn't get upset when she put a book back and bought it on Kindle.'

Light dawned. 'She has a tattoo on her upper arm.'

'That's her. I would never get a tattoo, but hers is nicer than most.'

'I couldn't tell what it was. I mean I could tell it was a tattoo, duh, but I couldn't see enough of it to make out the image.'

'It's a lizard.'

'A lizard.'

'A gecko, actually. It's supposed to look as though it's crawling up toward her shoulder.'

'To whisper in her ear,' I said, 'and sell her auto insurance. See, I make you laugh. That's important, Janine. Chloe thought you might like me, and it looks as though she was right.'

'Oh, Bernie.'

Oh, Bernie. There are a number of ways to deliver that line, and she picked the one that meant *Oh, Bernie, if only I'd waited for you to fall asleep we wouldn't have to have this conversation.*

'After I talked with Chloe,' she said, 'I walked past your bookshop. It must have been around three o'clock in the middle of the week and you were all by yourself in an empty store.'

'Just me and my adorable cat.'

'And I could see what Chloe meant.'

'When she said you would like me?'

'When she said you were cute.'

'But I guess you kept on walking.'

'Well, I was on my way to a meeting, Bernie. I just took a two-block detour to check you out.'

'And you thought, by God, Chloe's right.'

'Yes and no. A little bell rang.'

'You opened the door? I thought—'

'Not that bell, silly. The one that rings inside me when a guy is, well—'

'Cute.'

'Right. And it was still echoing when I heard the warning buzzer. "Not husband material."'

'How could you tell? I mean, how did the buzzer know to buzz?'

'It's intuitive, and I've learned to trust my intuition. So yes, I kept on walking.'

'And this afternoon you came back for another look.'

'I was pretty sure you weren't a marriage prospect,' she said, 'but I was in the neighborhood and it only seemed sensible to make sure.'

'And you came in and started a conversation about my cat.'

'It's a good opener.'

'It is, and you're not the first person to think of it, but it did get us off to a nice start. And you realized I might be husband material after all.'

'No.'

'But—'

'I decided you were cute,' she said, 'which I'd already established, and I also decided that you were hot. So I decided to sleep with you.'

'Just like that?'

'Well, hadn't you already made the same decision? I could tell the way you were checking me out. So I got you to ask me to dinner—'

'You never had a dinner date in the first place,' I said. 'The phone call was a ruse. Or did you even bother punching in a number? I bet you were just talking into a dead phone.'

'No, I was talking to Chloe, actually.'

'I suppose you told her you were going to sleep with me.'

'Well,' she said, 'I was right, wasn't I? But I didn't expect to get such a fabulous dinner out of it. When you suggested Italian, I figured we'd go to some red-sauce joint on Thompson Street.'

'And look where I took you. Maybe I was husband material after all.' She was shaking her head. 'No? Why not?'

'How could I even consider marrying a man impulsive enough to blow two hundred dollars on a meal?'

'Maybe I'm a gentleman of means,' I suggested. 'Maybe two hundred dollars is nothing to me.'

'Bernie, don't take this the wrong way. Your store doesn't do any business, and when your lease is up you won't be able to afford the rent increase.'

'For all you know,' I said, 'I own the building.'

'And for all you know I'm Queen Marie of Romania. No, everything I saw made it clear you wouldn't be standing next to me when I tossed my bridal bouquet. And that was kind of a relief, because it meant I could sleep with you.'

'And otherwise you couldn't?'

'Not on the first date, silly, and probably not on the second or third, either. But you and I were only going to have one date, so why not make the most of it?'

72

'Well, we certainly did that,' I said. 'You'd have thought you were trying to cram a whole relationship into a couple of hours.'

'I was.'

'And you're trying to deny it now,' I said, 'but the way you behaved in bed suggests that maybe you sensed more of a future for us than you let on.'

'You are so wrong.'

'I am?'

'Bernie, if I'd thought that, tonight wouldn't have been anything like this. We did some pretty wild things tonight.'

'No kidding.'

'Some of it, it's not the sort of thing you do with a future husband. It's not even the sort of thing you do after you're married, not for a couple of years, anyway.'

'Because you wouldn't want him to know what kind of woman you are?'

'Of course not. But if we've only got one night, and you're never gonna see the guy again—'

'Then what the hell, why not go for it?'

'Exactly. And one thing I knew, as soon as I knew we weren't going to get married, is that I wanted to try absolutely everything with you.'

'And I guess we did.'

She got a look on her face. 'Well,' she said.

'Well what?'

'Well, there's this thing I've never actually tried. I've just read about it, and you might think it's weird or sick or disgusting.'

'What is it?'

'If I tell you,' she said, 'you'll think *I'm* weird and sick and disgusting. But so what? We're never going to see each other again.'

She put her mouth to my ear, gave my earlobe a quick nibble, then whispered.

'Well, Bernie? What do you think?'

'I think you'd better take your blouse off,' I said, 'and come back to bed.'

* * *

'You'd better stay over,' I said. 'You'll never get a cab to Brooklyn at this hour, and God knows you don't want to take the subway.'

'Oh, Bernie.'

'You don't live in Brooklyn, do you?'

'I could have walked home from the restaurant. I made up Brooklyn so I could see your apartment.'

'And so I couldn't see yours?'

'Oh, Bernie.'

She was dressed now, and putting on lipstick, checking her reflection in the mirror on my closet door.

'I won't ask for your number,' I said. 'But you know how to get in touch with me.'

'I won't, though.'

'The husband hunt can't spare a couple of hours?'

'It's not that,' she said, and turned to face me. 'One night was fine. If I saw you again, well, we've already done everything, haven't we? It would almost have to be a letdown.' She lowered her eyes. 'Or if it wasn't, I might fall in love with you, Bernie. And that would be a really bad idea.'

TWELVE

'Straight women,' Carolyn said. 'I've never understood them and I always will.'

'Amen.'

'How do you feel, Bern? Used and abused?'

'If I had the energy to feel much of anything,' I said, 'that might be it. The first part, anyway. I can't really call it abuse.'

'No, a victim doesn't usually have such a good time. It was a real *Playboy* fantasy, wasn't it? She's hot and gorgeous, she does everything you can think of and a couple of things you can't, and then she's gone. It doesn't get any better than that.'

'It could have been better. Around four in the morning she could have turned into a pizza.'

'Hold the anchovies.'

'A pizza without anchovies,' said a voice from the doorway, 'is like an ointment without a fly.'

I looked up, even as Carolyn was closing her eyes, and saw a big man in an expensive if ill-fitting suit. His name was Ray Kirschmann, he's a detective in the NYPD, and over the years he has occasionally served as the fly in my ointment.

'Hello, Ray,' I said.

'Hello, Bernie. Hello, Carolyn.'

After a beat, just long enough to show her heart wasn't in it, Carolyn said, 'Hello, Ray.'

'Whatever that is you're eatin',' he said, 'I have to say it smells better than it looks. I guess it's some kind of Chinese, bein' as you're eatin' it with chopsticks, which I never got the hang of usin' myself.'

'That's just as well,' Carolyn said. 'I don't have an extra pair to offer you.'

'I wouldn't know what to do with 'em if you did.'

'I could probably suggest something,' she said, 'but never mind. There's no food left over, anyway.'

'Plus I already ate.'

'And yet here you are, Ray. And I'll bet you're going to tell us why.'

'A guy sets out to be friendly,' he said, 'and what does it get him? A guy walks in here, he doesn't make any nasty remarks about dykes, he doesn't even come up with any short jokes, although God knows he's got ample opportunity for both. And what does it get him?'

'The abuse he must unconsciously crave, or why else would he walk in the door?'

He shook his head. 'You're a piece of work, Carolyn. Bernie, where were you last night?'

'Last night?'

'That's right. That would be the little stretch of time between yesterday afternoon and this morning.'

'I had an early dinner,' I said, 'and then I was at my apartment.'

'Alone, I suppose.'

'No, I had company.'

'I suppose it was a lady,' he said, 'unless you've started pitchin' for the other team.'

'My preferences haven't changed,' I assured him, 'although I sometimes think it might be easier if they did.'

'Does she have a name? And how do I get in touch with her?'

'You don't.'

'You've got an alibi,' he said, 'but you want to keep it to yourself, and how can it do you any good that way? What is she, Bernie, married? Are you droppin' your load in some other man's Maytag?'

'That's the worst figure of speech I've heard in a long time,' I said, 'but never mind. Anyway, I'm not.'

'You're not what?'

'What you said. She's not married. Not yet, anyway. All I know is her first name, and I have a feeling it's not really hers in the first place. I don't have a phone number for her, or an address.'

'So how are you gonna see her again?'

'I'm not, and I don't care if she can't give me an alibi, because what in the world do I need with one?'

'They're useful,' he said. 'They come in handy for keepin' burglars out of jail.'

'I don't do that anymore, Ray.'

'Yeah, right. But if you did, an alibi wouldn't hurt a bit.'

'What happened last night?'

'What happened? Well, I'd say a few things happened. If he's to be believed, Mrs Rhodenbarr's son Bernard got lucky with a mystery woman. And, just playin' the odds, I'd guess that Mrs Kaiser's daughter Carolyn got drunk in one of the muff-type dives on Hudson Street.'

'If you've got nothing else going for you, Ray, you're just plain dripping with class.'

'Thanks, Carolyn. Let's see now, what else happened? Well, the Mets won and the Yankees lost, or maybe it was the other way around. And oh yeah, somebody killed a lady in a townhouse on East Ninety-second Street.'

'During a burglary.'

'Good guess, Bernie. Assumin' it was a guess and not a personal recollection.'

'Ray, you don't seriously believe I did it.'

'No,' he said, 'of course I don't. Give me some credit, Bernie. How long have we known each other?'

'A long time.'

'A long time is right, and I have to say I know you pretty good, probably better'n you think I do. I know you're still a burglar, no matter how you swear up and down that you've turned honest. A leopard don't change his stripes, and neither does a dyed-in-the-wool burglar.'

I sighed. 'I guess you'll believe what you want to believe.'

'Yeah, I guess I will, especially when it's the truth. But besides bein' a thief to the core, another thing you've always been is a gentleman.'

'Why, thank you, Ray. That's nice of you to say.'

'Don't get me wrong,' he said. 'You're still a lowlife deadbeat who breaks into people's houses and steals their stuff. But at the same time you're the last of the gentleman burglars. You wouldn't believe the kind of scumbags who've been moving into your profession.'

'I can imagine.'

'Instead of takin' the trouble to learn the art and science of pickin' a lock, they kick the door in. Instead of tiptoein' through a house, they wake up the occupants and force 'em to turn over their valuables.'

'And last night one of them killed a woman. Are you sure it was a burglar?'

He nodded. 'Unless she trashed the place herself. She was a widow, stayin' on in this big four-story brownstone after her husband passed on. Her kids wanted her to move to an apartment, and she was thinkin' about it, but where would she put all her art and antiques?'

'Oh.'

'Yeah. That'd be one load off her mind, if she was still around to appreciate it. She was at the opera, and it was a long one—'

'They all are,' Carolyn said.

'Well, it looks like we found one thing we can agree on, Carolyn, because how people can sit through them things is beyond me. This particular opera was by that guy Hitler was crazy about.'

'Wagner,' I suggested.

'That's the guy. Anyway, I guess Mrs Ostermaier could only take so much.'

'That's her name? Mrs Ostermaier?'

'Last name Ostermaier, first name Helen. She told her friend she was tired, and I guess all the screeching made it hard to sleep through. She went out and caught a cab, and she'd have been better off stayin' where she was.'

'I don't suppose you were able to locate the cabby.'

'Well, you're wrong for a change, Bernie. He turned up and he remembered the fare. He told us she read his name off the license and guessed he was from Haiti, which he was, and she told him all about a week she and her husband had spent there back when we were all of us a lot younger, herself included. He said she was a very nice lady.'

'And he dropped her at her door, and that's the last anybody ever saw of her.'

79

'Except for the guy who was waitin' for her. Philippe said he offered to walk her to her door, but she said she'd be fine. All the same he hung around at the curb long enough to make sure she got the door open, and only drove off after it closed behind her.'

We were all silent for a moment. Then Carolyn pointed out that there weren't many rich old ladies nice enough to talk to a cabdriver about his homeland.

'We can't afford to lose people like that,' I said. 'Ray, how was she killed?'

'See, I was plannin' to ask you that, Bernie. But if you didn't do it you probably couldn't come up with the answer.'

'You don't know the cause of death yet?'

'The cause is pretty clear-cut. The cause is breaking and entering. Otherwise she'd still have a pulse.'

'The medical cause, Ray, and don't tell me she stopped breathing.'

'Well, she damn well did,' he said, 'and that's about all we know for sure at this point. A couple of uniforms got the call and found her layin' in the middle of her living room floor. When I got there a gal from the medical examiner's office was standin' by to tell me she couldn't find a bullet hole or a stab wound or any bangs and bruises.'

'Maybe she had a heart attack.'

'First thing I thought of,' he said. 'She walks in, some mug's turnin' her house upside down, and she's scared and upset and she can't catch her breath.'

'Essentially,' Carolyn said, 'you're saying the poor woman was *verklempt*.'

'If that means what it sounds like, then that's what she was. And you always think of people as gettin' a big shock and fallin' over, but is that what gives you a heart attack? Then why are they always blaming it on steak dinners at Peter Luger's?'

'The shock comes when they bring the bill,' I said, 'and you find out they don't take plastic.'

'So it coulda been her heart, but it coulda been twenty other things, and that's why we're waitin' on the autopsy. But you know the law, Bernie. You'd have to, to break it as often as you do. Even if she died of a bee flyin' up her nose, the burglar's goin' down for murder.'

'"When the commission of a felony leads to a death, the perpetrator of that felony is guilty of homicide."'

'Felony murder,' he said. 'When I was at the Police Academy, they had an example that stuck in my mind. A guy's writin' out a forged check, and a drop of ink from the pen flies up in the face of the intended mark, and the guy has an allergic reaction and dies on the spot. And the forger goes away on a murder charge. Neat?'

'It couldn't happen nowadays,' Carolyn said. 'You'd pretty much need a fountain pen, wouldn't you?'

'I don't think it ever happened. The point's not what happened, it's how the law works.'

'Haphazardly at best,' I said. 'Ray, if you really think I had anything to do with this—'

'Aw, I know you didn't, Bernie. Let's say you were there. She pays off the cab, she walks in, and there you are, checkin' out the valuables.'

'And then what happens?'

'I dunno. I guess she flops on the floor. What else do you do when you get a heart attack?'

'Take aspirin,' I said, 'and call 911.'

'I guess she didn't get the chance. But that's the thing, Bernie. If you'd been there—'

'Which I wasn't.'

'Which I know, because what you woulda done is called 911 your own self. Am I right?'

'Well, I wouldn't just leave her there to die, Ray.'

'See? Case closed. You weren't there.'

'And yet you,' Carolyn said, 'are here.'

He nodded. 'I guess I was just wonderin' if you heard anything, Bernie.'

'As a matter of fact, I did.'

'You did?'

'Just now,' I said. 'Right here, from you.'

'Oh. For a minute there—'

'Well, how else would I hear anything? It's not as though I have friends in the business. I got locked up once, Ray, and one of the things they told me when they let me out was to avoid contact with other criminals.'

'And you took the advice to heart.'

'And followed it to the letter, because nothing could have been easier. I didn't hang out with criminals *before* I went away, and the ones I met on the inside didn't make me eager to continue the association.'

Ray nodded. 'If you weren't an incorrigible criminal yourself,' he said, 'it'd be hard to believe you were any kind of a crook at all. What did I call you before, Bernie?'

'I think you said I was the last of the gentleman burglars.'

'A vanishin' breed,' he said, 'although I don't know as there was ever too many of them around. You're the only one I ever met.'

'There was always Raffles,' Carolyn said.

'Raffles the Cat? Is this warming up to be some joke about cat burglars?'

'A. J. Raffles,' I said. 'He was the hero of a series of stories by an English writer named E. W. Hornung, who I believe was related to Sir Arthur Conan Doyle, who created Sherlock Holmes. It seems to me that Hornung was his brother-in-law.'

'One of 'em was married to the other one's sister.'

'I think so,' I said, 'but I may be thinking of someone else. I could look it up.'

'Later,' he said, 'when I'm miles away from here. What's this got to do with your cat?'

'My cat was named for A. J. Raffles,' I said, 'who'd been an outstanding cricket player in his school days, and who became equally distinguished as an amateur cracksman. In other words, a burglar.'

'And he was the hero?'

'He was suave and debonair,' I said, 'and apt to come to the aid of damsels in distress. And, like Robin Hood, he only stole from the rich.'

'Who else? They're the ones with something to steal. What kind of mope would waste his time stealing from the poor?'

'Landlords,' Carolyn said. 'And businessmen, and—'

'All right,' he said, 'give it a rest, Shorty. This Raffles, Bernie. This gentleman burglar you think so much of that you named your cat after him. He wasn't a real person, was he?'

'He was a very well-drawn character, Ray. People are still reading about him over a century later.'

'But he's a character, right? In a story?'

'Quite a few stories, actually.'

'Stories in a book.'

'More than one book.'

'So when you're lookin' to name a gentleman burglar,' he said, 'the best you can come up with is a made-up character out of a batch of stories. Case closed, Bernie. You're a vanishin' breed and you always were.'

THIRTEEN

Carolyn left a few minutes after Ray did, and I went back to pretending to be a bookseller. A few people came in, and a couple of them actually bought books, and a young man with cargo shorts and a Bruce Springsteen T-shirt opened up his backpack to offer me half a dozen current bestsellers that looked brand new.

I offered him ten bucks for the lot, and stood firm when he tried to bargain. He took it, as I'd been sure he would, and when he was out the door I found shelf space for them and priced them at $9.99 apiece. Not ten minutes later one of my regulars came in, a hygienist who works for a dentist in the neighborhood, and she was on the new S. J. Rozan like a mongoose on a cobra. 'Oh, I love her,' she said. 'I've been looking for her new one. If you hadn't had it I would have bought it new.'

So it was a good deal for both of us, I thought, and it was even an acceptable transaction for the Springsteen fan, because he'd no more come by those books honestly than I was Marie of Romania.

And then I remembered the last time I'd heard mention of that charismatic queen, and the context. And that put me right back in the mood I couldn't seem to shake.

A couple of hours later, after I'd talked through two rounds of drinks at the Bum Rap, Carolyn grabbed my wrist when I started to raise a hand for Maxine.

'No,' she said.

'No?'

She raised her own hand, but only to scribble in the air. Nobody ever signed anything in the Bum Rap, except possibly a ransom note, but the signal for the check is universal, and Maxine brought ours. 'I'll pay,' Carolyn said, 'because you're buying the bottle.'

'What bottle?'

'The fifth of scotch we're picking up on our way back to my place. You need to get drunk.'

'You're right,' I said. 'I don't usually get drunk. I have a drink or two, and sometimes I get a little tipsy, but I rarely let go and get drunk. But once in a while, it's what I need to do.'

'I know.'

'And tonight's one of those nights, and I didn't even realize it. But you could tell. Carolyn, you know me better than I know myself.'

'Well,' she said, 'somebody has to.'

Carolyn lives on Arbor Court, one of those little private streets in the West Village that tourists don't know about and cabdrivers can't find.

We got there and settled in, and I cracked the scotch while Carolyn put out cat food for Archie and Ubi. Then she put out people food for us, filling a couple of bowls with the corn chips and trail mix we'd picked up en route. 'Because we have to eat,' she'd said, 'but we don't have to make a whole production out of it.'

I got a pair of rocks glasses, added ice cubes, and covered the ice cubes with scotch. It was Teacher's Highland Cream, a cut below the top-shelf single malt that would have been my selection. 'That's for sipping,' Carolyn said, taking it from me, then giving it back because she couldn't reach the top shelf to put it back. 'Tonight is not a night for sipping, Bern. I'm not saying it's a night for swigging, exactly, but we don't want to devote too much time to appreciating the rich peaty taste. Besides, you don't want to run through Mr Smith's money faster than you have to. It might have to last a while.'

'I'm selling stolen bestsellers,' I reminded her, 'and making money hand over fist.'

We settled into our seats, drinks in hand, ice bucket within reach. I raised my glass and couldn't think of a toast.

'Happy days,' she suggested.

'You're a dreamer,' I said, and took a drink.

'Maybe it's time I got married.'

'Bern,' she said, 'I knew you were going to say that. I could see the subtitles crawling across your forehead.'

'Honestly?'

'Well, almost. Why do you think you ought to get married? So you can have a lifetime of perfect nights with Marie?'

'Janine,' I said.

'For me, Bern, she'll always be Marie of Romania, and I'd say that's as likely to be her name as Janine.'

'She looked about as Romanian as you do.'

'Oh? My grandfather on my mother's side was born in Bucharest.'

'Honestly?'

'No, and his name wasn't Marie, either. Or Janine.'

'You're mixing me up,' I said, 'and I wish you wouldn't. If I wanted to get married, it wouldn't be to Marie.'

'Janine.'

'Whatever. She's not the kind of woman I would marry.'

'Because she slept with you on the first date?'

'I wonder why we call it that,' I said. 'Believe me, there was no sleeping involved. But that's not why.'

'Then why? Because no man wants to marry a girl who does all the things he's spent his whole life hoping she would do?'

I frowned. 'Two drinks ago,' I said, 'I would have been able to make sense out of that sentence, and I might even have been able to respond to it. Look, I wasn't what Janine was looking for. She wanted a man of substance.'

'"A breakfast-eating, Brooks Brothers type."'

'That's from something.'

'*Guys and Dolls.*'

'Right. Well, I usually eat breakfast, and my blazer's from Brooks Brothers.'

'You told me you got it from a thrift shop.'

'Well, it didn't start out there. The first person who owned it got it at Brooks Brothers. It's in beautiful shape, too. I wonder why he got rid of it.'

'He was cheating on his wife, and she gave away all his clothes.'

'I hope so. I always figured he died, and I'd much rather believe he was out getting laid. What were we talking about, anyway?'

'Does it matter?'

'No,' I said. 'Hardly anything does.'

'You know,' I said, '*you* could get married. It's legal now.'

'Remember Randy Messenger? She wanted for us to get married.'

'That was years ago. It was nowhere near legal then.'

'Well, it's not like it was a criminal offense, Bern. They didn't lock you up for it. They just wouldn't give you a license. But there were plenty of gay weddings, and you and I went to one together.'

'Ginger and Joanne,' I said, remembering. 'In that church at the corner of West Thirteenth and Seventh. One of them wore a floor-length white gown.'

'Ginger.'

'And the other wore a tuxedo.'

'No, it was during the summer, and Joanne wore a white dinner jacket.'

'They looked sensational. Then they moved somewhere.'

'Rhinebeck.'

'And didn't one of them want to get pregnant? I suppose that would have been Ginger.'

'It was. They were looking for a sperm donor, but you weren't interested.'

'It seemed too weird. It doesn't seem that weird now, for some reason. Maybe I missed a good chance.'

'Maybe not,' she said.

'Oh? It might be nice to have a son. I could teach him my two trades.'

'Bookselling and burglary.'

'That way I wouldn't be the last of the gentleman burglars. He could creep along in my footsteps.'

'And if Ginger had a girl?'

'Who says a woman can't sell books? The guy who owns the Strand, his daughter's in the business with him.'

'And your other line of work?'

'So? Who says a woman can't break into houses?'

'Instead of the last of the gentleman burglars,' she said, 'she could be the first of the lady burglars.'

'Why not?' My glass had somehow emptied itself. I took care of that. 'What did Ginger wind up having? A boy or a girl?'

'A sex-change operation.'

'Huh?'

'It was after she and Joanne broke up,' she said, 'and they sold the house in Rhinebeck, and they both moved back to the city, but to separate apartments. Ginger realized she'd been suppressing her true self all along, and that was why she'd been such an over-the-top femme. Deep down inside, she'd always felt herself to be a man.'

'So she went and had the surgery.'

'The hormone treatments, and the counseling, and finally the surgery.'

'And it worked?'

'The person who used to be Ginger,' she said, 'is now a man named Jim. Matter of fact, you've met him.'

'I have?'

'At the Poodle Factory. We were in the middle of lunch and he brought in his Dandie Dinmont for a wash and set.'

'I remember the dog,' I said. 'Oh, Jesus – I remember the guy, too. That was Ginger?'

'Jim.'

'He came across as a regular guy.'

'He *is* a regular guy, Bern. He may not have started out that way, but that's what he is now.'

'Does he date? I mean, who does he date? I mean—'

'You mean does he go for boys or girls, and that hasn't changed. He's attracted to women.'

'Oh, he'd have to be,' I said. 'Nothing queer about our Jim. What does Joanne make of all this, do you happen to know?'

'Joseph,' she said.

FOURTEEN

'You're barely drinking, Carolyn.'
      'I'm drinking.'
'You're sipping,' I said. 'I should have bought the Glen Kirkatchacallit after all. But you talked me out of it.'
'What we're drinking is fine, Bern. Why waste the money?'
'It was only a few dollars more, and look what we saved by skipping dinner. And it would have been worth it. Remember what Thorstein Veblen wrote about conspicuous consumption?'
'What, Bern?'
'I was hoping you'd remember.'
'I don't even remember who he was.'
'Well,' I said, 'if you ever make it through *Swann's Way* with your eyes wide open, Veblen's your man. You ever find yourself in the path of a charging rhisonerus—'
'Rhinoceros.'

'Thank you. If you do, just whip out Thorstein Veblen and start reading. One paragraph and you'll stop that charging lion in his tracks.'

'A minute ago he was a rhino, Bern.'

'I didn't want to get my tongue all twisted up trying to say it. But you figured out a way around that, didn't you? Rhino. Two simple syllables, rhi and no. "Put 'em together and what have you got? Bippety Boppety Boo." Remember that song?'

'No.'

'Neither do I. Veblen wrote about conspicuous consumption, but the way you're drinking is more like inconspicuous consumption. But don't think you're fooling anybody, Carolyn. I see what you're doing.'

'What am I doing, Bern?'

'Playing the role of designated driver. We haven't got a car and we're not going anywhere, but that's what you're doing, isn't it?'

'I might be taking it a little bit easy,' she conceded. 'Even so, I'm way too far along to get behind the wheel, which is just as well, considering that I never learned to drive.'

'You want to learn? I'll teach you.'

'Not tonight, Bern.'

'No of course not,' I said. 'Tonight I'm the designated drinker.'

'I campaigned for gay marriage,' Carolyn said. 'I wrote letters to my congressperson, which some poor staffer had to read and respond to. I signed petitions, I went to fund-raisers. I marched, Bernie. I hate marching, I hate parades, I hate all that crap, and yet I marched for gay marriage.'

'I know you did.'

'And I danced in the streets when it passed in New York. If I'd been wearing a hat I'd have thrown it in the air.'

'You should have said something. I've got plenty of hats.'

'And then when the Supreme Court did the right thing, I celebrated all over again.'

'I remember.'

She leaned forward, lowered her voice. 'And now I'm going to
tell you something you must never repeat to another living soul.'

'No problem,' I said. 'I probably won't remember.'

'What I'm afraid of,' she said, 'is that you'll remember what I
tell you, but you'll forget that you're supposed to keep it to yourself. Well, I'm going to say it anyway. I'm not so sure gay marriage
is a great idea.'

'That's the scotch talking,' I said, 'and I guess you've had more
of it than I realized.'

'Oh, it's a right we should have, and we're way better off for
having it. And all the arguments for it are as true as they ever
were. And maybe it's different for gay men. But giving lesbians
the right to get married is a dangerous thing.'

'Why do you say that?'

'Bernie, what does a lesbian bring to a second date?'

'A U-haul,' I said. 'You told me that joke a long time ago.'

'And it still works,' she said, 'because it's true. We've got this
nesting instinct that's out of control. "Oh, you like me? Well, I
like you, too. And we've got so much in common! I see you've got
a cat. I've got a cat, too! Isn't that great? And our cats like each
other! Ooh, let's get a third cat and we can put our heads together
to come up with a really cute name for it!"'

'You're exaggerating.'

'Not by much. "Oh, let's move in together! We can share a closet
and wear each other's clothes. Don't you just love L. L. Bean?"'

'Those plaid shirts,' I said.

'And the worst thing about them is they last forever. "Hey, I got
an idea! Let's find a donor and a turkey baster and make a baby.

We can be mommies together, and it'll give us something to do when Lesbian Bed Death puts an end to our sex lives. Or maybe we should have *two* babies, so it'll be easier to divvy them up when we both fall in love with other people."'

'Oh, come on. That's not fair. There are plenty of lesbian relationships that last a lifetime.'

'I know.'

'In fact I'm not sure the odds are any better for a heterosexual marriage.'

'And how good is that? Bern, every marriage ends either in divorce or death. Did you ever think about that?'

'No,' I said, 'and I wish I didn't have to think about it now. What did Jim and Joseph do? I mean, when they were still Ginger and Joanne?'

'What did they do?'

'Well, they were married. We went to their wedding, we saw it happen. When they decided to split up, what did they do?'

'I told you, Bern. They sold the house in Rhinebeck, split up the money, and each of them found a place in the city. Well, Ginger did. Joanne wound up somewhere in Queens. I guess Joanne took the cats, because Jim's got a dog now.'

'The Dandie Dinmont.'

'Who happens to be show quality, though Jim's not crazy enough to go through all that rigmarole.'

'That's all there was to it?'

'Uh-huh, and that's kind of my point, Bern. They had a nice church wedding and lived together as wife and wife, and when it was time to split the blanket they didn't need to call their lawyers. But if a lesbian wedding has legal standing, when the marriage turns belly-up, you have to get a divorce.'

'A lesbian divorce.'

'Well, sure. A lesbian divorce used to be a simple matter of shouting and screaming and crying and figuring out who keeps the rent-stabilized apartment.'

'You'd still have that, wouldn't you?'

'Plus a little added something. It's not hard to understand why the Association of Matrimonial Lawyers was one of gay marriage's strongest supporters, is it?'

'All that new business,' I said. 'Think of the custody fights.'

'Maybe it's not fair to make you do all the drinking,' she said, and filled her glass. 'Not only is it gonna be more complicated to split up, but it gives couples something brand new to fight about, when one wants to get married and the other doesn't. Which just amounts to deciding whether to split up before or after the marriage ceremony.'

'I never thought of any of this.' And the thoughts kept right on coming. 'You know what? The next time we see *The Gay Divorcée*, it'll be a remake with a whole new slant to it.'

Once we'd each reached a particular peat-flavored plateau, the drinking lost its urgency and became a sort of background music for our conversation. The two of us found no end of things to talk about, and I'm sure the exchanges I don't remember were every bit as interesting as the ones I do.

'I can see why a person might want to get married,' I said, when that topic popped up again. 'You've met someone and you're in love, and you want a life together, with maybe a kid or two. And maybe that would involve a house in the suburbs—'

'Ugh.'

'—but maybe not, because if I was going to raise a kid I'd rather bring him up right here in New York. Right in my own neighborhood, so we'd be within walking distance of the American Museum of Natural History.'

'That's important, huh?'

'People go on about how they want to leave the city so their kid'll know what a cow looks like. So they move way to hell and gone, and the poor little bastard never gets to see a dinosaur.'

'I never looked at it that way. Bern, if they want all that, why do they have to get married?'

'They don't,' I allowed, 'but at the same time I can see why they might want to. But isn't that a step you decide to take after you've met the person and fallen in love? Janine had it the other way around.'

'Janine of Romania.'

'She had this picture in her mind – the house, the two kids, and her with a ring on her finger. That's what she wanted, so she was out hunting for the man to stand next to her in the picture.'

'And put a ring on her finger, and two buns in her oven.'

'It seems backwards to me,' I said, 'but maybe not. If you go ahead and fall in love first, suppose he turns out to be Mr Not Quite Right?'

'You've got your heart set on cows, and he's holding out for dinosaurs.'

'Whatever. It's something to think about.'

And, a little later:

'Bern, what's funny is the Romanian girl missed the point completely.'

'I don't really think she's Romanian.'

'I don't care if she's Etruscan, Bern. She looked at your clothes and your bookstore and your apartment, and everything screamed low rent.'

'Well, of course my apartment rent is low. The place is rent-controlled. I'd be an idiot to move.'

'Right.'

'And market rent on the store is as low as it gets, because I don't have to pay any. Otherwise it would be sky-high.'

'I know, Bern.'

'And my clothes – what's the matter with my clothes? I told you that blazer's from Brooks Brothers.'

'Via Housing Works, Bern.'

'It didn't say so on the label. You said she missed the point. What point did she miss?'

'The point that you were actually a pretty good prospect, at least from a financial standpoint. She thought you were irresponsible to pay two hundred dollars for dinner. What you were was a man celebrating a nice windfall. So what if the bookstore wasn't jammed with buyers? You'd just made thirty-five grand in a matter of hours.'

'Sure, but how often does that happen?'

'Often enough to keep you from missing any meals. And your apartment may not be packed full of high-ticket furniture, but there's a painting hanging on one wall that would bring a seven-figure price at auction.'

'If I could sell it.'

'It's worth the money, whether you can sell it or not. And the fact of the matter is that you could sell it if you wanted to. Not for full price, and not openly, but there are collectors who'll buy something knowing they can never show it to anyone. Like your Mr Smith with his manuscript.'

'So I was actually just the guy she was looking for all along, and she was too dumb to know it. I was that Scarsdale Galahad from the song, ready to buy her a split-level colonial in Westchester and support her in style by breaking into the neighbors' houses. And if anything went wrong, I'd be just half an hour away in Sing Sing.'

*

And later still:

'Carolyn, I don't want to get married.'

'I'm glad you told me, Bern. Here I was building up my nerve to propose, and you just saved me a lot of embarrassment.'

'Seriously, Carolyn?'

'Oh, God, of course not.'

'I didn't think so, but I wanted to make sure. You know what I want?'

'I hope it's not pizza. They're closed at this hour.'

'I want everything to stay the same,' I said.

'So do I.'

'I want to have lunch with you every day, and drinks after work at the Bum Rap. I want Maxine to keep that dead-end job forever, just so she can go on being our waitress.'

'She wouldn't dare leave. She knows I'd kill her if she did.'

'I don't want to sell books online. I want to keep the bookstore, even if most of the time it's just me and Raffles in there.'

'And some girl with a Kindle.'

'That girl with the Kindle,' I said, 'set me up for the hottest night I've had in years.'

'And when it was over—'

'I felt bad, but it was worth it. And I'll get over it, and do you know why?'

'Because there'll be other girls.'

'There will,' I said, 'and I'll keep thinking one of those relationships has a future, but it never will, and that's really the way I want it. One hopeless romance after another, with a lot of good times along the way.'

'Me too, Bern.'

'You want to know something? Even when I was in bed with her—'

'Janine.'

'Janine, Marie, whatever. Even when we were in outer space, smack in the middle of the asterisk belt, there was a part of my mind that knew I'd want to be rid of her sooner or later.'

'You want to hang on to that part of your mind, Bern. It's called sanity.'

'If you say so. Never mind marriage. I knew we'd be through with each other by the time the summer was over.'

'That soon?'

'With maybe the occasional one-nighter down the road, for old times' sake. Is the bottle empty?'

'I'm afraid so.'

'Well, that's okay. I guess we've had enough. Where was I?'

'Done with Janine, except for an annual reunion.'

'*Same Time Next Year.* That was a great play, and then it was a great movie. How often does that happen?'

'Not too,' she said. 'And what it really is, Bern, is a beautiful fantasy.'

'The best. Carolyn, I'm glad she's out of my life, I really am. But I'd give a lot for one more night with her.'

'It was that good, huh?'

'Yeah. It really was.'

She thought about it. 'I haven't even met her myself,' she said, 'but I think I've got a pretty good sense of her from you. And I think she's gonna find the guy she's looking for, and she'll get married.'

'Oh, I'm sure of it.'

'And she'll have two kids, and maybe even three, but my guess is she'll stop at two. And then they'll get a divorce.'

'Why?'

'Who cares? One way or the other, the odds are pretty good that the marriage will go in the toilet.'

'Well, I don't want her to be unhappy, Carolyn. I had a good time with her and I wish her well. I won't sit around praying for her marriage to fail.'

'But it probably will, Bern, with or without your prayers. And then she'll move back to the city, the way people do, and you'll get another shot at her.'

'Jesus.'

'Say the whole process takes seven years. She'll be what, thirty-five? She's sure to be a yoga-Pilates-personal trainer kind of girl, so she'll be in good shape. Of course, she'll be that much more experienced by then, so God only knows what kind of stuff she'll want to do in bed . . .'

FIFTEEN

I woke up on Carolyn's couch with a cat on my chest. Don't ask me which one. It was all I could do to determine the species.

A note on the kitchen table assured me that she'd feed Raffles on her way to work. 'Stay as long at you like. Food in the fridge if you can face it.'

I couldn't, nor could I face the world without a shower and a change of clothes. She'd anchored the note with a bottle of aspirin, and I got down a couple of tablets on my way out the door.

By the time I'd had a shower and a shave I felt surprisingly good. I remembered I'd been meaning to get a haircut, and left the barbershop with my appetite restored. I stopped at the diner, stayed for a second cup of coffee, and it was getting on for noon by the time I got downtown to my store.

Raffles did his oh-I'm-starving-feed-me number, rubbing against my ankles the way he learned in cat school. 'Not a chance,'

I told him. 'Carolyn already fed you. You think we don't talk to each other?'

Speaking of which. I called her to tell her I'd pass on lunch today, thanked her for the use of her couch, and for thinking to feed the cat. 'And for being such a good friend,' I said. 'I hope I wasn't too bad last night.'

'You were fine,' she said. 'You didn't puke, and you didn't even get particularly maudlin. I'd have given you the bed and taken the couch myself, because I'm a better fit there, but you, uh—'

'Passed out. Uh, am I remembering this right? Ginger and Joanne?'

'Jim and Joseph.'

'Do they stay in touch?'

'They're good buddies, Bern. They go to ballgames together.'

'Ballgames.'

'You know. Guy stuff.'

I had three visitors in the first twenty minutes, or five if you count the two out-of-towners who wanted directions to the Strand. I rang up a couple of sales, and then they cleared out and I picked up my book. I hadn't read a page before I was no longer alone.

'Well, it's about time, Bernie.'

'You think?' I looked at my watch. 'Good afternoon, Ray.'

'I was here two hours ago,' he said, 'and you weren't. You keepin' burglars' hours?'

'Carolyn and I stayed up late,' I said, 'drinking scotch and talking about sex-change operations.'

'Yeah? For you or for her?'

'We couldn't decide.'

'Well, you'd want to talk it over first. I guess it musta been late by the time you got home.'

'You're being sly, Ray.'

'How's that?'

'Asking trap questions. You evidently know I didn't get home until this morning, and that means you were probably looking for me late last night. Why?'

'Aw, last night I was sittin' in front of the TV, and I had this idea. And I was gonna call you, but it was late, and besides I figured it was probably a stupid idea.'

'And you let that stop you?'

'Then I woke up this morning,' he said, 'and the idea was still there, only it didn't seem so stupid. So I figured I'd come by your place, maybe catch you before you had your breakfast.'

'When was this?'

'Maybe eight, eight-thirty. I pulled up in front of your building and called you on the phone, and I got the machine.'

'Did you leave a message?'

'Why would I do that? What I did was I had your doorman ring your apartment, and that didn't get me anywhere either. So I went and had breakfast my own self, and then I went by the precinct and did a little of this and a little of that, and a little after ten I came down here, because I knew you'd be open.'

'But I wasn't.'

'No, you weren't. And that gave me more time to decide if my idea's stupid, and I think it probably is, but I can't seem to get it out of my head.'

'Perhaps it would help to share it.'

'What are you, Dr Phil? I was gettin' there.'

'Sorry.'

'It has to do with this other thing I can't get out of my head, which is Mrs Ostermaier up on Ninety-second Street.'

'You can't seriously believe—'

'Jesus, no, Bernie. I know you didn't have nothin' to do with it.

What I had was this feelin' that somethin' about the crime scene was starin' me in the face, and I just couldn't see it.'

'You want to describe it to me, Ray?'

He shook his head. 'What I want to do,' he said, 'is show it to you. You're a burglar, right?'

'I used to be.'

He gave me a look. 'What you are is a burglar, Bernie, and what I been thinkin' is you could give me a burglar's-eye view of the situation.'

'In what capacity? What would I be, some sort of civilian consultant to the NYPD?'

'I suppose you could think of it that way. What you'd be is doin' me a favor. Over the years I seen you pull plenty of rabbits out of plenty of hats, and a few people went away for murder on account of some quick thinkin' and fancy footwork on your part. Here's a nice woman got killed just because she had the sense to leave an opera before the fat lady sang, and that's not right.'

'No, it's not.'

'So what do you say? I'm parked next to the hydrant down the block, we'll take a quick run uptown on the FDR. I'll have you back here in two hours.'

'They're hours I can't spare,' I said. 'I just opened up, Ray. I've got a business to run.'

'Yeah, I can see how customers are stormin' the place. It's hard for you and me to have a conversation the way they keep interruptin'.'

'How's six o'clock? I'll skip drinks with Carolyn and go uptown with you instead. Does that work?'

'Actually,' he said, 'it's probably better. By then I'll have the autopsy results. Not that knowin' what killed her's gonna make it easier to work out *who* killed her.'

'Still,' I said, 'it can't hurt.'

Bells tinkled, my door opened, and a customer walked in.

'See?' I said. 'What did I tell you? I've got a business to run, Ray, just like I said. I'll see you at six.'

He left, and I waited until the door had closed behind him, then approached my visitor.

'Good afternoon, Mr Smith,' I said. 'How can I help you?'

SIXTEEN

The Ostermaier house was on the uptown side of 92nd Street, a few doors from Lexington Avenue. It fit the local definition of a brownstone, which isn't limited to edifices with façades of that color. This specimen was fronted with limestone, and I had to agree with the Ostermaier children; it was too big to be occupied by one woman living alone.

I followed Ray up the flight of stone steps leading to the parlor floor entrance. Yellow crime scene tape sealed the door, backed up by an NYPD-applied padlock.

Ray peeled back the tape and reached into his pocket. 'Now I know a man with your talents wouldn't need this,' he said, producing a key, 'but how would it look for the neighbors?'

Inside, the place smelled of air freshener, which was probably all to the good. The air held a trace of what the air freshener was there to mask, and you wouldn't mistake it for Chanel No. 5. We walked through a mirrored foyer into the large living room, and my eyes went to where the woman had been lying. There was no chalk outline, they don't even do that on TV anymore, but there might as well have been.

'On the chair,' I said. 'Is that the coat she was wearing?'

'Musta been. Took it off, dropped it on the chair.'

'Nice coat,' I said. 'Bottle green with a fur collar. She walked in the door, took off the coat, and she would have hung it up but instead she decided to drop dead on the carpet.'

'As far as anybody knows. Maybe she had it over her arm when she died, and it landed on the floor next to her.'

'And the intruder moved it? Maybe.' I had a closer look at where she'd fallen. 'The carpet's by Trent Barling,' I said. 'American, art deco period.'

'See, that's the kind of thing you would know, Bernie. But why bother learnin' about rugs? You have any idea what that thing must weigh? A man'd be better off stealin' a hot stove.'

On the other hand, the smaller orientals are readily portable, and there's an eager aftermarket for the better ones. But I didn't feel compelled to point this out.

'It's easy to see where you found her,' I said, 'because the rest of the carpet's covered with stuff. Books, knickknacks, framed photographs. And a nice clear space for a body. Her head was at that end? Was she prone or supine?'

'I can never remember which is which. She was layin' face up.'

Lying face up, I thought, but how many people get that right? 'Supine,' I said. 'Face down would be prone.'

'Like I'll remember, Bern. What's it matter, anyway?'

'It doesn't.' I knelt down next to a carving, three inches tall, of a man with Chinese features and a wispy beard. He was leaning on a cane.

'Ivory,' I said.

'You can't bring that stuff into the country. On account of the elephants.'

'You could back when this was made. She also had an elephant-foot umbrella stand, Ray. Over there next to the piano, and what do you bet the piano keys are ivory?'

'Not the black ones.'

'Ivory and ebony,' I said. 'They stopped using ivory for piano keys years ago. I wonder if they still use ebony. You can get it without killing elephants, but for all I know it's an endangered tree.'

'Everything's endangered nowadays,' he said, 'except for the crap nobody wants.'

'Playing cards,' I said. 'All over the place. Did anybody bother to count them? It's not hard to believe there are fifty-two of them here.'

'Assumin' she was playin' with a full deck.'

'An empty gift box,' I said, continuing the inventory. 'The lid's over there. I wonder what was in the box.'

'Take your pick, Bernie. Coulda been any of the crap that's all over the floor. Or maybe it was just an empty box she was keepin'.'

'See the tissue paper? I bet it was in the box. And there's a yard or so of blue ribbon. The box is light blue, so dark blue ribbon would be a good choice.'

'Bernie, what the hell difference does it make?'

'Who knows? You brought me here to observe, didn't you? So that's what I'm doing. Right now I'm observing a cigarette lighter, one of those sterling silver table lighters. Ronson must have sold a million of them.'

'My folks had one.'

'Mine had two. I remember we had one, and then somebody gave us another for a present, and my mother had to pretend it was just what she always wanted. You had to have lighters handy

107

for your guests, and plenty of ashtrays, and you'd have cigarette dishes on all the tables, with cigarettes in them, getting stale while your guests smoked their own.'

'They didn't get stale in our house, Bernie. You can probably guess who smoked 'em.'

'And you can probably guess who smoked ours. I remember when you quit, Ray. You had a tough time.'

'The worst. Did you ever smoke? I'm tryin' to picture you with a cigarette.'

'I quit when I went away.'

'You're not talkin' about college.'

'No, though some people call it that.'

'I guess you can get an education there. Why'd you pick that time to quit? You'd think they'd help pass the time. Couldn't afford 'em?'

I shook my head. 'They were too valuable to smoke. The joint I was in, cigarettes were currency. It would have been like burning up dollar bills.'

'It's like that now, and you don't have to be in the joint either. You seen what a pack goes for nowadays?'

We talked about the price of cigarettes, and the cost of a gallon of gas, and I started to feel like my father, remembering when a buck ninety-five would get you a four-course steak dinner in the dining room of the Hotel Claypool.

'All this stuff,' I said, waving a hand at it. 'How'd it get here?'

'The perp pulled things off the shelves. Yanked out drawers, turned 'em upside down. See that drawer? It came out of that end table there.'

'Nothing's broken.'

'Huh?'

'Look at all these china ornaments. Intact, every one of them. The little dog was broken once in the past, you can see where it's been mended, but nothing got damaged the other night. These are fragile items. You'd think at least one of them would have had a crash landing.'

'It's a soft carpet, Bernie.'

'Or they could have gotten crushed underfoot. How'd Mrs Ostermaier make it all the way to the middle of the carpet without stepping on anything?'

'My guess? Most of the stuff got tossed around after he killed her.'

'That's *if* he killed her.'

'It's hard to figure what happened,' he admitted. 'She had heart problems, and the autopsy said her heart stopped beatin'.'

'But we sort of knew that.'

'Yeah, bein' as she was dead. They said somethin' I never heard before. They said she had an empty heart.'

'What's that?'

'I'm not too clear on it,' he said. 'You know how your heart's a pump, and it pumps blood out your arteries, and then it flows back?'

'Through your veins.'

'Right. Well, if the veins don't pull their weight, blood can't get back to the heart the way it's supposed to. So there you are with an empty heart.'

'What would make that happen?'

'The veins dilate too much,' he said, 'or not enough, I forget which. The reason they do that, or don't do it—'

'Whatever.'

'—is different in different cases, but their best guess at this stage is a kind of shock.'

'Shock at spotting an intruder?'

'Naw, it's a certain kind of shock, and I can't think of the word. It's why they don't give you peanuts on airplanes.'

'Because that kind of random act of kindness would leave you with an empty heart?'

'No, because kids are allergic, and isn't that a hell of a thing? How can anybody make it through childhood without peanut butter?'

'Peanut allergy,' I said.

'Or any other kind, and there's a name for that kind of shock, and—'

'Anaphylactic.'

'Thank you, Jesus. That's the word I was lookin' for. It's the same thing you get from a bee sting, or whatever it is you're allergic to.'

'So maybe a bee actually did fly up her nose.'

'Huh?'

'Never mind,' I said.

'If it was an allergic reaction that induced anaphylactic shock,' I said, 'maybe she never saw the intruder.'

'How's that?'

'Say he came, found what he wanted, and left. Then she comes home – no, that doesn't make any sense.'

''Cause why's he leave the place lookin' like a bomb went off? Where's the sense in that?'

'So let's say she came home, and her house was just as she'd left it a couple of hours earlier. And she walks in, she takes off her coat, she sets it down—'

'And a bee flies up her nose.'

'Or a stewardess hands her a bag of peanuts. There's no way to know what happens, but something does, and she falls down dead.'

'All alone in her own livin' room.'

'And then, a little later, someone opens her door and walks

in on her. What's the time frame, Ray? How long was she dead before you guys got the call?'

'Coulda been a long time, Bernie. We know what time she got home.'

'From when she left the Met, and what time Philippe dropped her.'

'The cabbie, right. There was an intermission at 9:15, and that's when she left, and Philippe's trip sheet says he picked her up at 9:28 and dropped her ten minutes after that. A straight shot through the park, and no traffic to speak of at that hour.'

'So if she walked right in, and had time to take off her coat but not enough time to hang it in the closet—'

'That'd set time of death anywhere after say a quarter of ten. It was just past two in the morning when the daughter discovered the body.'

'What daughter?'

'The old lady's daughter. Who'd you think? The woman had four children, two of each. More or less.'

'Huh?'

'Well, one of the sons is a little light on his feet, but it was one of the daughters who walked in and found her mother. The younger daughter, Deirdre's her name.'

'She didn't live here, did she?'

'No, didn't I tell you the old lady lived here alone? They were tryin' to get her to move. But the daughter wasn't too far away. One of them high-rises on York Avenue. What she did, she tried to call her mother at half-past twelve.'

'That late?'

'Well, she knew she was gonna be at the opera, and it wasn't set to end until close to midnight.'

'No wonder Mrs Ostermaier left early.'

'Yeah, that's a long time to listen to all that screechin'. So if it ends around midnight, 12:30's a good time to call. She's home by then but she's still awake.'

'But there was no answer.'

'No, so she waited fifteen minutes and called again, and still no answer, so she tried her mother's friend, the one she went to the opera with.'

'And found out her mother should have been home hours ago.'

'"Oh, she left early, I bet she went straight to bed and never heard the phone." Except the daughter knows the mother's a light sleeper.'

'So she came over to check for herself.'

'Said she was too worried to sleep. She called again and let it ring a long time, and then she came over here and leaned on the doorbell, and finally she unlocked the door and walked in.'

'She had a key.'

'They all had keys. She used hers, and I don't think she messed up the crime scene much. She touched the body, of course, but she knew right away her mother was dead.'

'Cold to the touch.'

'Well, cool, anyway. She used her cell phone to call 911, and stayed here to let in the uniforms.'

'And I assume she was still here when you showed up.'

'Uh-huh. Anyway, there's your time frame. You got four hours between the woman gettin' home and her daughter showin' up. You coulda had all the burglars you want in that amount of time.'

I thought about it. 'So he comes in, and she's already dead. She's right there on the rug, she's got to be the first thing he sees. Why doesn't he turn around and walk out?'

'Must be somethin' he really wants, Bernie.'

'I guess.'

'And he's in a hell of a rush to find it and get out, which explains the mess. He hasn't got time to be neat.'

'So he takes a few extra minutes to make the place look like a bomb went off?'

'You don't want to leave without what you came for, do you? But you don't want to waste time lookin' for it, either. So you dump the drawers, you brush things off table tops—'

'And nothing breaks. And then what? You find what you came for and leave?'

'Or you don't find it,' he said, 'and you leave anyway, because not gettin' caught's even more important than findin' whatever it was.'

'And what do you suppose that was?'

'Jesus, Bernie. How the hell should I know?'

'You talked to the daughter.'

'The young one, Deirdre. I talked to her that night, and the rest of 'em yesterday. One son's a partner in a catering business, he lives with his partner in Chelsea. Not the catering partner, the living-together partner.'

'Okay.'

'His name's Boyd. The son, I mean. Not either of his partners. The other son's Jackson, he's a tax lawyer, married, lives in Brooklyn. Park Slope, I think it is. He works downtown at the Financial Center. And what the hell is the name of the other daughter?'

'I have no idea.'

'I wasn't askin' you, Bernie. I was tryin' to bludgeon my memory. The other daughter's married, but she keeps her old last name. Her and her husband live in Alphabet City on a block you wouldn't walk down a few years ago, and now you can't afford to live there. And her name's Meredith.'

'I guess that bludgeon worked,' I said. 'You must have been chasing all over town.'

He shook his head. 'Brought 'em all here, so I could get 'em to look around a little. Not too much, on account of it's still an active crime scene. I'm breakin' ten or a dozen rules havin' you here, by the way.'

'But I begged and pleaded and you just couldn't say no to me.'

'Hey, it's my idea, and you're the one doin' me a favor. But I'm still breakin' the rules.'

'I'm not about to rat you out, Ray.'

'No, I figured my secret was safe with you. What you were askin', nobody had a clue what the thief mighta been after. There's a wall safe upstairs in the bedroom, and she used to stow the good jewelry there when it wasn't in the safe deposit box at the bank. But after the husband died she said it was too much trouble chasin' back and forth to the bank, so she just left it there.'

'In the safe?'

'At the bank. Nobody quite said it, but I got the sense the safe was mostly for the husband's use. He was in real estate and worked with construction guys, and sometimes he had to be able to get his hands on serious cash.'

'And that's where he kept it.'

'Uh-huh. And when he died, the wife and kids made the cash disappear before the IRS took an interest. The safe's still there, and it's locked.'

'And nobody had the combination?'

'Written down at home, one of 'em said. I had a look at it, and either the burglar didn't know about it or he never got upstairs before she came home and surprised him. They kept a picture hangin' over it to hide it.'

'Because who'd ever think to look for a safe behind a portrait of a Spanish nobleman?'

'It's a woman,' he said, 'and don't ask me if she's Spanish. It's like these here. Not that one, Bernie. That's a couple of cows in a field.'

Black and white dairy cattle, with a barefoot milkmaid eyeing them. 'Holsteins,' I said.

'I guess he's famous,' he said, 'if you recognize the artist.'

'Actually,' I said, 'it looks like a Constable. Holstein's the breed of cattle.'

'I'll take your word for it. The rest are all pictures of people, and from the looks of them they've all been dead for a while. That guy over there looks like somebody stuffed him.'

Could that really be a Constable? At closer range I could see that I had the artist right, but that it wasn't a painting at all. It was a high-quality reproduction, the sort you find in museum gift shops, tastefully framed and ready to hang.

I studied it and the wall around it, and then I went over for a closer look at the portrait of the man. It, like others in the room, were what decorators call ancestors – though rarely of the people on whose walls they now repose.

'Stuffed,' I agreed.

'Or maybe embalmed. He's a pretty good match for the dame upstairs.'

'Then why isn't she down here keeping him company?'

'Somebody's got to hide the safe. I suppose the burglar coulda moved the picture and put it back, but would this guy take the trouble? The same guy who left the livin' room lookin' like a cyclone hit it?'

'That cyclone,' I said. 'Did it blow any bric-a-brac on top of Mrs Ostermaier?' When he looked puzzled, I rephrased my question. Had any of the living room litter been on the woman's body when she'd been found there?

'You'd have wanted to keep the scene intact,' I said, 'but you'd have had to clear off the body before removing it from the scene.'

'So was there anything layin' on her that got moved?' He

frowned, squeezing out a memory. 'I don't think so, Bernie. If there was, it'd be in the crime scene photos. Does it make a difference?'

'Does anything? But if he threw everything every which way, and nothing got broken and nothing landed on the dead woman in the middle of the Trent Barling carpet—'

'Or one of those china dogs hit her and bounced off. That's what woulda happened, Bernie.'

'You think?'

'We could try an experiment,' he said. 'You stretch out on the floor and I'll throw things at you.'

'Wouldn't we be compromising the crime scene?'

'And wastin' our time, but it might be worth it to peg that silver table lighter at you. And you'd get to stretch out on What-sisname's rug.'

'Trent Barling. Ray, a house like this, there has to be a burglar alarm.'

'Key pad's on the wall next to the door.'

I looked and wondered how I'd missed it. My eyes must have gone straight to the heart of the crime scene. 'Four digits, right? One-one-one-one?'

'One-two-three-four.'

'That would have been my second choice.'

'So Mrs O. turned it off when she walked in the door, or just as likely she never armed it in the first place. According to her kids, she didn't always bother.'

'When the daughter let herself in—'

'It hadn't been reset.'

'But it may not have been set in the first place, so that doesn't tell us much, does it? She came in, she threw her coat on a chair. He's already here, and she smells peanuts on his breath and falls on the floor with an empty heart.'

'Could that happen?'

'I have no idea. But if she walks in on him, why does she pause to take off her coat? Ray, it's hard to make sense out of this.'

'No kiddin'.'

'She walks in, and he's already been here and gone. The place is a mess. "What a dump," she says, just like Bette Davis, and she shucks her coat, clears off a place on the rug, and collapses. No, that's crazy. I'm just wasting our time, Ray.'

'No, you're doin' good, Bern. Don't stop now.'

'She comes home, she's all alone, nobody's been here. If she ever did set the alarm, one-two-three-four, she disarms it. Walks in here, place is the way she left it. Takes off her coat, puts it on the chair. Is that how you'd lay down a coat, Ray? Wouldn't you straighten it out more?' I dropped to one knee. 'Unusual buttons. I think they're porcelain, or some kind of ceramic.'

'Whatever you say.'

'Very ornate. Art nouveau, I'd say. And one's missing. See? There used to be ten of them, five on the left and five on the right, and one's missing. It used to be right there.'

'Maybe it popped off at the opera house. Or in the cab.'

'There'd be broken thread where it came off. No thread, so I guess it's not a clue after all. It's probably been gone for months. And she wouldn't have been able to replace it, because where would she find a button to match?'

'You know, Bernie, when you and I get to be her age—'

'We'll probably be missing a few buttons ourselves. I just thought it might have gotten torn off in a struggle, but then there'd be thread, and there isn't, so forget the whole thing. She puts her coat down, and then she has an allergic reaction to something. What?'

'Maybe she ate something at the Met.'

'What, popcorn? They have operas there, not movies.'

117

'I bet you can buy snacks at intermission. Maybe she got the peanut M&Ms instead of the plain.'

'Maybe. It would help if we knew more about anaphylactic shock. Whatever it is, it comes on fast. Next thing she knows she's on the rug.'

'Next thing she knows, she's dead.'

'Does it work that fast? Maybe. She's there, she's dead, an hour goes by. If she's dead at ten and the opera's supposed to get out around midnight—'

'Then a burglar could show up at eleven and figure he's got plenty of time to go through the place.'

'Instead he walks in on a corpse. Now he's in a hurry, and he tosses the place, and finds it or doesn't, whatever it is.'

Outside on the stoop, I finally got a good look at the lock. I straightened up and told Ray that our intruder had a key.

'It wasn't forced,' I said. 'It's a good lock, it'd be tough to pick, and you'd probably leave scratches around the keyhole. And would you want to stand out there in plain sight poking around at a lock? I'll bet he had a key.'

'Maybe he made himself really small, Bernie.'

'And slithered through the keyhole? Didn't Plastic Man do that in the comics?'

'It sounds like something he'd pull, all right.'

'And what would he see when he did?'

I stepped inside for a minute, and the air freshener smell hit me anew, along with its undercurrent. What the hell was that? Not the smell of death and decomposition, which you'd expect, but something else.

'Bernie?'

'Oh, right,' I said, and returned to the stoop. '"Rats, I can't take the carpet, because somebody went and left a dead woman on it. I'll throw things around until I find something else to steal.'"

'You're hipped on that carpet, aren't you? Is it really good enough to steal?'

'You tell me. Doyle auctioned a Trent Barling a lot like this for something like twelve thousand. And it was smaller, nine by twelve, and this one has to be twelve by fifteen.'

'If you say so.'

'And that was four or five years ago, so if you want a ballpark figure—'

'Twenty grand?'

'Close enough. Of course you'd need two men and a van, and somebody to take it off your hands. So I think I'll pass. No, if I was going to walk off with something it'd be the little Chinese gentleman.'

'That ivory thing? It's valuable?'

'It could be,' I said. 'The carving's fine enough. But I don't know orientalia, and most of it's pretty reasonable, and I'd frankly be surprised if it's worth more than a few hundred dollars. No, I'd take it because I like it.'

'You'd take it and keep it.'

'And put it on a shelf, and have to remind myself to dust it. But it's nice. I wouldn't mind having it around just to look at.'

He was replacing the crime scene tape, and paused. 'You want it, Bernie? You could slip inside right now and put it in your pocket, and I bet I wouldn't notice a thing.'

'Um—'

'You just did me a favor,' he said, 'and it's unofficial, plus I broke all those rules bringin' you here in the first place. So the city can't pay you a consultant's fee, so why don't you take a China-man's chance and bring home a souvenir?'

'That's very thoughtful of you, Ray.'

'Hey, it's not like it's costing me anything.'

'Even so, I appreciate it. But I think I'll pass.'

He finished reattaching the tape, slipped the padlock in place. 'You sure, Bernie?'

I said I was, and he snapped the padlock shut.

SEVENTEEN

Ten minutes later we were pulling up across the street from my apartment building. 'You wouldn't take the ivory doodad,' Ray said, 'and now you won't let me buy you dinner. Makes it hard to balance the books.'

'I'm not hungry, Ray. And after last night I really want to make this an early one.'

'Then I guess I'll have to owe you one, Bernie. You did me a favor, even if you don't come up with anything. But if you get a brainstorm—'

'I'll let you know.'

Upstairs in my apartment, I spent ten minutes on the phone bringing Carolyn up to date and ten more in the shower, washing away of what had certainly felt a lot like burglary, even if I'd done it in Ray's company.

I put on khakis and a blazer, this one from Bloomingdale's. (Would it have made a difference if Janine had known I owned more than one blazer? Probably not.) I made another phone call, and this time I had to check the number, because I had never dialed it before. It went straight to voicemail, and the message was generic, inviting me to leave a number.

But I didn't. Instead I got my tools from my hidey hole, stuck a pair of pliofilm gloves in my hip pocket, and went out in the hall to ring for the elevator.

But when it came I didn't get in, and when the doors had shut I went over and knocked on Mrs Hesch's door. No response. I could hear her TV, but sometimes she dozed off in front of it, and I didn't want to disturb her. I was about to turn when I heard the pitter patter of little old feet.

'So?'

'It's Bernie,' I said.

As far as I know, Mrs Hesch is the only one in the building who knows I have a second career. It's my good fortune that she's not bothered by it. As far as she's concerned, I live on the west side and prey exclusively upon the rich momsers on the east side, and what's so bad about that? Besides, I'm useful to have around, especially when she locks herself out.

'So,' she said again, drew the door open. 'I don't suppose you want to borrow a cup of chicken fat.'

'No, but I'd like to look out your window.'

'What's out my window?'

'I won't know until I look.'

'Ah,' she said, and stood aside. My own apartment is in the back, and Mrs Hesch, across the hall from me, looks out on West End Avenue. And a moment later so did I, from her living room window.

'So what do you see?'

'Nothing,' I said.

'This is good?'

'It's what I was hoping for,' I said. 'And what I expected, because why would he hang around? I guess I was just being paranoid.'

'What I always say,' she said, 'is you never know, and a person can't be too paranoid. You in a rush, Bernard? You got time for a piece of flanken?'

'I wish,' I said. 'But I've really got to go. Can I take a rain check?'

'Who knows? Maybe I'll eat it myself.'

This time when the elevator came I boarded it, but Mrs Hesch's words rang in my head. I rode it down past the lobby to the basement and let myself out the rear service entrance, mounted the steps to the rear courtyard, and made my circuitous way out to the street.

A person can't be too paranoid.

EIGHTEEN

They've been doing a lot of work on the subways lately, in a heroic effort to bring a late nineteenth-century system into the twenty-first century. The long-awaited Second Avenue subway is a work in progress, and likely to remain so for the next thirty years, while the lines that actually exist are having more work done than an aging beauty queen.

They're thoughtful enough to do this work at night, and after ten o'clock some local trains stop running, and some express trains run on local tracks, and some people take taxis who'd otherwise save the money, while others wind up in Midwood when they were hoping for Parkchester.

But it was just a little after nine when I got to the corner of Broadway and 72nd, so I had nothing to worry about. Not, that is, until I got off the One train at Sheridan Square.

That put me a few minutes from Carolyn's apartment on Arbor

Court, but that's not where I was going, nor did I look for her in any of her regular watering holes. Instead I headed for Testinudo's, where Janine and I had dined so well, if at such expense. I hadn't eaten since breakfast, and if I'd been a cat I'd be treating my owner to an ankle rub, but I wasn't on my way to dinner, either.

The house I was looking for was on the opposite side of the street from the restaurant, and twenty or thirty yards closer to Fifth Avenue. It was a brownstone, originally built to house a single family. Now it accommodated four in as many floor-through apartments, with the half-basement given over to a dealer in oriental antiques. The shop was closed for the night, but I took a moment to wonder what its proprietor would make of the little ivory gentleman I'd so admired on East 92nd Street.

I walked past the brownstone and continued past Testinudo's to University Place, where I chose a pizza parlor over a deli. I ordered a small pie with garlic, and the aroma (which was one of the reasons I'd picked it) wafted up out of my other reason, the unmistakable flat cardboard box.

What's less suspicious than a man bringing home a pizza?

The brownstone's entrance was half a flight up from the street. You didn't need a key for the door to the vestibule, where four mailboxes were mounted on the wall to my left, each with a name-plate and a little button to push, so the occupant could confirm over the intercom that your presence was an agreeable prospect, and buzz you in.

The third mailbox said Wattrous, and it was Melville Wat-trous whose number I'd dialed before leaving my apartment. If Mr Smith was to be believed, Melville and Cynthia Wattrous were chasing the midnight sun on a Seabourn cruise of northern waters. They'd be gone for another week, their yellow lab was at a kennel that cost almost as much as their stateroom, and their third-floor apartment was vacant.

But that hadn't stopped me from making the phone call, and it didn't stop me now from ringing the bell, and waiting a moment, and ringing it again. A friend, using their place during their absence, might have been instructed to let phone calls go to voice-mail, but would he feel obliged to ignore the doorbell?

No answer. The lock was what you'd expect, and I couldn't have opened it all that much faster if I'd had a key. I climbed two flights of stairs, one hand on the serpentine banister, the other gripping the pizza box. I hadn't seen or heard anyone since I entered the vestibule, nor did anyone make an appearance now, so I'd probably wasted a few minutes and as many dollars on my camouflage, but one does like to do things right.

The door to the apartment had a trio of locks, and they were all good ones. There was a Fox police lock, the kind you can't force because it employs a stout steel bar braced against the door. You have to turn the lock to move it, but if you've got the tools and the talent you can manage that without a key.

The other locks were a Rabson and a Poulard. The Rabson is a marvelous mechanism, and it's no slur on its good reputation to say I can open any model they ever made in no time at all. I've devoted a lot of time to it, I've given it a lot of study, and I know their complete line as well as old Leo Rabson himself ever did.

The Poulard is the one they advertise as pickproof. Well, most of the time it probably is.

It took me some time, standing there in front of the Wattrous door and working on the Wattrous locks. I'd have preferred being on the top floor, where no one going up or down the stairs could see me, but you have to play the cards you're dealt. I did hear a door open a flight below, and a brief conversation between the woman who lived there and the man who was going home to his family in Upper Montclair, New Jersey, and I held my breath while he went down the stairs and she went inside and closed the door, slamming it just a little harder than she needed to.

Then I opened the last lock, picked up my pizza box, and went inside.

According to my information, the Wattrouses had been gone for a little over a week. I could believe it. The most pervasive odor was the garlicky pizza smell I'd brought with me, but I could tell the air in that apartment had been there for a while, undisturbed by the opening of a window or door.

I'd closed the door upon entering, of course, and turned one of the locks. I blinked my flashlight a couple of times, found my way to a table lamp, and turned it on. Whatever light slipped past the living room drapes had better be nice and steady. That's less of an attention-getter than the dancing beam of a handheld flashlight.

And it left my hands free. They were gloved by now, so I could handle objects with impunity, should I feel the need to do so. But first I sank into the reading chair and got my bearings.

It was an oversized leather recliner, and I called it the reading chair because that was so obviously its *raison d'etre*. In another setting it could have played another role; plant it in front of a flat-screen TV among a patchwork of college pennants and football jerseys, and the only reading done within its embrace would be the ESPN news crawl at the bottom of the frame.

But if Melville Wattrous even owned a television set, he must have confined it to the back bedroom. Built-in bookcases took all the wall space on either side of the living room fireplace. Books filled them from floor to ceiling, and the rest of the room held their overflow – on tabletops between bookends, in rotating book-cases serving as side tables, and, in the absence of suitable surfaces, stacked on the floor beside a table or next to a chair or simply piled in a corner.

Was the fellow a customer of mine? He almost had to be, because how could a man with such a passion for books have lived five minutes from my shop without once crossing its threshold?

Melville Wattrous. I couldn't recall hearing the name before Mr Smith spoke it just a few hours ago, and it was distinctive enough (unlike, say, Smith) to have earned shelf space in my mind. If he'd been my customer, he'd never introduced himself, never tendered a check in payment.

Still, most of my business is cash, and most of my customers never have occasion to tell me their names. A framed photo might have settled the matter, but books took up the space where photos might have stood.

I'll tell you, it was hard to leave the embrace of that chair. I worked the lever to make it recline, and the footrest promptly ascended, taking my feet with it. My eyes closed of their own accord, and I felt all the tensions of the day draining out of me, and—

No. If they included an owner's manual with every set of burglar's tools, one of the first tips it would give you would be that you stay awake throughout the commission of a burglary. One ought never to nod off *in media res*.

I got up and went to work.

If you want to hide a book, or even if you don't, there's no place like a bookcase. If you think a needle in a haystack's likely to be elusive, imagine sifting through the thing looking for a piece of hay. And not just any piece of hay, mind you. A particular piece of hay, distinct from its fellows however much it may look quite like them . . .

And it would have been easier, I have to say, if the object in question had not been a book among books, and I a bookman myself. Here I was, trying to work my way through the hundreds of volumes as quickly as possible, and feeling like a ten-year-old with ADD who'd skipped his morning dose of Ritalin. I couldn't just dismiss a book from my consciousness when it failed to be the one I was seeking. I had to read each title and take note of each author and remember what I knew about the book and its author and recall if I'd ever handled that title, or other books by that author, and whether or not this particular volume might once have graced my shelves, and—

Hell.

What I longed to do, of course, was approach this library as if I'd been invited to appraise it. And that meant picking up and examining every book that caught me eye. Take this copy of *Of Mice and Men*, for example. It's a first edition, and a glance at the copyright page tells us it's a first printing. But is it the first *state* of the first printing? The press run was interrupted so that a change might be made in the text; in the first chapter, a sentence in the description of Lenny ends with the clause *and his heavy hands were pendula*. Perhaps an early reader or reviewer didn't know that pendula is the plural of pendulum, perhaps Steinbeck himself had another look at the proofs and decided that the phrase was, well, at least as heavy-handed as Lenny himself. In any event, the phrase was duly expunged before the press resumed operations.

Now John Steinbeck's less highly regarded these days (though I don't know why), and not that many people collect him, and for those who do, *Of Mice and Men* has never been a particularly difficult book. The early novels – *Cup of Gold*, *To a God Unknown* – are thin on the ground, and *In Dubious Battle* can be elusive, but *Mice* is all over the place, and you wouldn't have to take out a second mortgage to secure a pristine first-state-first-printing specimen, with a nice dust jacket.

And this copy didn't even have a dust jacket, nice or otherwise, and in other respects was a long way from pristine. It had been put to the use for which it was intended – i.e., people had actually read it – and thus wouldn't grade higher than, say, very good to fine.

So why did I have to leaf through the first chapter searching for heavy hands?

Not there. It wasn't a first state. I put it back where I'd found it, which was precisely what I'd have done if poor Lenny's hands had been as pendulous as anyone could possibly want them to be.

Of making many books there is no end. It says so right there in the Book of Ecclesiastes, and you get the feeling the fellow sighed as he wrote the line. Well, do you think looking at books is any different?

Did it take that long? I don't suppose it did, not really. I kept getting distracted, and I kept pushing the distractions aside and scanning the titles of the books in front of me. I still had to give everything a glance, because while Wattrous (or perhaps Mrs Wattrous) had tried to impose order upon the library, the organizational scheme kept breaking down.

The book I was seeking was non-fiction, so when I hit a stretch of novels I thought I could speed ahead, but then I ran into Maeterlinck's classic *The Life of the Bee* wedged between Evelyn Waugh's *A Handful of Dust* and Michael Arlen's *The Green Hat.* And *The Life of the Ant*, frequently mentioned in the same breath with *The Life of the Bee*, was one shelf down, bracketed by two early novels of William Faulkner. I'm sure Melville Wattrous would have said he knew where everything was and could lay hands on any volume at a moment's notice, but right about then he was somewhere between Tromso and Longyearbyen, so I had to manage this on my own.

And then there it was, the object of my quest, and I took it gently from its shelf. It was a small volume, just six inches tall and four inches wide, and bound in dark blue cloth, with the author and title stamped on the spine in small gold letters.

I sat down with it and opened to the title page. *Thomas Baird Culloden*, I read. *My Adventures with Colonial Silver.* I turned the page and confirmed that it had been privately printed at the Lattimore Press in Waterbury, Connecticut, in 1898.

There were only two hundred pages, but it had been printed on coated stock and was a little over an inch thick. Consequently its removal had left an inch-wide gap in the wall of books, and I took a moment to search a stack on the floor for a same-size volume to take its place.

I couldn't think of anything else I needed to do. I'd had my gloves on throughout, so there were no prints to wipe, nor would I be giving anyone reason to look for them. It was time to take my book and go home.

But how to carry it? I own a pair of chinos with cargo pockets, and it could have gone in one of those, but tonight's chinos were dressier, and the pockets would strain at a rack-size paperback. I could slip the book under my waistband, letting my blazer cover it, but I didn't want to do that, nor did I want to walk out with the bare book in my hand.

Everybody has paper and plastic bags in their kitchen, and I chose a Gristede's shopping bag. And while I was there I could hardly avoid remembering that I hadn't eaten since breakfast. I opened the refrigerator, but of course they'd left it empty before departure.

Rats.

And then I remembered the pizza.

When I left, I was carrying T. B. Culloden's book in the Gristede's bag, and I had an empty pizza box under one arm. On my way out I set up the police lock's steel bar, and took time to undo all my earlier work, turning each cylinder and locking all three locks. I went down the stairs, paused in the vestibule to transfer my gloves from my hands to my pockets, and went out into the night.

I turned left when I hit the street and left again at University Place, heading uptown. I dropped the pizza box in the first trash can I came to and the gloves in the second. At Eleventh Street I considered walking half a block and leaving the book at my store. What better place to hide a book than a bookshop?

But did I want really want to unlock my door at that hour? I had every right to do so, I was the store's lawful sole proprietor, but would I enjoy proving as much to a suspicious patrolman? And he'd have the right to stop and frisk me, even if I was neither young nor black, and what would he make of the flashlight and burglar's tools?

I had the Gristede's bag in one hand. I held up the other one, and hailed a taxi.

NINETEEN

'Juneau Lock!'

'Music to my ears,' I told her, wondering what sense the words would make to her. Not that I was required to say anything. She was already dishing out whatever today's treat might be, filling a couple of containers with something that smelled dangerously wonderful.

'Ver' spicy,' she said, shaking her head in mock warning. 'Juneau Lock spicy.'

'We love spicy.'

A smile lit up her face, and the whole room along with it. She was a slip of a girl, her face a perfect oval, her features as dainty and delicate as, well, a china doll. The shapeless smock she wore kept me from knowing what her figure was like, and it seemed to me that I was better off in my ignorance.

She was really adorable. Carolyn had assured me she wasn't

interested in girls, and that left boys, and if only we had a language in common I might have made an effort. But all I did was pay for the food, and we smiled and giggled at each other, and I walked out wondering how difficult it would be for me to learn Mandarin.

Or did she speak Taiwanese? There were people all over town advertising Mandarin lessons, but I couldn't recall any listings in Craigslist offering to teach you how to ask directions in Taipei. But didn't the Taiwanese all know how to speak Mandarin, the way the Scots all know how to speak English?

Maybe, come to think of it, just a little more comprehensibly than Scots speaking English . . .

'Juneau Lock,' Carolyn said. 'And just in time, because I'm starving. I didn't realize I was hungry until I got a whiff of the food. How come it always smells different, and yet it's always recognizably Juneau Lock?'

'That's one of life's mysteries,' I said.

'And the list keeps getting longer, doesn't it? Mmm, this does smell terrific.'

'Even better than pizza.'

'Is that what you were thinking of bringing today?'

'Never crossed my mind.'

'It can cross your mind,' she said, 'just so long as it keeps right on walking. This is a much better idea than pizza. Not that there's anything wrong with pizza, but there's a time and a place for it.'

We ate for a few minutes in silence, too involved with the food to talk, and then she asked why I'd mentioned pizza at all.

'Because of last night,' I said. 'You know what they tell people in National Parks? "Take only snapshots, leave only footprints." Last night I visited somebody a few blocks from here, and I don't think I left any footprints, but I did leave the smell of pizza.'

'And you didn't take snapshots,' she said, after I'd filled her in. 'You took a book and you left an odor.'

'I prefer to think of it as an aroma.'

'By the time they get back, Bern, it'll be too faint to notice. Or they'll think it came in from the street. Especially with no other evidence that anyone was in there while they were gone. But even if you left a note on the kitchen table, "Thanks for your hospitality, I had a great time in your apartment," would they be able to tell they'd been burgled?'

'Only if he missed the book,' I said.

'You think it's one of his favorites? Is colonial silver a big passion for Mel?'

I hadn't seen any silver, colonial or otherwise. 'I'm not sure he ever read it. His book-buying habits are all over the map. There's a lot of fiction, along with a whole lot of history. He's got Motley's *Rise of the Dutch Republic*, Trevelyan's three-volume *England Under Queen Anne*, Oman's *Britain Before the Norman Conquest*. A fair number of biographies. Natural history – he's got Archie Carr's definitive work on the turtles and tortoises of North America, side by side with *The Burgess Bird Book for Children*.'

'I had that book when I was a kid! And the one about animals.'

'The companion volume, both of them by Thornton W. Burgess.'

'I remember the names of the characters, Bern. Jenny Wren, Jerry Muskrat.'

'Billy Mink.'

'Right, Billy Mink! I haven't thought of Billy Mink in years. He was a mean little bastard, wasn't he? I loved those books. I wonder whatever happened to them.'

'Your mother gave them to the rummage sale,' I said. 'Like my comic books.'

'That must have been some rummage sale. A whole room full of childhood memories.'

We speculated on what else might be in that enormous room, and Carolyn guessed that the Burgess volume in Wattrous's library was his own copy from childhood, one that his mother had failed to purge. I said that was likely, as he still had his Oz books, and that sent Carolyn into a long riff on Frank Baum's fantasy world, and how she longed to go there.

'I got my hopes up,' she said, 'every time the winds reached forty miles an hour. I kept bugging my parents to move us to a house in Kansas.'

'You'd stand a better chance in a trailer park,' I pointed out.

'I guess. Bern, the book you took, I forget the author's name.'

'Culloden.'

'It's real valuable?'

'What it is,' I said, 'is extremely rare. It's never been reprinted, and none of the rare-book sites on the Internet have a listing. A few university libraries have copies, and for all I know there's one nobody knows about at the bottom of a box in the Galtonbrook basement.'

'Along with the last two movements of Schubert's Unfinished Symphony.'

'And the rest of *Kublai Khan*, and Dickens's solution to *The Mystery of Edwin Drood*. I had a look at Culloden's book. The writing's hard to get through, but I guess there's some good information there, if the fine points of American colonial silver is what keeps you up nights. And there's a whole section of plates illustrating noteworthy examples from the author's own collection. Which must have been something, before it was dispersed after his death in 1901.'

'That wasn't too long after he published his book.'

'Just three years. You asked if the book was valuable. The

answer's got to be yes, but it's hard to put a value on it. There's virtually no supply, but how much demand is there? It might sit on my bargain table for days without anybody giving it a second glance. Or two people who wanted it could show up at the same auction and bid the price up into four or five figures. But it's not going to wind up on my bargain table, or on the auction block, either.'

'I guess Mr Smith will give it a good home.'

'Not a chance,' I said. 'What would he want with it?'

An hour later I was back at Barnegat Books, looking at the sheet of paper on which I'd practiced my penmanship. I wadded it up, and the sound the paper made got Raffles's attention. I gave it a toss, and he pursued it and pounced.

If he'd been a dog he'd have brought it back, and I could have tossed it again. But he's a cat, and he did what cats do. He batted it around a few times, decided it was dead, recognized it as inedible, and left it there, returning to the sunny spot in the window.

I picked it up myself and dropped it in the wastebasket. Then I returned to my perch behind the counter and picked up the phone. When a woman told me I'd reached Edwin Leopold's residence, I asked to speak with Mr Leopold. She asked for a name, and I had one ready and gave it to her.

The phone clicked, and I was on Hold, our world's version of Limbo. At least there was no music, just silence, and it only lasted for a matter of seconds before she clicked back to ask what my call was in reference to.

'I'm a bookman,' I said. 'I've just acquired an item that I believe might interest Mr Leopold.'

'One moment, please.' *Click!*

It was a longer moment than the first one, but then there was another click, followed by a man's voice, speaking slowly in the

Old New York accent you don't hear much anymore, resonant with culture and good manners. It drew me back into that Childe Hassam painting of Central Park in winter, and carriage rides, and dinners at Delmonico's.

'This is Edwin Leopold,' he said. 'I'm afraid I didn't get your name.'

'It's Philip Lederer,' I said, 'although there's no reason you should know it, Mr Leopold. I'm taking the liberty of calling you because I've come into the possession of a book I've reason to believe might interest you.'

'So Miss Miller said. I'm not a book collector, sir, although I do have a small and highly specialized library. But why don't you tell me the name of this volume.'

'It's Culloden's work on colonial silver,' I said. 'That would be Thomas Baird Culloden, and—'

'Yes, of course,' he said. 'You actually have a copy in hand?'

'It's in front of me right now.'

'*Adventures With Colonial Silver*. No, I've got that wrong. *My Adventures With Colonial Silver*. There's a copy in the library of Trinity College in Hartford. Culloden's alma mater, he presented them with a copy and they seem to have kept it. They wouldn't be persuaded either to sell it to me or to have it photocopied. They said I'd be welcome to examine it on their premises. Well, that of course was out of the question. Your copy is sound, Mr Lederer?'

'Easily very fine. There's no dust jacket, but—'

'I wouldn't think there was one, would you? A private printing for private distribution? No need for a wrapper to prevent its getting shopworn if it was never to see the inside of a shop. The pages are all there?'

'Yes.'

'And the plates? Collotype plates, and there should be twenty-four pages of them.'

'They're all here.' I drew a breath. 'And there's an inscription.'

'Always unfortunate,' he said, 'but nothing one can't live with. *Happy Christmas to Celestine from Aunt Mary* – something along those lines, I would suppose.'

'*To Hester R. Longbranch*,' I read, '*to whose illustrious ancestor all of us owe so much.* And it's signed with his initials, T. B. C. I can only assume they're his initials, and that it's in his hand, although I can't verify the latter.'

'It would have to be,' he said. 'Hester R. Longbranch. The middle initial stands for Revere, her illustrious ancestor. Who else but Culloden could have written that inscription? He was honoring one of our greatest patriots, and surely colonial America's foremost silversmith. There's another for whom I have a special affection, but one cannot deny Paul Revere's greater prominence.'

'I don't know anything about silver,' I said. 'He's certainly the one I've heard of. One if by land and all that.'

'"Ready to ride and spread the alarm, To every Middlesex village and farm." Have you placed a price on your book, Mr Lederer?'

'I thought a thousand dollars.'

'A nice round sum. Hardly cheap for a volume no one's ever heard of, but not unreasonable for one on which no one's ever laid eyes. I'd want to see the book.'

'Of course.'

'I don't know what you may know about me, but I never leave my residence. I wish I could, but it's impossible. I could send Miss Miller, but could I ask you to hand a valuable book over to her? Of course she could bring you a check, or even cash, with the understanding that the book can be returned if it turns out to be unacceptable. Though I'm sure it will be just as you describe it, and I'll be pleased to keep it. How does that sound?'

Cumbersome, I thought, and not at all what I had in mind.

I said, 'I'll bring the book to you, Mr Leopold. I'm tied up for the rest of the afternoon, but I could come this evening. Say nine o'clock?'

After I'd ended the call, I had another look at the inscription on the book's flyleaf. *To Hester R. Longbranch* . . .

Who else but Culloden could have written those words? Well, I could, prompted by my man Smith, who'd jotted them down for me. I'd used a calligrapher's stylus and India ink, and copied them out in the Palmer Method penmanship Miss Rukeyser had drilled into me all those years ago. Wouldn't the woman be proud of me now?

Well, probably not, given the circumstances.

I picked up the phone, made another call. 'I'm seeing him tonight,' I said.

'Oh, good. One doesn't want these matters to drag out. Though he could hardly have said he'd be out, could he? Did he ask the price?'

'I told him a thousand dollars.'

'I rather think he'd have been persuaded to pay a bit more than that. Not that it makes any difference to me. Whatever he pays you is yours to keep. I did tell you that, didn't I?'

Indeed he had. Among other things . . .

TWENTY

It was the previous afternoon when Mr Smith had paid what I guess was his third visit to Barnegat Books. This time he wore a three-button suit of a medium-gray flannel over a red vest of what looked like silk, but may have been rayon. His tie was a lighter gray than his suit, with red polka dots. His shirt was white broadcloth, with a button-down collar.

He asked me if I knew anything about apostle spoons.

'Unless they're what Peter and Paul used to eat their porridge,' I said, 'I haven't got a clue. Why?'

'This may take a while,' he said, 'and we wouldn't want to be interrupted. There's a coffee shop on University Place that's relatively quiet at this hour.'

'It's always quiet,' I said. 'The food is lousy.'

'And are the portions small?' He drew a familiar envelope

from his pocket. 'To make it worth your while,' he said, 'to miss an hour's business.'

If it held hundreds, like his previous envelopes, then it felt like $5000. Even if they were singles, the next hour was well covered. I put the envelope away without checking its contents, turned the sign in the door from OPEN to CLOSED, locked up, but left the window gates open and the bargain table out on the sidewalk. Let them rob me blind for an hour. What did I care?

'May I ask you something?'

We had cups of coffee in front of us, and our slack-jawed waitress was out of hearing range. He nodded, and I asked him about the ¾-inch brass disc attached to his lapel.

'It's a button,' he said, and tugged one edge to show me that it was sewn to the fabric.

'What's the image?' I leaned closer. 'It looks like a little house.'

'A log cabin, and I'm not wearing it to indicate membership in the Log Cabin Republicans. It's a campaign button.'

'I've never seen one like it.'

'That's because you weren't old enough to vote in 1840. It was distributed to promote the candidacy of William Henry Harrison, hero of the battle of Tippecanoe.'

'And Tyler, too,' I said.

'John Tyler of Virginia was his running mate, and very shortly his successor. Old Tippecanoe delivered an inaugural address of which nothing was recalled later but its inordinate length. They swore in presidents in March in those days, not in January, but it was still very much winter that day in Washington, and the new president caught his death of cold.'

'That rings a bell.'

'He was born in a log cabin,' he said, 'of which his Whig supporters made much. Hence the image on the button.'

'You were wearing something similar before.'

'I would think so. Which suit was I wearing, do you recall?'

I had to think. 'Your suit was dark, with a chalk stripe,' I said, 'but that was the first time I met you. The next time you were wearing a Norfolk jacket.'

'And each lapel bore a button. You're an observant man, Mr Rhodenbarr. And indeed they were different buttons.'

'I guess they'd have to be, since they're sewn in place.'

'The one on the suit,' he said, 'is the same size as this one. The image is that of a plumed knight.' I thought of the man in the Galtonbrook's Rembrandt, until he added, 'It supports the 1884 Republican candidacy of James Blaine, who lost a very close election to Grover Cleveland. His supporters called him The Plumed Knight. The Cleveland crowd disagreed. "Blaine, Blaine, James G. Blaine," they chanted, "the highfalutin' liar from the state of Maine."'

'Politics was so much kinder and gentler back then.'

'The Norfolk jacket, Mr Rhodenbarr, is credited to an otherwise unremarkable Duke of Norfolk, although it is almost certainly his unremembered tailor whose design it was. "Be nice if you could make me one with a belt," His Grace may have mused, so perhaps it was indeed his inspiration. And the one you saw me wearing was the genuine article, in that the buttons which close the belt in the back may be undone, then refastened after the belt's been brought around to the front.'

'I always thought the belt was just for decoration.'

'And so it is,' he said, 'because all fastening the belt in front does is make one look foolish. The Duke would seem to have been a fop, and a ninny in the bargain, yet his jacket has established itself over time as a classic. Do you suppose there's a lesson there?'

I said it wouldn't surprise me.

'The button attached to my Norfolk jacket is also of brass, and

larger than the others, almost twice the diameter of Old Tippecanoe's log cabin. Did you note the image?'

'I couldn't make it out.'

'It's over two centuries old, and while it hardly circulated like a
coin, I'm afraid it sustained some wear over the years. Still, at close
range it's easy enough to make out the image and lettering. The
central figure is an eagle, its wings spread, a star above its head, its
breast bearing the shield of the United States. The surrounding
legend proclaims "March the Fourth 1789 Memorable Era."'

'March 4, 1789 . . .'

'The inauguration of our first president at the beginning of his
first term. Did I describe these curiosities as campaign buttons?
That's true of the others, but Washington never campaigned. A
memorable era indeed. Politics actually was kinder and gentler
back then, albeit briefly, and the presidency was Washington's
for the taking. So mine is properly described as an inauguration
button.'

I said, 'When I think of political buttons—'

'You picture the sort they hand out today, all bright colors
and photographs, with a loop of wire at the back enabling one
to pin it in place. Pin-back buttons have predominated since
McKinley's first face-off with Bryan in 1896. But political clothing buttons lasted in a small way for another half century. I own
a brass button with a bear on it. You can probably guess the
candidate.'

'A Teddy bear? Theodore Roosevelt?'

'Quite right, but how about a possum?'

'A possum. That was George Jones's nickname, the country
singer, but I don't believe he ever ran for office.'

'I might have voted for him if he did,' Smith said. 'But the button's for William Howard Taft, evidently known to some of his
admirers as Billy Possum.'

'He was? Do you happen to know why?'

'No idea. I have a matched set of four clothing buttons from the 1932 election, bearing photos of Herbert and Marion Hoover and Franklin and Eleanor Roosevelt. And there's a clothing button from 1948 with Harry Truman's photo, and—' He stopped in mid-sentence, frowned. 'I'm telling you far more than you need to know. More than anyone needs to know.'

'It's interesting.'

'Every passion is interesting to him who suffers from it. And one sometimes feels impelled to inflict it on others.'

'Political campaign buttons you can sew on your clothes,' I said. 'I never knew such things existed. Do you collect the other sort as well? With the pins?'

'Pin-back buttons. Yes, of course, and they constitute the great bulk of my collection. I'm especially fond of third-party buttons. Debs is my favorite, Eugene Victor Debs. He was the standard-bearer for the Socialist Party in four consecutive elections from 1900 through 1912. A man named Benson took over in 1916, but in 1920 Debs was back again. He was serving a prison term for opposing the war, and his campaign button reads "For President: Convict No. 9563." And just under a million voters chose him over Harding and Cox.'

Something clicked.

'Buttons,' I said.

'Yes, and I can't seem to stop nattering on about them, can I? I do apologize.'

'Benjamin Button. Well, why else would you collect that particular story? You don't think much of its author and you're openly contemptuous of the story itself, but you paid me handsomely to spirit the manuscript out of a museum basement. And why? All because of the character's surname. If Fitzgerald had called him Zachary Zipper, he'd be nothing to you.'

'Or to Brad Pitt, I suspect. The name Benjamin Button does have a nice ring to it.'

'What's the matter with Zachary Zipper? Never mind. Are political buttons the only sort you collect? They're not, are they?'

He smiled. 'I have all types of buttons, Mr Rhodenbarr. If an article may be called a button, I'm apt to take an interest in it. Do you know of that curious subset of London Cockneys called the Pearlies? They favor clothing thoroughly festooned with pearl buttons; if those buttons were rhinestones, they could be Elvis impersonators. I own the costumes worn by the couple who reigned as King and Queen of the Pearlies in 1987.'

'Was that a particularly good year for Pearlies?'

'Vintage, I'd say. Do you like comedy albums, Mr Rhodenbarr?'

'You mean like record albums?'

'A curious phenomenon,' he said. 'Pay the price and you can own in permanent form the routine you paid not a penny to watch George Carlin or Steve Martin perform on TV. So that you can repeat the experience over and over? I suppose people bought them to entertain visitors. It saves having to force conversation when you can treat your guests to somebody else's wit and wisdom. I own one comedy album myself. Can you guess what it might be?'

I had a hunch he'd tell me.

'It's by Bob Newhart. It was his first album, recorded during a live performance in Houston, and it went straight to the top of the Billboard chart when Warner's released it in May of 1960. It's still funny all these years later.'

'I heard it years ago,' I said. 'There was a bit about a warship with an odd name.'

'*The Cruise of the USS Codfish.* And a routine where a marketing type is explaining to Abner Doubleday why baseball can't possibly catch on with the American public. Do you remember the album's title?'

I didn't.

'Newhart wanted to call it *The Most Celebrated New Comedian Since Attila the Hun*, but the chaps at Warner's had something they liked better. *The Button-Down Mind of Bob Newhart.*'

'That's right. I remember now.'

'It was such a great popular success that even now it's not hard to find a copy. Mine's a little special. It's signed by Newhart, of course, but what makes it particularly desirable is that it's inscribed to Jack Paar, who was hosting the *Tonight Show* at the time.'

'You always wear shirts with button-down collars,' I realized. 'Well, I've only met you three times, so I don't know about "always," but—'

'Always,' he said.

'Buttons,' I said. 'Why buttons?'

'Ah, always the beautiful question. But not the one you should be asking at the moment.'

'And what would that be?'

'It's a two-parter,' he said. 'What on earth are apostle spoons? And how do they come into the picture?'

TWENTY-ONE

You know what a spoon is, right?

An apostle spoon is one with its handle terminating in the figure of one of the twelve apostles. Since relatively few photographs of the Last Supper survive, each likeness is rendered identifiable by the presence of a particular emblem linked to that apostle. An X-shaped cross for St Andrew, a pilgrim's staff for St James the Greater, an axe for St Matthew, a cup (the cup of sorrow) for St John, and so on, all the way down to a bag of money for Judas Iscariot. St Peter gets a sword or a key, or sometimes a fish. (St James the Lesser gets a fuller's bat on his spoon, but don't ask me what a fuller's bat looks like, or how James felt about being designated the lesser of two apostles.)

Apostle spoons originated in Europe in the early 1400s, and were always a safe choice if you needed a present for a godchild.

Just get a local silversmith to turn one out with the likeness of the child's patron saint, and St Robert's your uncle.

(Look, if you already know all this, skip ahead. It was all news to me. I kept interrupting Mr Smith with questions, and a verbatim report of our conversation would take more space than I want to give it. I'm just summing it up here, but my feelings won't be hurt if you choose not to read every precious word.)

While an individual spoon might be made as an individual gift, they were more often produced in sets, sometimes of twelve but more often of thirteen. The thirteenth spoon, often larger than its fellows, was the Master, and depicted Jesus, with a cross and orb as his symbol. (There's an early sixteenth-century set in the British Museum, with the thirteenth spoon showing the Virgin Mary.)

Tableware was more important to folks back in the day, even if most of what they got to eat wasn't all that tasty. Precious metal, generally silver but sometimes gold, was how one kept one's wealth – and showed it off at the same time. You couldn't tuck away extra cash in a Roth IRA, or buy shares of Renaissance.com, and if you engaged someone to paint your portrait, it was so your descendants would know what you looked like, not in the hope that your likeness would appreciate in value.

It would have been tacky to keep bags of coin lying around, and a temptation to servants. So you put your wealth on display in the form of bowls and plates and chargers – and in your forks and spoons, some of which might be piously ornamented with the images and emblems of holy men.

If you were prosperous enough to own a set of apostle spoons, you'd very likely make special mention of them in your will. One Amy Brent did so in 1516, though I couldn't tell you to whom she bequeathed them, or what's become of them since. (If they wound up in the basement of the Galtonbrook, I never saw them.)

Beaumont and Fletcher, the Kaufman and Hart of their day,

mentioned such spoons in at least one of their plays, as did Ben Jonson, Thomas Middleton, and a fellow named Shakespeare in *Henry VIII*. (Act Five, Scene Three. Bishop Cranmer tries to weasel out of serving as sponsor for young Elizabeth, claiming he can't afford it. 'You could spare your spoons,' Henry tells him.)

More than you needed to know, huh? Well, look at it this way. If I had to hear it, and at greater length and with more detail than I've rendered it here, why should you get off easy?

TWENTY-TWO

When I returned to my bookshop, my bargain table was where I'd left it. No one had walked off with it. Nor, as far as I could tell, had any of its contents gone astray.

Books, I thought. Nobody even wants to steal them these days.

In fact, I found, there was more on my table than there'd been when I left it there. A note, carefully block-printed on a small sheet of lined white paper, its three jagged holes indicating it had been torn from a notebook. WHY ARE YOU ALWAYS CLOSED?

Well, I'm open now, I thought. And took the note into the shop with me.

A day had passed since then, plus an hour or so. I was closed again, and sitting across the table from Carolyn.

'Perrier,' she noted. 'Well, that answers that question.'

'What question?'

'The one I don't have to ask, because you already answered it. Question: What are you going to be doing tonight, Bern? Answer: Something criminal.'

'Am I?' I thought for a moment. 'Yes, I guess you'd have to say I am. On the one hand, I'm just visiting a gentleman at his invitation to sell him a book.'

'But since you're not the book's lawful owner—'

'Yeah, that's what makes it criminal. Although you could argue that it'd still be criminal if I'd come by the book honestly.'

'How do you figure that, Bern?'

'Well, this man I'm visiting.'

'Mr Leopold.'

'Edwin Leopold. He has something that Mr Smith wants.'

'And I suppose it would be too simple for Mr Smith to buy it from him.'

'It's not for sale.'

'And Smitty couldn't just send you there, the way he sent you to the Galtonbrook?'

'He didn't think I could get in.'

'Does he know whom he's dealing with here? Bernard Grimes Rhodenbarr, the man who could get into Fort Knox if he had to?'

'I'm just as glad I don't have to,' I said, 'although your faith in me is heartening.' I took a sip of bubbly French water. 'Edwin Leopold has one of the two penthouse apartments on the twenty-fourth floor of a brick building on Fifth Avenue and Eighty-fifth Street.'

'That's almost directly across the street from the Metropolitan, Bern. He must have some view.'

'I would think so.'

'He could look down on the museum and all of Central Park.

152

How tall are the buildings across from him on Central Park West? Could he see New Jersey?'

'I don't know,' I said, 'and I'm not sure why he would want to. But it's good he has a terrific view, because that's all he ever gets to see.'

'Because he doesn't leave his house.'

'So I understand.'

'You know, Bern, they've got wheelchairs these days that can just about make their way over a steeplechase course. And he's got someone working for him, doesn't he? The woman who answered his phone?'

'Miss Miller.'

'If he was going to send her to pick up the book, why couldn't he get her to take him for a walk in the park?'

'I don't know that he *can't* leave his house. I think it's more that he chooses not to.'

'Like Bartleby the scrivener?'

'"I would prefer not to." Yes, sort of like Bartleby.'

'Or like Nero Wolfe. He never leaves his house on business, but it's a different matter entirely if there's an orchid show he wants to check out. And didn't he go all the way to Montana in one book?'

'Was it Montana? Yes, I believe it was. But I also believe that it's different for Mr Leopold.'

'Business or pleasure, he stays put.'

'Right.'

'He's got his silver, the same as Wolfe has his orchids, but if they had an annual silver show at Madison Square Garden—'

'Our Mr Leopold would pass it up.'

'Well, then, it's good he's got his view, and a nice spacious apartment in a good building, and Miss Miller to take care of him. Is there a Mrs Leopold?'

'Not that I know of.'

153

'Does he have kids who visit him regularly?'

'Carolyn—'

'This is all stuff you don't know, huh?' She picked up her scotch, studied the melting ice cubes, took a drink. 'I suppose if you never get out, I mean absolutely never, it would be a comfort to be fixated on something.'

'In his case, early American silver.'

'Including a spoon,' she said, 'by one of the cops Ed McBain wrote about.'

A little earlier:

'Carolyn, have you ever heard of Myer Myers?'

'Of course.'

'You have?'

'You're surprised? Meyer Meyer, of the Eighty-seventh Precinct. There must have been fifty of the books, maybe more, and it seems to me he was in every single one of them, along with Steve Carella and Bert Kling and all the rest of those guys. Ed McBain wrote about them for fifty years.'

'I'm talking about Myer Myers.'

'Right,' she said, 'only you're getting the name wrong. There's no S on the end of it. It's Meyer Meyer.'

'No, it's—'

'Please,' she said, 'there's no end of things where you know more than me, Bern, but this is one of those rare times when I'm right and you're wrong, and I can prove it to you. Meyer Meyer was completely bald, right?'

I just looked at her.

'Not a hair on his head,' she went on. 'And do you know why?'

'Because of his father,' I said.

'Exactly. His father thought it would be a great joke, giving him the same name for a first name as he had for a last name, and of course all the kids teased him, the way kids do.'

'And that traumatized the kid,' I said, 'and his hair fell out.'

'Never to return. But do you remember what the kids used to chant at him?'

'Yes.'

'"Meyer Meyer, Jew on fire." You know what that sounds like?'

'"Liar liar, pants on fire"?'

'Exactly. That's probably what gave the little bastards the idea. I mean, kids aren't all that original. But if it was Meyer *Meyers*, the way you're insisting it was, then it'd have been "Meyer Meyers, Jew on fires," and what sense does that make?'

'Rather little,' I said.

'Well, there you go,' she said, and frowned. 'We're not talking about the same people.'

'No, we're not.'

'I'm talking about Meyer Meyer, a fictional cop, and you're talking about somebody else.'

'Myer Myers.'

'Who wasn't fictional at all.'

'He was a silversmith,' I said, 'born in 1723 right here in old New York. And I'd never heard of him myself until Mr Smith told me about him.'

And earlier still, in a really lousy diner on University Place:

'Myer Myers, Mr Rhodenbarr. Without question the most prominent Jewish silversmith in the American colonies. In fact, his ritual and secular silver is the largest body of extant work by a Jewish silversmith from anywhere in Europe or America prior to the nineteenth century.

'And a patriot. As you might imagine, wealthy Tories made up most of his customer base. Nevertheless, he supported the Revolution.

'In 1776, that pivotal year, Myers moved his business and his family to Norwalk, Connecticut, thinking it would put him out of harm's way. Three years later British troops burned the town. Myers lost his tools and his house, moved up the coast to Stratford, and didn't get back to New York until 1783 when the war was over.'

His business, I learned, was never what it had been. His more important customers tended to be rich people, and the rich are rather less likely to rally 'round the flag of revolution. The larger one's fortune, the less inclined one seems to be to pledge it (along with one's life and one's sacred honor) to abstractions like life, liberty, and the pursuit of happiness.

Samuel Cornell was one such Tory. For Cornell and his wife Susannah Mabson, Myers had fashioned a dish ring and bottle stands, whatever those may be, that remain the only surviving colonial examples thereof. Cornell had his property seized during the Revolution, and anyway by 1781 he had died, so Myers couldn't expect anything from him in the way of future commissions.

'But not every rich colonist remained loyal to King George,' Mr Smith said. 'The Livingston family was genuinely wealthy, and of staunchly republican sentiments. Among them was Henry Beekman Livingston.'

At the Bum Rap, Carolyn had finished one drink and started in on a second. I was still working on my first Perrier, and I'd just begun recounting what I'd learned about Livingston.

'I've heard of him, Bern. Dr Livingston I. Presume, right? He got lost in Africa, and Stanley Kubrick found him.'

'That was David Livingstone, with an E on the end, and Henry Morton Stanley. And it was a century later.'

'Oh,' she said.

Henry Beekman Livingston, I went on, was born in 1748 and

was thus twenty-eight years old when his kinsman Philip Livingston signed the Declaration of Independence. He'd married Sally
Wells in 1774, and he celebrated the birth of their first child by
joining the American Revolution. He held the rank of major, and
commanded the New York Regiment from 1776 to 1779.

In 1783, two years after Cornwallis surrendered at Yorktown,
Sally Livingston died. She'd borne four children, and left Henry
to raise them alone. In 1793 he married Jane Patterson, and had
four more children with her. He led a blameless life, as far as
anyone can tell, and he spent his time writing poetry while he
watched all those children grow up.

'Poetry? Was it any good, Bern?'

'He wrote mostly for his own amusement,' I said. 'And he
didn't publish much of anything, but there's one poem of his that
received a fair amount of attention. A lot of people know it, and
you're one of them.'

'I know a poem of his? Bern, a minute ago I mixed him up with
the guy who swam up the Congo and got lost. What makes you
think I know his poetry?'

'I'll quote the first two lines,' I said, 'and you let me know if it
rings a bell. "'Twas the night before Christmas / And all through
the house."'

'Bern, I know for a fact that was somebody else. He lived in
Chelsea, and there's a building there with a plaque on it, and I can
come up with his name if you give me a minute.'

'I'm sure you can.'

'Moore,' she said. 'That's his name. One of them, anyway.
Something Something Moore.'

'Clement Clarke Moore.'

'That's the guy. He wrote *'Twas the Night Before Christmas*,
except the actual title was something else.'

'*A Visit From Saint Nicholas*.'

'There you go. He just about invented Christmas, if you stop and think about it. He was the one who named the reindeer. Of course he didn't know about Rudolph, but he got all the others right.'

'All true,' I agreed. 'Except it was actually Henry Beekman Livingston who wrote the poem. The names of the reindeer were those of the horses in Henry's stable. Do you remember *Primary Colors*, the political novel published by Anonymous a while back?'

'Of course I do. I hope you're not going to tell me Henry Livingston wrote that one, too. Because everybody knows who wrote it. Joe Klein wrote it.'

'And do you remember who outed Joe Klein?'

'Some guy who analyzed the text. It was pretty interesting the way he worked it out. But I don't remember his name.'

'It was Donald Foster.'

'I'll take your word for it, Bern.'

'And the same Donald Foster ran the same kind of textual analysis of *A Visit From Saint Nicholas*, and guess what?'

'Henry Beekman Livingston wrote it?'

'It certainly looks that way. According to him there's no way on earth Clement Clarke Moore could have written that poem.'

I told her some more – more than she needed to know, I have no doubt – about how Livingston made a habit of writing Christmas and New Year poems, and how this one was published anonymously in an upstate newspaper, and how Moore read it to his kids but later on was never able to show working drafts of it, explaining how it had all come to him word for word in a dream, and he just rushed to his desk and wrote it down in finished form, and – oh, never mind. Carolyn didn't really need to hear the whole story, and neither do you.

'Bern,' she said, when I finally stopped talking, 'this is all very interesting.'

'You honestly think so?'

'Up to a point,' she said, 'I do. But here's my question. What's all of this got to do with apostle spoons and Myer Myers?'

'Livingston would be pretty interesting,' I said, 'even if he hadn't written the poem. He had a wide range of interests, a great intellectual curiosity, and a spirit of quiet adventure. He kept a low profile, so there's a lot we don't know about him, but among the things we do know is that he was acquainted with Myer Myers, both the person and the work. Relatives of his had commissioned work from Myers, and an inventory of his widow's estate includes a pierced silver bowl that was almost certainly Myers's work.

'And he knew what apostle spoons were. There's a 1792 letter that survives from a neighbor in Poughkeepsie with the report of a visit from "Henry and Jane, she well recovered from her recent illness, and he so taken with the St Jude spoon I felt moved to press it upon him, but he too much the gentleman to accept it, for which I remain quite glad, as it should pain me to part with it."

'It wasn't long after that social visit that Henry made a journey to New York that included a stop at Myer Myers's shop. There he arranged an unusual commission – a set of fifteen silver spoons "fashioned in the manner employed for the depiction of the twelve apostles, but each showing rather a contemporary exemplar of civic virtue, selected to represent the thirteen original colonies."'

'I thought you said fifteen spoons, Bern.'

'One for Vermont. It was part of New York when the colonies declared their independence, and it declared its own independence a year later in 1777, proclaiming itself the Vermont Republic and issuing its own coins. In 1791 New York recognized the secession, allowing Vermont to join the union as the fourteenth state. A year later, when Livingston ordered his spoons, he felt moved to include Vermont.'

'That's fourteen.'

'Number fifteen was George Washington. He could have been on the Virginia spoon, but that would have meant leaving out Thomas Jefferson. Livingston's reasoning was that Washington, first as Commander-in-Chief of the Continental Army and now as President of the United States, ought to stand not for one state but for the nation as a whole.'

'So he got a spoon of his own. Just like Jesus.'

'I'm not sure Myer Myers would have put it that way,' I said, 'or George Washington either, as far as that goes. I suppose Livingston must have decided who would represent each of the states, although he may have talked it over with Myers. A lot of them were men who had signed the Declaration of Independence, like Samuel Adams of Massachusetts and Maryland's Charles Carroll of Carrollton, and of course Philip Livingston of New York. But Henry Livingston was a soldier, and he evidently admired military men, because he selected Nathanael Greene for Rhode Island and Francis Marion for South Carolina. Marion was known as the Swamp Fox, and his spoon showed him with a little fox at his feet, posed like man's best friend.'

'More like man's slyest friend,' she said.

'And for Vermont, well, there weren't any signers from Vermont, and the choice was another military hero, Ethan Allen.'

'What did Myer Myers put at his feet, Bern? A love seat? A ladderback chair?'

'I don't know. He captured Fort Ticonderoga, so maybe it was a pencil.'

'Myer Myers,' she said. 'You know, when you first mentioned the name—'

'You thought for sure I meant the Ed McBain character.'

'Well, can you blame me? But it just this minute hit me, Bern. Myer Myers, right?'

'So?'

'And Roda Roda?'

'Oh.'

'It's like we keep ducking into an echo chamber. I think I'll go to the jukebox and play some Duran Duran. Or go home and watch reruns of *Mary Hartman*, *Mary Hartman*. Or—'

'Stop.'

'Okay. You probably think I was going to mention Walla Walla, but it never entered my mind. Myer Myers made the spoons, right? All fifteen of them?'

I took out the Culloden book, opened it to Plate XVI.

'That's George,' she said. 'He's probably the only one I'd have a chance of recognizing. What's he holding?'

'I forget what it's called, but it's an instrument surveyors used. He did a lot of surveying, when he wasn't busy crossing the Delaware.'

'A hatchet would be better, Bern. For chopping down cherry trees. I don't think I've ever seen a spoon shaped like that.'

'Myers went retro,' I said. 'The bowl like a teardrop, the long straight handle – he must have been inspired by the typical apostle spoons of a century or two earlier.'

'I like it,' she said. 'I guess you'll be looking at the original in a couple of hours.'

I shook my head. 'Not unless I go a few blocks north of Leopold's place to the Museum of the City of New York. That's where George has been ever since a Livingston descendant died and left it to them.'

'I thought Mr Leopold had the whole set.'

'Not even close. The Charles Carroll of Carrollton spoon wound up in the collection of the Baltimore Historical Society, and—'

'Bern, why do they always call the guy Charles Carroll of Carrollton?'

161

'I have no idea. Not that I haven't often wondered myself. You could look it up.'

'I could,' she agreed, 'but probably won't. He's in Baltimore, huh?'

'Well, his spoon is. I couldn't tell you what became of the man himself. The other spoons are scattered, some in public collections, some in private hands. Two or three have vanished without a trace. Every so often manipulation sends the price of silver skyrocketing, and every time it does, a lot of collectible silver goes to the smelter. Gone, never to be seen again.'

'If there was ever a Judge Crater spoon, I bet that's what happened to it.'

'Of the original fifteen,' I said, 'our Mr Leopold has four of them.'

'And you're going to take them.'

'Only one,' I said. 'The one with the button.'

TWENTY-THREE

The book got me into the building.

That, of course, was why Mr Smith had sent me to steal it in the first place. Access to the Wattrous apartment, itself easily gained, could give me access to the far more formidable fortress uptown.

And I'd have had a hell of a time without it. Many of Manhattan's wealthiest citizens are essentially immune to burglary simply because the buildings they inhabit are impregnable. Edwin Leopold lived in such a building, and if he hadn't sent down word earlier that I was expected, I'd have been sent speedily on my way.

A liveried doorman, built like a tight end, was stationed out in front. I gave my name, along with Leopold's, and he passed me on to the concierge, a slightly smaller man in a similar uniform, the jacket cut to cloak but not entirely conceal the bulge of a shoulder holster.

Or maybe he was just glad to see me. He looked me over – my suit, my muted necktie, the briefcase I was carrying. I gave my name, and he nodded in recognition, checked a list to confirm his memory, and then called upstairs on the chance that Mr Leopold might have changed his mind, and no longer welcomed my company.

'Mr Lederer,' he announced, and listened. 'Very good, sir,' he said, and gave me a smile, though not a terribly warm one. 'The front elevator,' he said.

I'd noted a camera mounted above the building's entrance, and another above and behind the concierge's desk. From where that gentleman sat, he could monitor a bank of a dozen screens, which suggested that there were at least that many closed-circuit cameras busily recording the activity in all of the building's public spaces.

I spotted one in the elevator, along with its operator, an older fellow with a bulldog jaw and, yes, a maroon uniform with gold piping, a match to those I'd seen on the concierge and the doorman. He whisked me two hundred feet closer to heaven and dropped me at a hallway some ten feet square. There were paintings on both side walls, rural landscapes in matching frames, while opposite the elevator was the door to the Leopold penthouse.

Behind me, the elevator operator held his position, and I knew he wouldn't budge until my host let me in. I transferred my briefcase to my left hand and knocked with my right, and a male voice asked my name.

'Philip Lederer,' I said, and locks began to turn.

Several of them. Two cylinders showed on the outside of the door, but there was also a massive sliding bolt, and a Fox lock at least as sturdy as the one I'd encountered on Tenth Street.

The locks were a surprise. As a general rule, the easier it is to get into a building, the harder the residents make it to get into their apartments. The Wattrous apartment, swaddled by Rabson and Poulard and Fox, was a perfect example. Anyone armed with a butter knife could get past the downstairs door, so the brownstone's tenants hung industrial-strength locks on their doors.

But here on Fifth Avenue, with a gun-toting concierge and a doorman who could double as the Rock of Gibraltar, you'd expect a more casual attitude toward locks. If no one could get into the building in the first place, why put oneself to the trouble of carrying all those keys and turning all those locks?

My heart would have plummeted at the sight of all those locks, especially once he'd let me in only to relock every one of those contrivances. You can't be too paranoid, Mrs Hesch had advised me, but she'd never met Edwin Leopold.

So the locks would have lowered my spirits, but they were already somewhere below sea level, and I was just glad I had the book with me, and that we'd already set a price for it. Because that thousand dollars was all the money I'd ever see for my efforts.

He didn't need all those locks. He didn't need a single one of them. He could have fastened his door with a piece of string, or left it open altogether. It didn't matter.

It wasn't Fort Knox, but it might as well have been. There was no way I'd be getting anything out of that building.

Edwin Leopold had a firm handshake, and treated me to it after we'd introduced ourselves. The handshake came as a surprise, but then so did everything else about the man's appearance. All I knew about him was that he had a passion for old silver and an extreme disinclination to leave his apartment, and the mental picture I'd formed was of a pale little slug of a man, possibly corpulent, possibly chair-bound, looking as if he'd crawled out of a cartoon by Charles Addams.

He was my height but looked taller, perhaps because his posture was better than mine – and indeed better than just about anyone's.

His shoulders were broader and his waist trimmer. His made-to-measure suit was understated, but the functional buttons on its cuffs were a custom touch that Mr Smith would have appreciated.

And his skin, firm and unlined, boasted a deep coppery tan. I supposed he could have obtained it on a terrace, but the terrace would have had to be in Miami. It was only June, and it would take all of a New York summer to turn him that color.

'I hope you'll excuse this silliness with the locks,' he said, after capping the performance by arming his Kaltenborn alarm system. He took my arm and led me to a small table set for two, holding a thermos of coffee and a plate of cookies. 'But if I fail to lock every last one, and set the alarm even though I'm sitting this close to the door, I assure you I'll be able to think of nothing else. Are you phobic, Mr Lederer?'

'I don't think so,' I said. 'Still, I wouldn't say I'm fearless. There are certainly things that make me uncomfortable.'

'There's a difference between discomfort and paralysis. If you were phobic, you'd realize it. Do you know the word *agora*?'

'From crossword puzzles. I think it means market.'

'In the sense of the Greek marketplace of old, which would have been an open public area where merchants laid out their goods. Thus agoraphobia, which is literally a fear of open spaces. Have one of these cookies, Mr Lederer. They're from the Hungarian bakery on Second Avenue.'

'Delicious.'

My seat gave me a good view of the glassed-in triple cabinet off to my right. It reached to within a few inches of the ten-foot ceiling, and light glinted off the silver objects on its shelves. A quick glance didn't show me any spoons, but that didn't mean they weren't there to be seen.

'I call them,' he said of the bakery, 'and they're good enough to deliver. New York is remarkably considerate of the agoraphobic.

166

One can have virtually anything brought to one's home.'

'How long—'

'Have I been like this? I'm sixty-two years old, Mr Lederer.'

'You look younger.'

'Do I? I try to stay in shape. I ran five miles this morning. A normal man would have gone across the street and done his running in the park. I used a treadmill. I'm assured my cardiovascular system can't tell the difference.'

He'd had one room converted to a gym, with other machinery to keep the treadmill company, along with an assortment of free weights. And he'd had a sauna installed – it didn't take much space, or use that much electricity. And a sunlamp, which accounted for the tan.

'All of this,' he said, 'to accommodate a deplorable neurotic condition. You asked how long I've suffered from it. When I was thirty years old, I was a world traveler, even an explorer. I camped out in the Taklamakan desert in western China. Have you been there?'

Curiously enough, I hadn't.

'A miserable place. This vast expanse, and it looked as though someone had set out to pave it and ran out of tar. And there I was, sleeping under the stars, all alone in the middle of nowhere. And quite comfortable, if you can believe it.'

'What happened?'

'I honestly don't know. All I can say is that something happened. I had a trip planned to Italy, a region of that country that was the closest thing to a second home to me. I woke up one morning and realized I didn't want to go. I canceled the trip, and I've never been out of New York since.'

'I see.'

'Do you? Because I don't. This is the apartment I grew up in, it was my parents', and my mother was still living then. I moved back in with her, and went on living here after her death. At first I was comfortable anywhere in the city, but gradually my world grew smaller. I learned to stay in the immediate neighborhood. The day came when I crossed the avenue, intending to sit for a few minutes in the park, and instead I turned around and came right back. I never crossed Fifth Avenue again.'

He poured himself some more coffee. 'I was seeing a psychiatrist,' he said, 'but then I could no longer go to his office, and he felt he'd be enabling my phobia if he came to me, so that was the end of that. Not that he'd been doing me any good. I wondered, though, where it would all end. There was a period of a month or so when I couldn't leave the building, but was still able to go downstairs for my mail.'

'And then you couldn't?'

'They were good enough to bring it to me. And now of course Miss Miller goes down for it. I don't leave the apartment. I don't even step out into the hall, and when I do open the door, well, you've seen how quick I am to lock everything up again.'

His eyes held mine. 'One expert holds that the agoraphobe is an unindicted co-conspirator, that I could force myself to face my fears rather than accommodate them. That sounds good, doesn't it? All I can say is it's as useful as telling a depressive to cheer up. I'm just grateful my condition seems to have stabilized. I have the run of the entire apartment.'

'That's something.'

'It is, because I've read of men and women who become incapable of leaving the bedroom, and eventually of leaving the bed. I don't know what I would do if that happened to me.' He smiled. 'I make it a point,' he said, 'to pay a daily visit to every room in the apartment. Like an animal, staking out its territory. Thus far I haven't felt the need to mark the perimeters with urine.'

'That's probably just as well.'

'Yes, I'd say so.' He'd been leaning forward, and now he straightened up. 'And now,' he said, 'you surely would welcome a change of subject. And I do believe you've brought me a book. Do you suppose I could have a look at it?'

TWENTY-FOUR

I'd been a little concerned about the inscription. It had seemed to me like gilding the lily. The book was what he wanted, and would he want it any more ardently because the author had signed and inscribed it? Probably not, and suppose the signature looked phony to him? It was supposed to have been signed over a century ago, and to me it looked like yesterday's work.

He glanced at it, nodded in appreciation, and turned the page.

The two dozen pages of plates got most of his attention. He studied them, frowned at them, smiled upon them, and even talked to them, mumbling about this piece or that one.

'He did think the world of Revere,' he said, 'as who does not? But he doesn't give short shrift to my favorite, either.'

I had a hunch I knew who that would be.

'A man named Myers,' he said. 'I doubt you've even heard of him.'

Whereupon he told me everything I'd already learned about Myer Myers, and a bit more besides. I did a good job of appearing interested, and I didn't need to show too much enthusiasm to make him happy.

He told me, for example, that Myers had formed a partnership in 1756 with one Benjamin Halsted, and that the two were the first to devise a joint monogram as a hallmark for their wares. Other silversmiths who joined as partners used their individual marks, but Myers and Halsted linked their initials with an ampersand, and their mark was 'H & M' in a rectangle.

'I'll show you,' he said, and took me to the glassed-in cabinet that had caught my eye earlier. Its various sections were fitted with locks, simple affairs one can pick with a hairpin, but he didn't need a hairpin, having the appropriate one-size-fits-all key in his pocket. He used it to unfasten a mullioned cabinet door, picked up a six-inch bowl by its edges, and turned it to show me the hallmark. And there it was, all right, stamped into the bowl's underside: a rectangle three-eights of an inch across, with an ampersand joining the team's initials.

'Their innovation,' he said reverently, as if Halsted and Myers had invented the wheel.

'And the initials caught on,' I found myself saying. 'They came into use again years later for the trains running underneath the Hudson River.'

'I beg your pardon?'

'The H&M Tubes,' I said. 'Oh, they call it the PATH train now, have done so for years. But there are places where you can still see the original logo. H&M.'

'For Hudson and Manhattan,' he said.

'Yes, of course,' I said. 'But I've a feeling I'll always think of it henceforth as Halsted and Myers.'

*

And what was I doing, turning so playful?

Well, hell, why not? I'd come here with the intention of leaving with one of Edwin Leopold's silver spoons – if not this evening, then at a later visit facilitated by what I discovered here tonight. Perhaps, I'd thought, after I handed over the book and accepted my thousand dollars, I could find some spot in the building that would serve as a hiding place; then, while everybody slept, I could let myself into the apartment and raid the silver cabinet.

Or perhaps I could do as I'd done at the Galtonbrook, building in a back-door entrance that I could use at another time. Or maybe—

Never mind. I could go on in this vein, but why? All the possibilities were in fact impossible. The building was too well staffed, the closed-circuit TV cameras were everywhere, and any stratagem I might devise was doomed from the start. The locks, the alarm, the fact that at any hour of the day or night he'd be inside the apartment, it all added up to the certain knowledge that my buttoned-up and buttoned-down Mr Smith was going to have to get along without his silver spoon.

And the realization was oddly liberating. If I couldn't steal from this charming eccentric, then I was free to relax and enjoy his company. I only regretted having given him a false name at the onset, and now whenever he called me Mr Lederer, I had the urge to correct him. *It's Rhodenbarr*, I longed to say, *Bernie Rhodenbarr, and I have a store you can never visit, since it would be impossible to do so without leaving your house, but I can certainly supply you with books you might find interesting and look for any titles you may be seeking and—*

But how could I say all that without having to explain how Rhodenbarr had become Lederer in the first place? I couldn't work out an approach that wouldn't make me appear at least as eccentric as my host. So I let him go on calling me Mr Lederer, and wondered what I'd do if he were to ask me whether people called me Philip or Phil.

But we never got all the way to first names. He remained Mr Leopold, and went on calling me Mr Lederer.

Which, as it turned out, was just as well.

I was standing at the cabinet, looking through glass at four matched spoons with teardrop bowls. Could I ask for a closer look at them?

'But I've kept you far too long,' Leopold said, and took my arm, and drew me away from the spoon with the button on the handle. 'One thousand dollars. Do I remember correctly? Is that the price you mentioned?'

'Yes. You called it a nice round sum.'

'And so it is. Do you mind a check?'

'Well—'

'Then cash it is.' He drew an envelope from his breast pocket, took a mix of fifties and hundreds from it, and asked me to count them. I did, and confirmed the sum.

'And now I have a question. How did you come to call me, Mr Lederer?'

'Well,' I said, 'a book scout brought the book in, along with a dozen or so others he'd rescued from thrift shops. The rest were nothing special, but I understood you'd want the Culloden, and—'

'That's my question. How did you happen to know that?'

How indeed? 'I'm afraid I'm not free to say,' I told him.

He nodded, as if I'd confirmed his suspicion. 'Roundtree,' he said. 'He'd know, and he'd be a natural for you to call. I'm just surprised he gave you my number instead of buying the book from you himself. It was young Geoff, wasn't it?'

'Sir, I really—'

'Can't say,' he finished for me. 'And so you've said nothing, but I'll regard that as confirmation enough, if you've no objection.' He smiled. 'Geoffrey Roundtree, of the New-York Historical Society. It's curious, isn't it, the way they're so attached to that hyphen? At the slightest provocation they'll launch into their justification for retaining the hyphen, despite the fact that the city's name has been hyphenated nowhere else for centuries. When you point out the illogic, they take shelter beneath the umbrella of tradition. The New-York Historical Society. They're over on the other side of the park, you know, and a few blocks down. I used to be able to see their building from here.'

I must have looked puzzled. What could have sprung up to block his view? No construction could have intervened, and what trees could have grown anywhere near tall enough?

'From my terrace,' he said. 'But of course I'm no longer able to set foot on it.'

He went on, telling me how the hyphenated institution coveted his silver, and hoped he'd bequeath it to them upon his death. No doubt young Geoff would call him in a day or two, congratulating him on his acquisition of the Culloden book, and taking credit for steering it his way, all to curry favor. But they all wanted his silver. The New-York Historical Society, hyphen and all, and the Museum of the City of New York, properly unhyphenated, and as far as the Myer Myers pieces were concerned, the Jewish Museum. All fine institutions, certainly, with good people in their ranks, and—

And I'd quit listening. A terrace? Did the apartment really have a terrace? He might not be able to set foot on it, but could I?

I removed myself mentally from the apartment to the street below, sent myself across Fifth Avenue, and imagined the view from that vantage point. I couldn't recall noticing a terrace, but what I did remember was that Leopold's building was taller than the ones on either side. That meant I couldn't reach his terrace from a neighboring roof.

And could I get onto the building's own roof, and clamber down from there onto the terrace? The clambering, I thought, would be the easy part; getting past locks and alarms and security cameras in order to get onto the roof would be extremely difficult, and probably impossible.

And even if I somehow brought it off, clambering and all, I'd be on a terrace, and on the other side of a door that would be trebly locked and wired into that damned Kaltenborn alarm. So forget the terrace, and curse the bloody man for mentioning it at all.

'—no hurry to add codicils to my will,' he was saying, as I pulled myself in from my imaginary perch on his terrace. 'I am, after all, a comparatively young man, and in good health. Did I mention that I ran this morning?'

'Five miles, I believe you said.'

'On my treadmill, and one gets as good a workout that way as one could manage in the park. I'm healthy and youthful, and I have the same physical needs as any man. You may have been wondering about that.'

I hadn't, but now that he'd mentioned it, I wished he hadn't, and recalled the way he'd twice taken hold of my arm. I hoped he wouldn't do that again.

'I'm a normal man with normal desires,' he said, conveniently answering a question I hadn't asked. 'I require a woman's company from time to time, and my condition precludes my going out in search of it.'

I was relieved. Not that he gave off a gay vibe, but I'd recently learned that I lived in a world in which two lesbians could follow a church wedding with sex-change surgery.

'There are escort services,' he said. 'You visit a website, you choose from an array of photos, you input your credit card data, and the young woman you've selected comes over and, well . . . '

St Robert's your uncle, I thought.

'And yet there was something unsavory about those transactions,' he said. I guess when you don't get out much, you make the most of a captive audience. 'And once Miss Miller came to work for me, it became awkward. I could hardly bring in some professional escort when my assistant was on the premises. You haven't met Miss Miller.'

'No.'

'She lives here,' he said. 'She takes courses at Hunter College, so this is quite convenient for her, and her hours are flexible. But when she's not at school, or on an errand for me, she's apt to be here. You can see my problem. Can you guess the solution?'

I supposed I could, but I'd as soon he kept it to himself.

'Miss Miller,' he said, 'is studying American history and literature at the moment, but it's not the only subject she's pursued. One day I complained of sore muscles, and the next thing I knew I was stretched out on the sofa and she was giving me a massage. It turned out she was a skilled masseuse.'

'How fortunate for you.'

'The very next day I gave her some cash and had her purchase a folding massage table. Now every day after I've finished with the treadmill and the free weights, Miss Miller gives me a massage.' He smiled. 'Are you familiar with the term *Happy Ending*?'

'Every story should have one,' I said.

'And every massage. It's not really sexual, you know. It's simply the manual relief of a physical urge. And yet I know I'd enjoy it less if Miss Miller were not such a physically attractive young woman.'

'Um,' I said.

'The massage begins with me in a prone position. And then she'll have me roll over and lie on my back.'

'Er.'

'And it's just a massage, you know. Until she strips to the waist. And it's *still* a massage, but her touch, previously so firm, becomes so remarkably soft. And I look at her breasts, which are quite beautiful, and her tattoo, and, well, I'm sure you can imagine the rest.'

Right.

TWENTY-FIVE

'Of all the dyke bars,' Carolyn Kaiser said, 'in all the streets of New York, you walk into mine.'

'They're all yours,' I pointed out. 'This is the fifth place I've been to, and it's the same story everywhere I go.'

'It's still the same old story,' she said. 'A fight for love and glory. We're still in the movie, Bern, and the hopes and dreams of a couple of little people like you and me don't amount to a hill of beans.' She looked at the glass she was holding, noted that it was empty, and frowned at it. 'Bern, *what's* the same old story?'

'I walk in the door, and every eye turns toward me, and the tension's so thick you could cut it with a knife.'

'Or a silver spoon,' she suggested, 'if you'd been born with one in your mouth.'

'And I say, "Is Carolyn here? Carolyn Kaiser?" and all the tension goes out of the room. "Oh, you just missed her," someone says. "Try the Duchess. Try Paula's. Try Swing Rendezvous."'

'Those joints all closed years ago, Bern.'

'Well, they're the only ones left on my list. I've been everywhere else. Where are we now? Mytilene? I never even heard of this place, until a woman at the last place told me how to find it.'

'Poor baby. And I'll bet you've had a drink in every place you've been.'

'I haven't had a drink in *any* of them,' I said. 'I had a cup of coffee and a Hungarian cookie on Fifth Avenue, and before that I had a Perrier at the Bum Rap.'

'And that's all?' She turned. 'Sandy, this is my friend Bernie. He's okay, except he's in desperate need of a drink. So bring him what I've been having, and bring me—' She stopped, took a breath. 'No,' she said. 'Bring him a double scotch. Bring me a cup of black coffee.'

I worked on my scotch. Carolyn worked on her coffee. All around us, women of varying ages with varying estrogen levels drank, talked, laughed, cried, danced, paired off, broke up, and drank some more.

And I talked.

By the time I stopped, my drink was gone and so was her coffee. 'I feel a lot better,' I told her.

'And I feel sober,' she said, 'although a traffic cop might not see it that way. Bern, lots of people have tattoos.'

'I know.'

'If you look around this room, you'll spot a whole lot of ink. Go ahead, take a look.'

'They'll think I'm staring at them.'

'So? The worst thing that could happen is somebody'll beat you up. That was a joke, Bern.'

'Ha ha.'

'Okay, so I'll look around, because they're used to me staring at them. Tons of tats, Bern.'

'I'll take your word for it.'

'And that's not counting the ones you can't see. Like the little butterfly way up on the inside of Rosalie's thigh, or Denise's frog, and why anyone would want a frog there is beyond me, but—'

'Okay,' I said. 'I get it.'

'Do you? Because the mere fact that your Mr Leopold's Queen of the Happy Ending has a tattoo doesn't mean her first name is Chloe.'

'But—'

'She's not the one, Bern. Of all the bookstores in all the streets of New York, she didn't walk into yours. She probably doesn't even own a Kindle, and if she ever heard of *The Pit* I bet she thinks Edgar Allan Poe wrote it.'

'She's studying American literature and history at Hunter.'

'And massage at the House of the Rising Sun. What's Miss Miller's first name?'

'It's Chloe.'

'Did he tell you this?'

'I didn't ask.'

'Why not?'

'Because it would have been awkward. "My assistant gives me the most wonderful hand jobs." "Oh, really? What's her first name?"'

'Well, I can see where that might have been a little awkward.'

'You think?'

'But so what, Bern? You already wrote off the evening and you're never going to see him again. What's awkward gonna cost you? He won't let you have any more Hungarian cookies?'

'We'd finished the cookies by then.'

'There you go. What was Hungarian about them, by the way?'

180

'They came from a Hungarian bakery. I didn't ask her name because I didn't have to ask her name. I *knew* her name.'

'Chloe.'

'And you knew this because anybody with a tattoo pretty much has to be named Chloe.'

'If the tattoo's on her left arm, above the elbow.'

'Lots of tattoos—'

'And if it shows a gecko.'

'Oh,' she said.

'I didn't ask her name,' I said, 'because that would have been awkward. But I did ask about the tattoo. "My friend Carolyn has a tattoo," I told him. "It shows a snake, all wrapped around her arm."'

'You used my name, Bern?'

'It was the first name that came to mind. What difference does it make? He doesn't know you.'

'He will, the minute he spots my tattoo. Except I don't *have* any tattoos, Bern.'

'I know that.'

'Yeah? How do you know for sure? I could have a butterfly like Rosalie or a frog like Denise, and how would you know it?'

'You'd tell me.'

'Yeah, I probably would. So you told him about my snake, and he told you about Chloe's gecko.'

'Right.'

'There's probably more than one gecko tattoo in New York City.'

'Probably.'

'But we both know it's her.'

'I'd say so, yes.'

'You met her, Bern. In the bookstore. Then you spoke to her when you called Leopold. Did the voice sound familiar?'

181

'No, but—'

'But you weren't looking for similarities. You just wanted to talk to Leopold. Bern, the woman you met. Can you picture her performing that particular service for him?'

'Vividly.'

'She's the type, huh?'

'She turned up at Barnegat Books,' I said, 'and picked an item out of my stock, booted up her Kindle, ordered the eQuivalent from Amazon, and reported her accomplishment with innocent pride. And then she steered Janine of Romania my way, allowing that enterprising young woman to take me out for a test drive. So yes, I'd say she's definitely the type to put her hands to good use in order to keep her boss happy. If she worked at the Bronx Zoo, she's probably do the same for the elephant.'

'I suppose I could have waited until morning,' I said. 'But all I could think of was that victory was there, waiting to be snatched from the jaws of defeat.'

'And you wanted to share it with somebody.'

'With you, Carolyn.'

'One more lesbian club,' she said, 'and you'd have shared it with the bartender. You were like Chloe herself, Bern, after she'd snatched Frank Norris from the jaws of Amazon.'

We had left Mytilene, with Rosalie's butterfly and Denise's frog still unseen, and walked the few blocks to Arbor Court, and I was telling her it was a little different. 'In my case,' I said, 'victory is still unsnatched.'

'And that's where Chloe comes in.'

'I can't get into Leopold's building again. I had to steal a book to get in there the first time, and a fat lot of good it did me. The only way I could leave his apartment was in the attended elevator, and it took me straight to the lobby, where the elevator operator watched me walk to where the concierge and doorman were waiting.'

'Buildings like that,' she said, 'don't make it easy.'

'They don't. I'm sure Leopold's apartment has a service entrance, where the porter picks up the trash and whisks it away on the service elevator, but what good would that do me? And, knowing Leopold, it's probably got three or four locks on it, too.'

'And a moat around it, Bern.'

'Complete with alligators. You know, I might have had a chance. When it was time to pay me, I was hoping he'd have to get the cash from a wall safe.'

'What were you gonna do, Bern? Hide in the safe?'

'It would be in another room,' I said, 'and he'd probably have to take down a framed painting to get at it, and work a complicated combination. That might have given me enough time to pick the lock on the china cabinet.'

'And grab the spoon.'

'And possibly even lock up again before he got back. But possibly not, and what happens if he comes back right in the middle of things?'

'Not good.'

'Not good at all. But he had the money all ready for me, all he had to do was reach into his pocket for it. Then I thought maybe he'd get a call of nature. He had a couple of cups of coffee, and he may be in great shape but he's had the same bladder and prostate for over sixty years, so you'd think sooner or later he'd have to pee.'

'Would that give you enough time?'

'I don't know. Probably not, but I never got the chance to find out. I guess all those happy endings have kept his plumbing in good shape. He never left the room.'

'And then he told you about Miss Miller.'

'Miss Miller,' I said, 'and her manual dexterity. And her tattoo, which served to identify Miss Miller for me. She could do it, Carolyn.'

'And evidently she did, on more or less a daily basis, but—'

'Not that. She could steal the spoon. All she'd have to do is get hold of the key, and she might already have one of her own. When those remarkably soft hands aren't otherwise occupied, don't you suppose they're occasionally put to use polishing silver?'

'You want her to steal the spoon for you.'

'What could be simpler? She opens the cabinet, she removes the spoon, she pops it into her purse.'

'Where it can keep the Kindle company.'

'Whatever. Then the next time she has a class at Hunter, I'm there at the classroom door.'

'You could just walk right into the college?'

'Or I'll meet her on the corner, or wherever she wants.'

'And she gives you the spoon.'

'Right. But here's the problem, Carolyn. How do I find her?'

'How do you find her?'

'The first time,' I said, 'she showed up at Barnegat Books, just walked in off the street. But who knows if that'll ever happen again? But I happen to know someone who knows her.'

'Janine.'

'Janine. She'll know how to get in touch with Chloe. I bet she's got Miss Manual Dexterity on speed dial. But I don't have a number for Janine, or an address, and she never told me her last name, and I'm pretty sure the first name she gave me is bogus. So how do I find her?'

'She said she lives just a few blocks from your store.'

'What do I do, go door to door?'

'Maybe Ray could help,' she said. 'You've been helping him with Mrs Ostermaier, haven't you?'

'I haven't been all that much help.'

'But you've been trying. Maybe he could sit you down with one of those police artists, and you could describe her.'

'And the guy'll draw a pornographic picture.'

'Bern—'

'All right, I sit down with an artist, and together we come up with a sketch that looks about as much like Janine as that sketch of the Unabomber looked like the guy they caught.'

'He got the hoodie right. And anyway, they caught him, didn't they?'

'His brother turned him in.'

'Well, all that counts is they caught him. And you probably got a better look at Janine than anybody ever got of the Unabomber.'

'I got a very good look at her, Carolyn.'

'So maybe your sketch'll turn out better.'

'And then what? Ray puts out an APB of it? We run around taping it to lampposts? The woman didn't do anything.' I thought about that last sentence. 'Nothing illegal, anyway. Well, considering all the things people do in private that are technically against the law—'

'Bern.'

'Sorry. I don't think a police artist is the answer. Maybe an ad.'

'You mean like Missed Connections in Craigslist?'

'I was thinking more of a personal notice at the bottom of the front page of the *New York Times*.'

'They still have those? The only one I ever see is to tell Jewish women to light Shabbos candles. What would you put?'

'I don't know. "You said your name was Janine. There's something I need to ask you. Call me at the bookshop."'

'Would you put the number? No, because this way you'll only hear from somebody who knows which bookstore to call. I suppose it might work.'

'I don't know. I'd probably stand a better chance with a Ouija board. Those ads probably work when a person's waiting to get a message that way, but who else actually reads them?'

'People with a lot of time on their hands, Bern. Not people who are busy day and night looking for a husband.'

I stood up. 'I'm going home,' I said, 'to sleep on it. There's got to be a better way to reach her, Carolyn. We're just not thinking of it.'

I went home, I went to bed, I woke up. And I caught the phone midway through the first ring. 'We're both stupid,' I said.

'I can't believe how stupid we are, Bern. You only had one drink, too.'

'It was a double.'

'I had more than that, but then I stopped and switched to coffee. I don't think we were drunk.'

'No, just stupid.'

'I can see one of us being that stupid, but—'

'Which one?'

'Either one, depending on circumstances. But both of us? I think the French have a word for it.'

'*Stupide*?'

'No, it's a phrase. *Folie a deux*, I think. You know, when two people get stupid together.'

'Really stupid, in this case.'

'Boneheaded, brainless-type stupid. All the schemes we kept coming up with.'

'Craigslist,' I said. 'The *New York Times*.'

'Sitting down with Ray and a police artist.'

'Going around the neighborhood putting up fliers and knocking on doors.'

'Stupid. When all along—'

'I knew her name—'

'Chloe Miller.'

'And where she lives and works.'

'I've even got her number. And you know something else, Carolyn?'

'What?'

'If it's not Chloe, if it's some other young woman with remarkably soft hands—'

'But we figured out that it has to be her.'

'And it does,' I agreed, 'but on the remote chance that it isn't, so what? Even if her name is Madeleine Miller, or Rachel Miller, or, I don't know—'

'Janine Miller?'

'Whatever. She still lives there, and works there, and polishes the silver. And can come and go as she wishes.'

'With a spoon in her bag. Did you call her yet?'

'I was just about to,' I said. 'I wanted to wait until I had a chance to brush my teeth.'

'Ewww,' she said. 'You're talking to me and you haven't brushed your teeth yet? That's gross, Bern. I'm hanging up.'

TWENTY-SIX

'Edwin Leopold's residence.'

'Chloe?'

Her pause was confirmation enough. When she didn't tell me I had the wrong number, I knew I had the right one.

'My name's Bernie Rhodenbarr,' I told the silence. 'We met recently.'

'We did?'

'In my bookstore. I have a store on East Eleventh Street, and you came in looking for Frank Norris.'

'I don't think I know a Frank Morris.'

'Uh—'

'Wait a minute. Frank *Norris*? The writer? Now I remember. What did you say your name was?'

'Bernie Rhodenbarr.'

'No,' she said. 'I mean, I'm not saying it's not your name. You'd know that better than I would, wouldn't you?'

'Uh—'

'But I don't think I ever *got* your name. The store had an un-usual name. Book Barn? No, but it had barn in it.'

'Barnegat Books.'

'Right.'

'The previous owner had a summer place at Barnegat Light, in New Jersey.'

'So?'

'So that's how the store got its name.'

'Oh,' she said. 'How did *you* get *my* name?'

'From a friend of yours.'

'A friend of mine? You want to narrow it down a little?'

'Her name's Janine.'

'It is, huh? And who's she supposed to be, Frank Morris's sister? I don't know anybody named Janine.'

This was not going well. 'That's the name she gave me,' I said, 'after she realized I wasn't husband material. I had a feeling it wasn't her real name, but what was I supposed to do, go through her purse?'

'Wait a minute.'

'Okay.'

'Her name's not Janine.'

'There's a shock.'

'Look, if you're trying to get in touch with her, I'm afraid I can't help you.'

'I'm not.'

'Because if she wanted to hear from you she would have given you her number, and – you're not?'

'No. You're the one I'm trying to get in touch with.'

'Me? You mind telling me why?'

'Well, to thank you, for one thing. Your friend and I spent a few very enjoyable hours together, whatever her name might be.'

Her voice softened. 'So she said.'

'And all because you told her I was cute.'

'Yeah. As a matter of fact—'

'What?'

'Well, she had some nice things to say about you.'

'Oh?'

'And I sort of thought I'd come say hello if I was in the neighborhood. But the one time I got down there you were closed, and—'

'I got your note.'

'What note?'

'On my bargain table.'

'I didn't leave a note. Why would I leave you a note?'

'It must have been somebody else,' I said. 'Look, Chloe, I think we should meet. I can't go into this over the phone, but there's an opportunity that you don't want to miss.'

'An opportunity?'

'With the prospect of considerable financial reward.'

A pause. 'How did you get this number?'

'I told you, your friend said—'

'The only number she could have given you is my cell. She doesn't even *have* this number.'

'Ten minutes,' I said. 'That's all it'll take.'

'You're way downtown. I can't—'

'Your neighborhood is fine. You give me ten minutes and I'll give you five thousand dollars.'

'For what?'

'For listening. Pick a place that's convenient for you, set a time, and I'll be there.'

'Oh, God, I can't think. And he just got off the treadmill. Five minutes in the shower and he's going to want his massage. I have to get off.'

'I guess you're not the only one.'

'Huh?'

'Never mind. Say where and when.'

'Five thousand dollars? Just for listening?'

'That's right.'

'Two-thirty this afternoon. Is that okay?'

'It's fine. Where?'

'The only place I can think of is Three Guys.'

'I think you mean Two Guys.'

'Jesus, don't you think I can count? It's Three Guys, it's a coffee shop on Madison Avenue.'

'I'm sorry, I thought—'

'Three Guys at half past two,' she said. 'And if you show up at Two Guys at half past three, the hell with you.'

It was a gecko, all right, and a dead ringer for the TV gecko with the Australian accent. She was wearing a denim jacket over a sleeveless pink blouse, and she'd slipped off the jacket even as she'd slipped into the booth opposite me.

I'd been there for almost ten minutes when she showed up right on time. 'Well, you're here,' she said. 'Just like you said. That's not all you said.'

'Oh, right.' I handed her an envelope. It was the last one my client had handed me, the one I'd put away unopened. This morning when I fetched it from the store I checked its contents, and she did the same now, holding the bills in her lap and giving them a careful count, while I kept one eye on the little lizard on her arm and the other on the coffee shop entrance.

I was fairly sure the gecko would stay put, and more anxious about who might walk through the door. It wouldn't be Leopold, not unless someone had come up with an instant cure for agoraphobia, but a woman like Chloe could probably count on more than a tattoo for protection.

'It's five thousand dollars,' she said.

'I'm a man of my word.'

'Well, have you got any more words? You said this was for listening. I guess you've got my attention.'

While I talked, she held the money in her hand and kept her hand in her lap, making a fan of the bills, then gathering them together. When the waiter brought more iced tea, she shifted her bag to block his view of the cash. When he withdrew, her hands resumed their play.

When I stopped, she returned the bills to the envelope. She said, 'Suppose I say no. Then what?'

'Then I'll be disappointed, but it won't be the first time.'

'And?'

'And my client will be disappointed, but he'll have to learn to live with it.'

'Do I have to give back the money?'

I shook my head. 'You earned it when you showed up.'

'But I could have a lot more. Just for one spoon.'

'That's right. But not just any spoon. I'm not sure if you know the one I mean, but—'

'There are four of them,' she said patiently, 'in the cabinet with the rest of Whatsisname's stuff.'

'Myer Myers.'

'Uh-huh. Caesar Rodney from Delaware with the horse he rode in on. Benjamin Franklin from Pennsylvania with a key, because of that experiment with the kite. And John Hart from New Jersey, with a deer's head, antlers and all. I don't know who he was or what the deer's about.'

'I don't know who he was either, but I think it's a pun. A hart is another name for a male deer.'

'I bet that's it,' she said, 'because the fourth spoon's a play on the name, too. Button Gwinnett of Georgia, and it's got, duh, this little button. That's the only one you want? You don't care about the others?'

'Just that one.'

'And I bring it to you, and then what happens?'

'You get twenty thousand dollars.'

'And that's not counting what you just gave me. That's twenty more, for a total of twenty-five.'

'I see you're good at math, too.'

She gave me a look. 'Look,' she said, 'what I am basically is this slacker drifting through life and not amounting to anything, okay? I keep taking college courses, one or two a year, but I'll never get a degree, and I don't want one because it would just make me overqualified.'

'For what?'

'For anything. I could teach yoga, except I hate teaching, and I'm a massage therapist qualified in Swedish and shiatsu and Coblenz reflexology, but I found out I hate touching strangers. You saw what I was doing with the money you gave me?'

'After you counted the bills? Shuffling them, it looked like.'

'I was playing with them,' she said. 'I never had anywhere near that much cash before. So if I played with it then it was play money and I didn't have to be scared of it. What am I supposed to do with it?'

'Whatever you want.'

'Like put it in the bank?'

'You could.'

'But you wouldn't.'

'Well, somebody someday might want to know where it came from.'

'Got it. So I should keep it in cash, but someplace safe.'

'That's what I always do.'

Her eyes narrowed, and I could see her mind working. 'That was you last night,' she said. 'When I got home he was all excited about the book he'd bought. But last night you were using a different name.'

'I was.'

'An alias, I guess they call it.'

'That's if you use it with some frequency,' I said. 'In this instance it was just a name I assumed for the occasion.'

'She thought you were this nebbishy low-rent guy with a store and a cat.'

'Janine.'

'Yeah, alias Janine. "You'd have fun with him," she said. Like she's going places, and I'm not, so I could afford to waste my time with a loser.'

'Like me.'

'Uh-huh. Like you, Joe Loser. Meanwhile you've got all this cash that you know enough not to keep in a bank.'

'I'm not exactly rolling in it.'

'But when you want some, you find a way to get some.'

'Well, it tends to work out that way.'

'You make money the old-fashioned way. You steal it.' She took a deep breath, let it out. 'Okay,' she said.

'Okay? You mean you'll do it?'

She nodded. 'How long am I supposed to think about it? I'll get it out of the cabinet tonight and bring it to your store tomorrow afternoon. Twenty thousand dollars?'

'I'll have it ready.'

'Great.' She stood up, hesitated. 'Uh, my iced tea . . . '

Joe Loser told her he'd take care of it.

TWENTY-SEVEN

Why buttons?

I'd held off as long as I could, but eventually I'd had to ask.

'Why does anyone collect anything, Mr Rhodenbarr? I'm familiar with all the theories, as I trust are you. To create the illusion of order in an unordered universe. To accumulate objects which will in some way reflect a flattering image of oneself. To present oneself with a challenge, and rise to it; to get hold of every different kind of stamp or coin or book or widget, to possess the finest specimen, or the rarest sub-variety, or otherwise outdo one's fellow collectors.

'Many men take up collecting late in life. They've been successful, they've made all this money, and they want to spend some of it in a gratifying fashion. Why buy another stock certificate when one can buy a painting? "My art collection," Mr Puglash can announce, gesturing offhandedly toward what's on his walls. When he runs out of wall space, he can lend pieces to museums. *From the Russell N. Puglash Collection*, the little brass plate will state, and he can bask in its reflected glory.'

'But you started collecting early,' I guessed.

'I was born with the impulse,' he said. 'I tried different hobbies, as boys will do. Brought home rolls of pennies from the bank, sorting for different dates and mint marks. Picked up bottle caps off the street, trying to see how many different ones I could find.' He sighed. 'And then one day an aunt gave me a handful of buttons. Odd ones that had come off coats and dresses, I suppose. The sort of buttons that accumulate in a corner of a sewing box, never to be either used or discarded. "Buttons for you, my little Button."' His eyes met mine. 'My name,' he said, 'is not actually Smith.'

'I'm shocked.'

'It's actually Burton Barton the Fifth.' He looked off into the middle distance, remembering. 'My great-great-grandfather was the first Burton Barton, having been given his mother's maiden name for a first name. He liked the name well enough to pass it on to his first-born son, my great-grandfather, who went through life answering to Junior. His only son was my grandfather, Burton Barton the Third, called Burtie in childhood and Burt thereafter, and by the time that gentleman had given the world a son, the family was forever in thrall to tradition. A third Burton Barton could only be followed by a fourth.'

'Your father.'

'Known to one and all as Buster. "I'm Buster Brown, I live in a shoe." An inane slogan, but one remembers it, so perhaps it sold shoes. My father was more bluster than buster, but he gloried in the nickname, and perhaps it suited him. In any event in the fullness of time he took a wife, and she produced a male heir. I've told you the inevitable name I was given, and you can probably guess the nickname that soon followed.

'"He's just as cute as a button," some female relative said, and that was that. I suppose it's more remarkable that it took five generations of Burton Bartons for that name to pop up. I liked the nickname well enough. I was happy enough to bear it.'

So an aunt's handful of buttons had grown into a lifelong passion. In due course the penny collection was spent, the bottle caps discarded. Friends and relatives were advised to set aside attractive or unusual buttons for young Button, who sought them for his collection.

And one thing led to another. Political buttons. Benjamin Button.

And Button Gwinnett.

TWENTY-EIGHT

With the devil-may-care attitude I seemed to have acquired, I'd left my bargain table on the sidewalk when I went to meet Chloe. On my way back downtown I wondered if it would still be there. It would make a nice kitchen table, once you got rid of the books.

But it was right where I'd left it, and so, alas, were the books. And there was a note, a mate to the one I'd found before, printed in block capitals on a small sheet of lined notebook paper, but with a longer message this time: *GONE AGAIN! I SNUCK OUT OF WORK AND STILL NO LUCK. SOMEBODY LEFT YOU TWO DOLLAR BILLS. GOOD THING I AM HONEST. I PUT THEM WHERE THEY WON'T BLOW AWAY. CZECH AROUND AND SEE.*

Huh?

I read it through a second time, noted the spelling of the first word in the last sentence, and reached for a battered copy of the Lonely Planet guide to Czechoslovakia. The depreciation rate for travel books is pretty fierce, and anything more than a year or two old is essentially worthless. Still, wouldn't some passerby be whimsical enough to snap up a guidebook to a country that no longer existed?

Evidently not. I found the promised pair of dollar bills inside the book's front cover, considered leaving them there to reward whimsy, decided whimsy was its own reward, and gave them a home in my wallet.

Inside, I looked around for the first note, and was comparing it to the second when the bell announced a visitor. 'You gotta get that fixed,' Ray Kirschmann said. 'Way it is now, it makes that little tinkling noise every time I open the door.'

'It's not just you,' I told him. 'It makes the same noise no matter who walks in.'

'And here I thought I was special, Bernie. Whatcha got there?'

'Two notes,' I said, 'written days apart, and left on my bargain table.'

'Looks like the same paper. From one of them little notebooks.'

'It does look the same, doesn't it?'

'Same pen, too, from the looks of things. Blue felt tip with a fine point. This here was written first.'

'It was,' I said. 'How'd you know that?'

'Notice how these letters are thicker? The felt tip's a little worn down.'

'Right you are, Ray. I hadn't noticed.'

'Well, I'm a trained investigator, Bernie. I'm supposed to notice things like that. Far as how much earlier this note was written, that I couldn't tell you.'

'You couldn't? I'll bet Sherlock Holmes could.'

'Yeah, and so could those geniuses on CSI. Give 'em fifteen

minutes and they can bounce a DNA sample off a data base and tell you how much the writer weighs and what she had for breakfast. Of course that's TV.'

'And we're down here in the real world.'

'Where they just this morning finally worked out what killed the old lady.'

'Mrs Ostermaier.'

He nodded. 'It wasn't a bee flew up her nose,' he said. 'It was peanuts.'

'Peanuts flew up her nose?'

'Flyin' peanuts,' he said. 'Nobody ever thought of that. It'd explain it, too.'

'Explain what?'

'Why her blood work showed peanuts but her stomach contents didn't.'

'How could that be?'

'It couldn't. We oughta be on television, Bernie. That'd be the clue that broke the case, but we're here on Planet Earth and all it means is the crime lab missed somethin'. There was peanuts in her stomach, or she had peanut oil in her salad dressing, or some food that was cooked in it.'

'I guess nobody's perfect.'

'Not in the real world. Anyway, it's peanuts that killed her.'

'I read up a little on anaphylactic shock,' I said. 'Out of curiosity. A surprising number of people die of it, and sometimes there's no prior history of allergic reaction, or not enough to pay attention to. Maybe you got stung by a bee once, and you had a red bump for a day or two, and then it went away. Then two years later another bee stings you and your heart stops.'

'Well, Mrs O. was allergic. She had a bunch of allergies when she was a kid, and peanuts was one of 'em. Then she outgrew 'em, the way kids'll do.'

200

'And then what? It came back?'

'Two, three years ago. She got shingles, which sounds like it oughta be funny, with a name like that. "Oh, you got shingles? What are they, cedar? You gonna paint 'em or leave 'em natural?" Only my uncle had 'em and there was nothin' funny about it. But he was fine once he got over it. When she got over the shingles, she had allergies.'

'To peanuts.'

'And a couple of other things, but peanuts was the main one. She carried a little syringe in her purse in case she got a bad attack. I forget what was in it.'

'Epinephrine.'

'I guess you did read up on it. Yeah, that sounds right. It was still in her purse, so I guess she never got a chance to use it.'

'It must have hit her hard all at once.'

'Or she thought it was something else. "I'm a little woozy, I'll just put my coat down, see if I can't catch my breath."'

'And by the time she realized what was going on—'

'It was too late, assumin' she ever realized it at all. But you know what this means, don't you, Bernie?'

'What?'

'It's not homicide. You already figured out that the burglar got there after the woman was dead. And if the death was from natural causes, and you can't get much more natural than a peanut, and if it all happened before the burglar was on the scene, then you can forget all about felony murder.'

'Because the death and the felony had nothing to do with one another.'

'Right.'

'It was just a coincidence,' I said, 'that an intruder turned up an hour or so after she had one peanut too many.'

He frowned. 'A coincidence on TV,' he said, 'is a bad sign.'

'While in real life—'

'It still gives me a headache. But there's got to be such a thing as a coincidence or how would we happen to have a word for it?'

TWENTY-NINE

'Like unicorns,' Carolyn said at the Bum Rap. 'If they didn't exist, where did the word come from? Let me see those notes again.'

'For a while,' I said, 'I wondered if the first note might be from Chloe. It didn't make any sense, but I couldn't shake the feeling.'

'But when you found the second note—'

'I knew it wasn't her, because it would have been left while I was sitting across a table from her in Three Guys.'

'After having had lunch with me,' she said, 'from Two Guys. How's that for a unicorn?'

'It's a nice one.'

'Maybe that's what the mystery meat was this afternoon.'

'Unicorn? I hope not.'

'So do I. I try to avoid eating endangered species, let alone myth-ical ones. You thought it was from Chloe because you wanted it to be. You couldn't get those remarkably soft hands out of your mind.'

'No,' I said. 'I got the first note the day before I set foot in Edwin Leopold's penthouse. I didn't even know about Miss Miller's magic fingers, or that they shared an arm with a gecko. I saw the whole tattoo today, by the way. If a person has to have a tattoo, it's not a bad one.'

'But fortunately,' she said, 'a person doesn't. You could have been thinking about her anyway, Bern. You just saw her the one time, when she bought Frank Norris for her Kindle, but then Janine mentioned her, and that could have got you thinking.'

'I was wondering if she'd ever stop in again,' I admitted.

'And she didn't, and now she's gonna steal a spoon for you. Just like that.'

'Unless she chickens out.'

'You think she will?'

'No,' I said. 'I think she gave the whole business about twenty seconds of serious thought and made her decision. And she'll stick with it.'

'She lives with this man—'

'She lives in his house. That's not the same as living with him.'

'They have a relationship, Bern.'

'He's her employer. One of the services she performs has a sexual element to it.'

'No kidding.'

'He calls her Miss Miller,' I said, 'and she calls him Mr Leopold. She's a licensed massage therapist.'

'Who doesn't like touching strangers.'

'Which he's not, since she sees the man seven days a week, but neither is he a lover. Once a day he hops off the treadmill, takes a shower, and lies down on the massage table. The massage is therapeutic.'

'So why does she take her top off? To make it more therapeutic?'

My glass was empty, and our conversation was making me thirsty. I guess Maxine somehow sensed this, because she appeared with a fresh drink without my having summoned her. 'You're a mind-reader,' I said, and drank deep. To Carolyn I said, 'So maybe Chloe's a little bit of an exhibitionist. Maybe she doesn't want to get her blouse all sweaty. Maybe she figures it won't take as long if she gives him something nice to look at. Why are you all hipped on this all of a sudden?'

'I don't know,' she said, and thought about it. 'Maybe I'm jealous, Bern.'

'Of her?'

'Of him, with his daily rubdown and his daily happy ending.'

'Is that something you'd want?'

'No,' she said, 'it's not, not at all, and that's why I'm jealous. Not just that he gets to have it, but that he gets to want it. The son of a bitch, I'm *glad* she's stealing his goddam spoon.'

A drink later, she said, 'I wonder who left the notes.'

'A stranger. Someone I don't know, and will evidently never get to meet, since she only comes around when I'm not there.'

'Twice.'

'Probably more than that. Look at the first note. *WHY ARE YOU ALWAYS CLOSED?* Meaning every time she comes by I'm closed, but this time she could leave a note because my table was on the street.'

'And she saw your table, so that made her come over, and then you were closed, and she was really pissed.'

'Well, disappointed, anyway. And the same thing happened again today, and she left another note.'

She sipped her drink. 'We keep saying "she,"' she said. 'How do we know it's a woman?'

'We don't, not really. The writing is plain block capitals. There's nothing gender-specific about it.'

'And yet a woman wrote it, and we both know it.'

'Yeah,' I said. 'And Ray made the same assumption, come to think of it. He said "she," and I barely noticed.'

'So she's a woman, Bern. If all three of us know it, who cares why we know it? She's a woman. What else do we know about her?'

'She carries a little notebook.'

'And a blue felt-tip pen.'

'And she tears sheets out of it without taking the time to open the three little rings.'

'Why bother? She's gonna leave the note on your table, not put it back in the notebook. She printed both notes. Maybe her hand-writing's lousy.'

'You think? Her printing's very neat.'

'Good point. You know what I read somewhere? A lot of kids these days aren't being taught cursive writing. They're using a keyboard all the time, so printing's good enough when they actually have to use a pen or pencil.'

'Goodbye, Palmer Method,' I said. 'What about SpeedWriting?'

'I guess it's SpeedPrinting these days.'

'"F U CN RD THS, U CN GT FKD,"' I said. 'Remember those ads in the subways?'

'I thought the message was something about getting a good job. I guess there were different versions.'

'Must have been. Remember SpeedReading?'

'Evelyn Wood, Bern. Read a whole book as quickly as you can turn the pages.'

'I wonder if anybody ever took both courses. SpeedWriting and SpeedReading.'

'Maybe that woman who writes twenty reviews a day for Amazon. I forget her name.'

'You must have read it too quickly. Skimmed right over it.'

'I guess.'

'Or she left out the vowels. "F U CN RD HRRT KLSNR, U CN GT A GD RVW."'

'Bern, we're getting off the subject here. All we know is she prints. What else?'

'She's honest.'

'Because she didn't take the two dollars. She's more than honest, she's considerate.'

'Because she put them out of sight, so nobody else would take them.'

'And said so in the note, and spelled it "Czech" so you'd know to look in the book.'

'So she's clever, too, and given to wordplay.'

'Are you gonna leave her a note?'

'You think I should?'

'It's only polite, Bern. Besides, you're wondering about her. You're hoping she's cute.'

'Don't be ridiculous,' I said. I drank some of my drink, which was mostly melted ice. 'I thought about a note,' I admitted, 'when I was closing up. But I couldn't leave my table out all night. That would be suggesting that I wanted somebody to take it away.'

'Or you'd get a summons for littering. You could tape a note to the window.'

'"SORRY, STILL CLOSED."'

'Maybe not. Next time you leave the table out—'

'I'll leave a note. If I remember.'

'So it wasn't murder,' she said.

We'd left the Bum Rap, and not a moment too soon, and were walking in the general direction of Arbor Court, which was also the general direction of the Seventh Avenue subway.

'It was natural causes,' I said.

'And a burglar with a key just happened to pick that time to show up.'

'Whoever the intruder was,' I said, 'and whatever he was looking for, there was nothing wrong with his timing. It was *her* timing that threw things off. If she hadn't left the opera early—'

'She'd still be alive?'

'Maybe,' I said, 'and maybe not, depending on how she got the peanuts into her system. But she wouldn't have been home and on the floor when he unlocked her door.'

'It sounds as if you're blaming the victim,' she said, 'but how can you blame anybody for giving up on Wagner?'

'Oh, I don't know. Mark Twain said his music's not as bad as it sounds.'

'I thought Mick Jagger said that about Barry Manilow.'

'You may be right. Something bothers me.'

'About Chloe? You think she might get caught?'

'No, she won't get caught.'

'About the woman who left you the notes?'

'No, either she'll turn up or she won't, and either way it's not important. No, what bothers me is the whole way she died.'

'The peanut lady.'

'Mrs Ostermaier.'

'Right. Well, of course it bothers you. It's sad, a nice woman like that. And you know what's really terrible, Bern? It'd be funny, except a woman's dead, so how can it be funny?'

'What are you talking about?'

'The song,' she said. 'The goddam song, the ad jingle. I can't get the damn thing out of my head.'

'What song?'

'Oh, like I'm the only one with the jingle running through my mind? *"I wish I was an Ostermaier wiener, that is what I really want to be, 'cause if I was an Ostermaier wiener, everyone would be in love with me.*" Come on, Bern. Don't tell me it's not running in your head the same as it is in mine.'

'Well, it is now,' I said. 'Thanks a lot.'

THIRTY

When you can't get a song out of your head, when it's muzak and your mind's the elevator, when it keeps repeating on you like a decimal or a bad burrito, there's a word for it. You've got what's called an earworm, and sooner or later it will go away. But until it does, well, it doesn't.

Carolyn's take on the Oscar Meyer jingle grabbed a hold and wouldn't let go. The subway was crowded and noisy – I know, it's hard to believe – and I didn't get a seat until it thinned out some at Penn Station. I tried to divert myself with the ads, but not even Dr Zizmor's offer to improve my complexion could stifle the Ostermaier Wiener.

I got off at 72nd Street, and I don't suppose it was entirely co-incidental that I stood at the counter at Papaya King and let a pair of hot dogs serve as dinner.

I went home and played music, which didn't help, and tried

TV, which didn't help either. I picked up a book and read about Bill Bryson's adventures in Australia, and kept finding passages I'd have read aloud, if I hadn't been alone in my apartment. I went on reading, and I chuckled some, and nodded in occasional agreement, and all the while the earworm went on burrowing in my consciousness.

I tried other jingles, the most annoying ones I could recall. That seemed dangerous, because what if the cure proved more enduring than the disease? I tried the Pepsi jingle, a bare childhood memory (*Pepsi-Cola hits the spot / Two full glasses, that's a lot*) and my mind quickly segued into the parody (*Christianity hits the spot / Twelve apostles, that's a lot*) and that sent me back to apostle spoons, and Button Gwinnett, and Chloe Miller, and I did a certain amount of thinking and worrying and wondering, and underneath it all was the Ostermaier jingle, ever the relentless background music to my rumination, and harder to shake than a summer cold.

I got undressed. I had a shower. I got in bed with the Bryson book and a cup of chamomile tea, read one and drank the other. When I closed the book and switched off the lamp, my earworm was still hard at work. I decided it must hold the secret of the universe, and I meditated upon it one word at a time, and while I was at it I fell asleep.

When I woke up it was gone.

I opened up around ten. After my usual chores on Raffles's behalf (spooning out cat food, freshening his water dish, flushing the toilet) I dragged my bargain table out onto the street. When I got back inside the phone was ringing.

It was Ray. 'I called ten minutes ago,' he said. 'You didn't pick up.'

'I wasn't here.'

'That's what I figured. You know, I almost called you late last night.'

'I wasn't here then, either.'

'At home.'

'Well, you'd have reached me there, but if it was late I can't say I'd have welcomed your call. I went to bed early with an earworm.'

'That's a hell of a thing, Bernie. A man takes his life in his hands when he leaves the city, and if it's not Lyme disease or bees flyin' up your nose, it's worms in your ears. Where'd you pick it up?'

'Actually,' I said, 'I got it from Carolyn.'

'From Shorty? I can't say I'm surprised, the places she goes and the degenerates she hangs out with. You seein' a doctor?'

'It's all better now, Ray.'

'You sure? A thing like that, if it comes back—'

God forbid. 'I'll take measures,' I assured him. 'You said you almost called last night. Why?'

'I had somethin' on my mind, and I couldn't stop thinkin' about it.'

'I know the feeling.'

'And it's from somethin' you said.'

'Oh?'

'Or didn't say. This Ostermaier case, which isn't even a homicide anymore, on account of you can't get an indictment against a peanut.'

'It'd be different,' I said, 'if it was a ham sandwich. What was it I said?'

'Intruder.'

'Huh?'

'What you figured out,' he said, 'and all credit to you for it, because it's helpful, is that the old lady was already dead when the burglar got there.'

'Well, it certainly looks that way to me, Ray, but—'

'No, it does to me, too, now that you laid it out for me. She came home and dropped dead, and an hour later he came callin'. The intruder.'

'So?'

'That's what you called him, Bernie. The intruder.'

'Well,' I said, 'he was intruding, wasn't he?'

'You never once called him a burglar. And it's not like it's a word you've never heard before, bein' as you been one yourself for all the years I've known you.'

'I always called him an intruder?'

'Every time.'

'And never a burglar.'

'Not once, Bernie.'

I looked over at Raffles, who had been stalking something invisible to the human eye, and who was now gathering himself to pounce on it.

'It must have been unconscious,' I said.

'So I should just forget about it?'

'No, because it has to mean something. Ray, I guess I just don't think of the guy as a burglar.'

'Because he had a key.'

'There have been times,' I said, 'when I had a key.'

'You're sayin' this was different.'

'All those objects scattered around.'

'The cigarette lighter. The little ivory Chinaman. The figurines.'

'Everything,' I said. 'And nothing broken, as though they'd been deliberately arranged that way.'

'Why would anybody do that?'

'To make it look like a burglary,' I said. 'And the only reason anybody would carefully stage a scene to look like a burglary—'

'Is if it wasn't.'

'Right.'

'Four children,' he said.

'They all must have had keys.'

'They used to live there, Bernie. And why wouldn't they have keys to their mother's house?'

'It would be interesting to know more about them.'

There was a pause. 'Well, I was gonna type up a report,' he said, 'and it's too nice a day for that. I already talked to all of 'em once. Maybe I'll talk to 'em some more.'

A few minutes later the phone rang again. I'd thought it might be Chloe the first time, and I thought so again, and this time it was Mowgli. 'Just wanted to make sure you're open,' he said. 'Okay if I come by in like five minutes?'

It was more like ten, and he didn't spend much more time than that in the shop, scanning my shelves with a practiced eye, picking out ten books and paying the marked price without a murmur. Then he left, and the phone rang a third time, and it was Carolyn.

'Barnegat Books,' I said, and she asked me what was the matter.

'I'm sorry,' I said. 'Was I snarling? I didn't mean to. I keep expecting it to be Chloe, and it keeps being somebody else.'

'That's why I was calling, Bern. To see if you'd heard from her, but I guess I know the answer.'

'She didn't say she'd call,' I said. 'She said she'd come by, and sometime in the afternoon.'

'But it's on your mind.'

'It's hard not to think of all the things that could go wrong.'

'I can imagine. Look, the other part of why I'm calling is I know it's your turn to pick up lunch and bring it over here, but why don't I switch with you? You want to be around if the phone rings.'

'Or if the door opens,' I said. 'Thanks, I appreciate it.'

214

'Not a problem. Uh, as far as what kind of food—'

'Surprise me,' I said.

'Juneau Lock,' I said, an hour or so later. 'What a surprise.'

'You don't look surprised,' she said, 'but you don't look disappointed, either. I was all set to go somewhere else, and I had this vision of Chloe turning up sometime this afternoon.'

'I hope it proves prophetic.'

'No you don't, Bern, because in the vision she's wearing handcuffs, and there's a cop on either side of her.'

'Oh.'

'And they take you away,' she said, 'and what did you have for your last meal as a free man? A soggy Reuben sandwich from the deli? Some vegan slop from Transcendental Tofu?'

'You did the right thing,' I said, 'right up until the point where you told me about your vision.'

'Oh, it's not really a vision, Bern. Just a fleeting thought. By the way, our girlfriend at Two Guys seemed surprised to see me. I think she keeps track of whose turn it is.'

Lunch was almost good enough to take my mind off Chloe and the silver spoon, which could turn up someday as the title of a children's book, but probably won't. If she did show up handcuffed to a cop, I'd have a lot of explaining to do, and how would I explain the $20,000 I was carrying?

'If everything works out,' I told Carolyn, 'then it's a good investment. I give her twenty thousand—'

'Plus the five you already gave her.'

'Right. And Barton pays me fifty thousand for the spoon.'

'So you double your money without having to do anything.'

'It seemed that way,' I said, 'when I thought of it. I'd been to Leopold's apartment, I knew I couldn't possibly spirit the spoon out of there, and I was ready to give up. Then all of a sudden there was a way after all, and she'd do the work and run all the risk, and I'd split the money with her. But I forgot my number one rule.'

'Never have a partner.'

'Especially an amateur,' I said, 'and particularly an amateur who's never done this before. There's only one thing that gives me hope.'

'What's that?'

'Her attitude,' I said. 'I think she just might be a natural-born thief.'

The phone rang once during lunch, and I moved more quickly than usual to get to it. A woman wanted to know how long I'd be open. I said five-thirty, and she rang off without another word.

I reported the conversation to Carolyn, and she asked if it could have been Chloe.

'It didn't sound like her,' I said. 'And why would she be so cryptic?'

'Maybe Leopold was standing next to her and she didn't want to give anything away.'

'Well, she didn't,' I said. 'Not to him and not to me either. Anyway, her voice is deeper than the one I heard just now. That's four calls today, which is more than I usually get in a week.'

'The Universe knows you're expecting a call,' she said, 'and it's doing all it can to fulfill your expectations.'

'Did you really say that? You know, if this food didn't taste as good as it does, I'd think you picked it up at Transcendental Tofu.'

THIRTY-ONE

I had two more phone calls within an hour of Carolyn's depart-ure for the Poodle Factory and a pressing appointment with a Kerry blue terrier. One was a wrong number, a drunk who couldn't believe I wouldn't put the mayor on the phone. 'I know he's there,' he said. 'All right, never mind the high-hat sonofa-bitch. Lemme talk to FDR.'

I would have liked to hear what else he had to say, but I wanted to keep the line open. And, sure enough, the phone rang again a few minutes later, and this time it was my client.

'I hope I'll have some news soon,' I told him.

He would have liked a more informative answer, but that was all he was going to get.

I picked up a book, read two pages, put it down again. I walked over to a bank of shelves and rearranged some books. I crumpled a ball of paper and tossed it to Raffles, who ignored it utterly.

And then the door opened, and there she was.

'Hi,' she said.

'I was wondering if you'd come.'

'What time is it?' She glanced at her wrist and answered her own question. 'I'm right on time. In fact it's two twenty-eight, so I'm two minutes early.'

'So you are,' I said. 'But you didn't call.'

'Was I supposed to?'

She was wearing jeans, though lighter in color than the pair she'd worn to Three Guys, and she'd left the denim jacket home. Her top was a man's dress shirt in French blue, and my client would have approved of the button-down collar. I've called it a man's shirt, but it had clearly been cut for a woman, and I suppose it had the buttons on the other side.

And who do you suppose thought that one up? *'Now here's my idea, Chuck. For guys, whether it's a shirt or a coat, we'll put the buttons on the right and the buttonholes on the left. And with women, see, we'll do it the other way around. Why? Gee, I dunno. It just, like, feels somehow right to me, ya know?'*

'No,' I said. 'But I thought you might, although I don't suppose there was any reason why you should. I guess it's just that I was concerned that something might have gone wrong. That you'd change your mind, or that you might, um, encounter some difficulty.'

'Like get caught in the act, you mean?'

'Or get away with it, only to have him notice the spoon's absence.'

She nodded, thinking about it. 'Well, first of all,' she said, 'I didn't change my mind. I knew I wasn't going to, but there was no way for you to know that, so I can see why you might worry. But I didn't. Didn't change my mind, I mean, but what I also

218

didn't do was worry. I just went ahead and did what I said I was going to do.'

'And the spoon is—'

She patted her handbag. Somewhere within its confines was an eReader with a Frank Norris novel on it, and a spoon with a teardrop-shaped bowl.

'You brought it,' I said.

'Yeah, isn't that what we said? I'd bring the spoon and you'd have the money for me?' Her brow clouded. 'That didn't change overnight, did it? The price?'

'No, no,' I said. 'I have it. Here, with me.'

It was just too straightforward and simple, I thought. Too easy.

'What happens,' I wondered aloud, 'when he notices that it's missing? That there are only three spoons where there used to be four?'

'Oh, he knows,' she said.

'He knows?'

'Sure,' she said. 'I told him.'

'You told him.'

'Yeah, I told him right away. That was the first thing I did. Well, not the first thing, but almost.'

Was this a set-up? Was she wearing a wire? Was there a white van parked across the street, bearing on its side panels the name and address of some nonexistent construction firm in Maspeth? And were its occupants even now listening to our conversation and laughing hysterically?

'I waited until I heard him on the treadmill,' she said, 'and I got my key and unlocked the cupboard and took the spoon and locked up again and tucked the spoon away in my bag. Hey, I hope I got the right one. Gwinnett, the signer from Georgia? With the button on it?'

I just nodded. Let the cops in the truck make what they wanted out of a silent nod.

'So I was all set,' she went on, 'and he was still getting his five miles in. Then when he got out of the shower and dried off I went in and gave him his massage. That always puts him in a good mood.'

'I'm sure it does.'

'And then I said, "Say, I was wondering. Did you loan out one of the Signer spoons? Because I looked in the log book and I couldn't find a notation." See, sometimes he'll lend a piece for a museum show, and there'll be a note to that effect in the records of the collection, along with the letter from the institution, thanks for letting us display this exceptional specimen, di dah di dah di dah.

'And he said no, all four spoons were in the living room cabinet where they belong. And I said the last time I polished them I noticed there were only three, and I meant to mention it to him, but I kept forgetting. So we went in and checked, and Button Gwinnett was missing, and he said that was funny, he could have sworn they were all there the other night, and I said no, it must have been a good week since I noticed one wasn't there, and I really meant to mention it, but I wasn't really worried because I took it for granted he'd let his buddy at the Historical Society borrow it, or the other museum up the block, or there's a lady in Philadelphia at Independence Hall who's always bugging us about stuff related to the signers. By the time I left for my class, we'd pretty much agreed that he must have let somebody borrow it, and it was a matter of figuring out who it was. Why are you looking at me like that?'

'I'm in awe.'

'Yeah? I don't know how stuff like this is supposed to work, but I thought I better be the one who notices it's missing. If he spots it first, who's the first person he looks at?'

220

'It makes perfect sense.'

'Plus I didn't want him thinking it was you that took it, even if he doesn't know who you are. "There was a fellow here the other night, a Mr Lederman." *He* said Lederman, but that wasn't quite right, was it?'

'Lederer.'

'So he remembered it wrong, which is even better. "A nice fellow, brought me the Culloden book. But I made sure he was never out of my sight."'

'All that coffee,' I remembered, 'and he never once went to the bathroom. His back teeth must have been floating by the time I got out of there.'

'So he knew you couldn't have taken it, but now he knows it went missing before you came over. So you're clear, and so's Lederer, and Lederman, too, as far as that goes.'

'I'll let them both know,' I said. 'It'll be a load off their minds.'

'He'll have me write letters,' she said, 'to a couple of museums. And then something else'll go missing, and when it turns up he'll realize he misplaced it, and he'll decide that must have been what happened to the spoon. And he'll wait for it to turn up.'

'But without any great sense of urgency.'

'No, because it's not like he needs it to stir his oatmeal.' She took a deep breath. 'Well,' she said. 'I guess you'd like to see the spoon.'

'That would be good.'

'And I'd just as soon get it out of my purse.'

She passed it to me, swathed in tissue paper. I unswathed it, and it wasn't Ben Franklin with his key or Caesar Rodney with his horse. I wrapped it up again, slipped it in a pocket.

'Um,' she said.

'Oh, right.' I fetched envelopes from my cash box. 'You'll want to count these. It'll be more private in back.'

She disappeared into my back room. I took one more look at the spoon, ran my thumb over the refined features of the gentleman from Georgia and his eponymous Button.

Then, the spoon back in my pocket, I went to the window and looked outside. No white van, no van of any sort.

Not that I expected one. But you can't be too paranoid, can you?

'Twenty thousand dollars,' she said.

'I gather it was all there?'

She nodded. She seemed perfectly calm, but there was excitement in her eyes. 'Plus the five thousand you already gave me.'

'Yes, we don't want to forget that.'

'I'll say. It's as much as I earn in a year.'

'Twenty-five thousand?'

'*Five* thousand,' she said. 'Well, fifty-two hundred, to be exact. I get a hundred a week.'

I found myself computing the average cost of a happy ending, and some of that may have shown on my face.

'It's not much money,' she said, 'but I've got a better deal than a whole lot of people. I have my own room in an amazing Upper Fifth Avenue apartment, and I have my meals, and my hours are very flexible. But it's hard to put any money aside, you know?'

'I can imagine.'

'What I want to do,' she said, 'is go to Europe. I had it worked out that ten thousand dollars would give me a year in Europe. You don't think so? I couldn't have a real job over there, but I don't have a real job here, do I? I could find ways to make money. I could teach ESL. You know, English as a second language? Which never made sense to me, calling it that, because if English is your first language, nobody has to teach it to you. You just pick it up from your parents.'

222

'I never thought of it that way.'

'Or something else'll turn up. Something always does, and it's always an education, you know? I mean, I didn't know anything about silver until I started working for Mr L. And now look at all I've learned about silver, and about American history.'

'And now you can learn all about European history.'

'I was going to take a course in the fall. Europe Since 1815. In other words, after Napoleon. Then later on I guess I'd have to go back and learn something about Napoleon.'

'Before you know it,' I said, 'you'll be back in ancient Rome.'

'That's on my list of places to go. Rome, I mean. Ancient Rome, I'd need a time machine. But for modern Rome, I could go tomorrow.'

'I don't think—'

'Oh, I know! I'll stay right where I am, at the very least until the end of August.'

'That's a good idea.'

'And I won't spend one dime of this money, and if I see something in a shop window that I'll just die if I don't buy it, I'll do what I do now.'

'What's that?'

'I won't buy it,' she said, 'and I won't die, either.' She patted her handbag. 'I'll keep this until it's time to go. I'm not stupid.'

'I can see that.'

'Except I am, in a way, because until yesterday it never occurred to me that I could make money this way.'

'By stealing,' I said, partly to see if she recoiled at the word.

'Right. I mean, I had the thought that this stuff was worth money, and it wouldn't be hard to get out the door with it. But then what? So that's as far as the thought ever went, until you came along.'

'In shining armor.'

223

'Yeah. Um, this works out to be a good deal for both of us, right? You'll make money, too, won't you?'

'About the same amount as you. And without the risk.'

'What about the risk that I'd chicken out and go whining to the police? No, you took a chance. We both did, and we both get a payoff, and I think that's really neat. I owe you a lot, really. You opened up a whole world for me.'

'Well—'

'I wish there was something I could do, and do you know what? There is.' She walked to the door, threw the bolt, and turned the sign in the window from OPEN to CLOSED. 'You're not exactly packed with customers,' she said, 'and I saw you've got a couch in the back room, and I'm a trained masseuse. So why don't you let me give you the best massage you ever had in your life?'

THIRTY-TWO

***

THIRTY-THREE

And what did I know about Button Gwinnett?

A good deal more than I'd known a month ago. Back then all I knew was what most people know – he'd been one of the fifty-six signers of the Declaration of Independence, and he'd written his name infrequently enough to make his signature far and away the rarest of the lot. The signers have always been a popular topic for autograph collectors, and it's not hard to understand why; signing their names, after all, was the source of fame for these men, and if you could manage to get all fifty-six—

Well, see, you couldn't. Not without Button Gwinnett, and that's what made his signature hugely expensive.

That's about all I knew. Since then I'd learned, from my client and from my good buddies Google and Wikipedia, a fair amount more. For one thing, I learned that he'd come by his first name honestly. He'd been born in 1735 in England to Welsh parents, and his mother's maiden name was Button. He went to school in Gloucester, where his name may have gotten him teased by the other boys, but maybe not. Maybe the kids were nicer there than the ones I knew in Ohio.

He set up as a merchant, got married, emigrated to the colonies, and moved from Charleston to Georgia, where he bought land and started a plantation. He was politically active, and became the bitter rival of another Georgian, one Lachlan McIntosh.

John Hancock of Massachusetts was the first man to sign the Declaration of Independence, and we all learned how he wielded his quill pen with a bold flourish while announcing that King George wouldn't need his spectacles to read it. And everybody recognizes that signature, although the man himself has about as much connection to the insurance company as Ethan Allen has to the furniture. What you don't know (or at least I didn't) is that Button Gwinnett was the second person to put his name on the Declaration.

Remember Lachlan McIntosh? Gwinnett was in line for the command of the First Regiment of the Continental Army, but McIntosh beat him out. This didn't sit well with Gwinnett, and the possibility exists that he didn't handle disappointment well. And, on the 16th of May in 1777, less than a year after he'd made himself immortal by signing his name, he proved his mortality on the physical plane by losing a duel to that same Lachlan McIntosh. He died of his wounds three days later, on the 19th of May.

Or it may have been eleven days later, on the 27th of May. Sources, as they say, differ.

'Whenever the man died,' I told my client, 'he lingered for a minimum of three days.'

'Not uncommon at the time, you know. A wound we'd

nowadays regard as superficial would lead as often as not to an untreatable infection.'

'But he'd have been conscious in the days before he died, wouldn't he?'

'For the most part, I'd think. Why?'

'Well, it's too late now,' I said, 'but it occurred to me that someone with a little foresight could have handed him a pen and a stack of index cards.'

There was a long pause. 'I suppose that's an interesting area for speculation.' His tone was the careful sort one uses when speaking with someone who's off his meds. 'Was there anything else?'

'Yes, as a matter of fact.' My bell jingled, and my cat perked up his ears, and I looked up at my visitor and shifted conversational gears abruptly. 'Some good news, Mrs Hawkins. I've got a lead on a nice copy of his first novel. Let me check and get back to you.'

I rang off and looked up at Ray Kirschmann. 'Now I'll duck around the corner and buy the book at the Strand,' I said, 'and I'll call her back tomorrow and tell her she's in luck.'

'It's nice to see you makin' an honest livin', Bernie. And all you got to do is walk around the corner, instead of chasin' all over town.'

'You talked to the Ostermaier children.'

'Yeah, and I gotta say I don't see any of 'em lookin' good for the intruder.' He pulled a notebook from his back pocket. 'Let's see now. Meredith, that's the older daughter, lives in Alphabet City.'

'With her husband.'

'Right. The two of them head up a little theater company, what you call off-off-Broadway.' He frowned. 'Isn't that a double negative, Bernie? If somethin's off-off-Broadway, doesn't that put it back *on* Broadway?'

'I don't think so.'

'Well, you'd know better'n me. He's a producer-director and she's some kind of manager, and they're in rehearsals for a new play by a guy whose name I couldn't write down without askin' how to spell it, which I didn't want to bother. They were both at the theater from late afternoon until one or two in the mornin', with a whole cast of actors who could swear to it, not to mention the playwright.'

'And the son in Chelsea was busy passing hors d'oeuvres at a party in Tribeca.'

'What'd you do, talk to him yourself? That'd be Boyd, and it wasn't Tribeca, it was Murray Hill. He and his partner were catering a company dinner. That'd be his business partner.'

'And it ran late?'

'Past ten, and it was close to eleven by the time he got out of there. His other partner picked him up, and they went to a club and had some drinks, and then they went to the gym and buffed their lats and their pecs and their quads, and then shared a bench in the steam room until the sun came up.'

'Better them than me.'

'My thought exactly, Bernie. His brother's the tax lawyer in Park Slope.'

'Jackson.'

'You got a good memory. Jackson Ostermaier. He didn't get home until around the time his mother was bailin' out on Wagner, but once he did he was in Brooklyn for the rest of the night. He'd been workin' late at the office, but not as late as he told his wife.'

'He's got a girlfriend?'

'He took this drawin' class, and she was the model. Now he pays the rent on her two rooms in Boerum Hill, and he's the only one who gets to see her naked.'

'At least as far as he knows.'

'Right. Anyway, she's in Brooklyn, like two subway stops from him. It's a regular thing for him to stop for an hour or so on the way home, and that's what he did the other night.'

'I guess that leaves Deirdre.'

'The younger daughter,' he said, 'and she coulda been the intruder, but we already got her at the scene discoverin' the body a little after two o'clock. And she was home from midnight on, because she made all those calls to her mother before she went over there.'

'That's all four,' I said. 'Meredith, Boyd, Jackson, and Deirdre.'

'And none of 'em's the intruder.' He looked at me. 'And you're not surprised, are you? You already figured as much. So why'd I waste my time checkin' 'em out?'

'Suppose they didn't have alibis, Ray. Suppose each of them had the opportunity to sneak into the Ostermaier house late that night. Who'd have a reason?'

'All of 'em. It was drivin' me crazy, all those solid alibis, because all four of 'em have plenty of motive, and it's the best motive there is.'

'Money,' I guessed.

'There you go, Bernie. You ever happen to notice how nobody's ever got enough? First glance, everybody's doin' okay for theirselves. Take a closer look and you see four serious cases of the shorts.'

'Catering business isn't going so well?'

'No, and the partners don't get along too great. What Boyd wants to do is buy his partner out. That'd be his business partner, not—'

'Not his life partner. I get it, Ray.'

'Well it's confusin', the same word croppin' up all over the place. Best thing about gay marriage is we can stop callin' 'em partners all the time. The caterin' business is him and his partner, the steam room is him and his husband. Which also sounds strange, *him and his husband*, but I figure I'll get used to it.'

'In time.'

'Anyway, that's Boyd. Next up is Meredith. The off-off-Broadway theater keeps losin' money.'

'There's a surprise.'

'Ready for another one? The landlord wants to raise their rent. Plus their apartment's gonna be too small when the baby comes.'

'She's pregnant?'

'That you could work your way around, you know? Keep the kid in a dresser drawer for a few months. No, they got an adoption in process, and the agency says their apartment's not big enough. Anyway, same story. Not enough money.'

'And Jackson's got a wife and a girlfriend.'

'And kids in private school, and last year's bonus wasn't so hot, and two other guys want him to join them and start their own firm.'

'And Deirdre?'

'Keeps spendin' more'n she brings in. She's out of work, and the work she's out of don't pay much anyway. Workin' part-time at day-care centers is a slow way to get rich, and her credit cards are pretty much maxed out at this point.'

'All four of them need money,' I said, 'or want it, anyhow. And there's this big house on Ninety-second Street with just one person living in it.'

'No mortgage on it, either. Mr Ostermaier paid it off years ago.'

'And left it outright to Mrs Ostermaier?'

'Nope. Didn't have to. He was in the kind of business where you play it safe by putting things in your wife's name. So it was all hers, free and clear.'

'A house like that, in today's market—'

'Gotta be ten, Bernie. Might go fifteen.'

'Million.'

'Well, yeah.'

'Say twelve, and split it four ways—'

'More'n enough for a caterer to buy out his partner. His business partner, I mean.'

'He could probably buy out his husband, too. Three million would let a lawyer pay his girlfriend's rent and his kids' school fees, too.'

'You could start a day-care center easy.'

'If you still wanted to. You could move to a larger apartment, and keep your theater open.'

'So we got four people sharin' a hell of a good motive,' he said, 'but none of 'em coulda done it. And nothin' got done to begin with except breakin' in after the woman was already dead, and what's the point of that? Bernie? You payin' attention?'

'Sorry,' I said. 'I was thinking of something.'

'Tryin' to work out who's the intruder?'

'Oh, I already know that,' I said. 'I'm trying to figure out who's the murderer.'

'She died of peanuts, Bernie. Remember?'

'I know,' I said. 'Don't put your notebook away yet, Ray. There are a few more things it'd be good to know.'

THIRTY-FOUR

After the door closed behind him, and the bell marked the occasion with its usual jingle, I waited before I went to the phone. And it was just as well, because in less than a minute Ray was back, holding a small piece of paper.

'On your table,' he said. 'I read it on the chance it might be a clue.'

'And was it?'

'Same blue felt tip,' he said, 'but see the thickness of the letters?'

'I guess the tip's showing a lot of wear.'

'What I'd guess,' he said, 'is that she pressed really hard on it, just to show you how pissed off she is. You gotta treat your customers right, Bernie, if you expect to make a go of it in a legit business.'

I said I'd keep that in mind. He left again, and the bell jingled again, and I went and made my phone call.

*

'I have to apologize,' I told Burton Barton the Fifth. 'Someone came into the store, and I didn't want our conversation overheard.'

'I assumed as much. You have the, uh—'

'Book,' I supplied.

'Yes, let's call it that. It's in your possession?'

'It is, and I'd rather it were in yours.'

'As would I. Shall I come to your shop?'

'I think it may be under observation.'

'By your earlier visitor? And might he be a government worker?'

'Yes,' I said, 'and yes. Why don't I bring the, uh, book to you?'

'To me?'

'At your residence. Or your place of business, as you prefer.'

He considered it, or at least paused as if so doing. 'No,' he said at length. 'No, I wouldn't want you to put yourself out.'

'It's no problem, really.'

'It would be a problem for me,' he said. 'I'll come to you, as I've done in the past. But not to the store, not if it's being watched. We adjourned to a coffee shop recently.'

'Yes, and once was enough. Let me think,' I said, and at least paused as if so doing. 'There's an establishment on the corner of Eleventh and Broadway where no one will take undue notice of us. It's not fancy, but it's comfortable enough. It's called the Bum Rap.'

A few minutes later my store was closed for the night and I was two doors down the street at the Poodle Factory, tapping away at Carolyn's laptop.

'Shit,' I said.

'No luck, Bern?'

'No.'

'Bern, your problems are nothing compared to this poor woman's. *"CLOSED? WHAT DO YOU MEAN, CLOSED??? YOUR LIGHTS ARE ON AND I KNOW YOU ARE IN THERE! YOU HAVE A BOOK I NEED!! BUT YOU ARE NEVER OPEN!! JUST FOR THAT I AM STEALING CZECHOSLOVAKIA!!! TOMORROW I WILL COME BACK FOR LONELY PLANET GUIDE TO ATLANTIS!!!"* All those exclamation points, Bern.'

'I know. She probably wants me to sell her a Robert Ludlum novel.'

'The Lonely Planet Guide to Atlantis. Did she actually take Czechoslovakia?'

'Somebody did.'

'She's enjoying this, Bern. She's frustrated that you're always closed, but she's making the most of it. When did she leave this? Not during lunch.'

'When Chloe came over.'

'You locked up?'

'Chloe did. She wanted to spend a few minutes in the back room.'

'Oh?'

'She was expressing her gratitude.'

'I'll just bet she was. And did her expression have a happy ending?'

'Carolyn, I'm trying to concentrate.'

'Always a problem,' she said, 'when one has been recently drained of one's precious bodily fluids. I'll let you be.'

She let me be, but I couldn't get anywhere. I gave up and used her phone. Two miracles happened in quick succession: I remembered Ray's cell phone number, and he answered it.

'I have a phone number,' I said, 'and I need an address. And I know they've got reverse directories online, and I tried them all and got nowhere.'

He told me to give him the number, and I did. 'I'll call you back,' he said. 'You're at Carolyn's, right?'

Jesus, was he watching me after all?

'How did you know that, Ray?'

'A secret cop trick,' he said. 'My phone rang, and I looked at it, and it said "Poodle Factory" on it.'

'Oh, right. You want the number?'

'That popped up, too. Gimme a minute, I'll check that other number for you.'

It was more like five minutes, and he came back with a blank. 'It's a burner,' he said. 'You buy a phone for cash and use it until the minutes are up. Then I suppose you could burn it, but it'd make a hell of a stink, so you'd most likely just toss it. No name, no address, not that we can get hold of, anyway.'

I thanked him and ended the call, and Carolyn asked me what it all meant.

'It means I need your help,' I said. 'I've got a meeting at six at the Bum Rap.'

'With the button man?'

I nodded.

'And you want me there?'

'Not exactly,' I said.

THIRTY-FIVE

I was a thoughtful seven minutes early. I took a table and seated myself so that I could watch the door, and I'd barely settled in my chair when Maxine glided over with two glasses on her tray. One was tall, one short, and both held an amber liquid, a bit paler in the tall glass.

'Carolyn won't be coming,' I said.

'She won't?'

'As a matter of fact she may be along later,' I said, 'but she won't be joining me.'

Maxine's face clouded. 'You two okay?'

'We're fine,' I said, 'but I have a business meeting. A gentleman will be meeting me here in a few minutes.'

'Got it,' she said, and began to place the taller of the two glasses in front of me, but I waved it off.

'Perrier for you, huh?'

'Right.'

'And your friend?'

'He'll have to let you know,' I said.

It means something to Carolyn when I pass up scotch for Perrier, but I don't think Maxine attaches any significance to it beyond its demonstration of my charming eccentricity. She took the booze away and returned with the soda water, and when I raised it I was looking over the brim of my glass at my client. He was honoring the season in a blue and white seersucker suit, and carrying a slim briefcase.

When Maxine appeared, he asked me what I was drinking, raised an eyebrow, and told her what he'd like was a very dry martini, straight up, made with Gray Goose vodka and garnished with a lemon twist. That's a little more specific than most drink orders at the Bum Rap, and I wasn't sure what he'd get, but what showed up was the right color and served in a martini glass, and if it was Georgi instead of Gray Goose, I don't think he noticed the difference.

Our business took hardly any time at all. He had a long look at the spoon, turned it over to examine the mark (MM in a narrow rectangle), ran his thumb over the low relief effigy of Gwinnett and the eponymous button, drew a breath and let it out in a soundless whistle.

'It looks just like him,' he said.

Button Gwinnett is depicted in the classic engraving of the signing, but the artist hadn't been there for the event, and did his work long after the fact, often basing his likenesses on portraits. He may have had a look at a portrait of Gwinnett by one J. Chancelling, of whom little is known, including what the J. may have stood for. He was evidently a Charleston native, painted a few portraits in South Carolina and Georgia, and vanished.

And so did his portrait of Gwinnett, which had long since

disappeared before the rarity of the man's signature moved a lot of people to wonder what he looked like.

So how could my illustrious client say that Myer Myers had done well by his subject? Well, I once heard a woman make the very same observation about a painting of Jesus Christ. Perhaps his obsessive interest in the man had blessed my Button with a comparable mental image of that earlier Button.

Of course there was another explanation that I liked even better . . .

'Triumph,' he was saying, 'is tragedy. I know how Alexander felt.'

'When Aaron Burr shot him?'

'Alexander the Great, when he looked around and realized there were no lands left to conquer. It is every collector's fate, and it happens over and over and over.'

'You can't have run out of things to collect.'

'No, hardly that. There are always more items to find and acquire. Buttons, for heaven's sake. Human civilization has produced an essentially endless quantity, and one keeps finding new examples.'

'The one on your jacket—'

He touched it, a small brass disc with an American eagle as its central figure.

'A fairly recent acquisition,' he said. 'I don't know if you can make out the lettering. The top line is Harrison, the lower Morton.'

'The Log Cabin guy?'

'Tippecanoe's grandson, Benjamin Harrison, who interrupted Grover Cleveland's two terms by beating him in 1888, though without winning the popular vote. Levi P. Morton was his running mate.'

He told me more about Morton, who'd been an unsuccessful

candidate for his party's nomination in 1896. And, wouldn't you know it, he had a lapel button from the fellow's campaign. I said something encouraging, and he got back to Alexander the Great.

'The more you want something,' he said, 'and the harder it is to get your hands on it, the greater the sense of accomplishment. But then you've achieved your goal, and for months or even years you've been in part defined by it.' He patted the pocket with the spoon. 'I'm glad to have it. But I'm sorry I can no longer aspire to it. Want implies lack, doesn't it? One can only want what one does not have. I can treasure the spoon, and I shall. But I can't yearn for it, I can't seek it, I can't move heaven and earth to lay hands on it. And it's hard not to suspect that I've lost as much as I've gained. If not more.'

'There must be other objects you want just as keenly. Gwinnett's signature, for instance.'

He beamed.

'You already have it?'

'And not on some index card thrust upon him on his death bed, as you were going on about earlier. I was very fortunate several years ago. I won't go into details, but a curator at a small museum in – well, never mind where. It was an institution that made inadequate provision for a gentleman's retirement, and, ah, we came to a private arrangement. I treasure it, I cherish it. But I no longer have it to stalk through the corridors of space and time.'

He fell silent for a moment, and I kept him company. Then he straightened in his chair and put the briefcase on the table. It was full of envelopes, similar in size and shape to the others I'd received from him – and, come to think of it, to the ones I'd handed to Chloe Miller. I reached in, lifted the flap of one of the envelopes, and confirmed that Benjamin Franklin was once again well represented.

He told me I was welcome to count the money. 'You know,' I said, 'let me just examine one envelope.' I glanced quickly around the room. 'But without an audience. I'll take it to the men's room. I won't be long.'

'I'll be right here,' he said.

A moment ago Carolyn had appeared in the doorway. Our eyes met, and she'd given me a nod and slipped outside again. I rose, holding that one envelope casually at my side, and headed for a door at the rear. The sign on it said GENTLEMEN, but I didn't let that stop me.

I locked myself in a stall and took the time to count the envelope's contents. It came to an even five thousand dollars; should the briefcase hold nine more just like it, then his count would be correct. But I didn't know now many other envelopes there were, and I had a feeling it wasn't going to matter much.

After I'd counted the bills a second time I waited a few minutes, and before I left I used the squalid little room for its intended purpose. It was likely to be a long night, and Perrier goes through one's system so rapidly it barely has time to lose the bubbles.

When I got back to my table, Burton Barton the fifth was gone. And so was the briefcase.

THIRTY-SIX

When I asked for the check, Maxine told me my friend had taken care of it. 'Left me a big tip, too,' she said. 'Classy guy, but I knew that when I saw the suit he was wearing.'

'He's a real seersucker,' I said.

'Well,' she said, 'I have to say it shows.'

Okay. No time to waste.

I bought a cell phone on Fourteenth Street, a burner that might have been the twin to my buttoned-down client's. It came with a hundred minutes, and I couldn't imagine that I'd use more than ten of them.

Then I went home and tended to my hidey-hole, stowing $5000 where $20,000 had been that morning. I wondered idly why we're not supposed to cry over spilled milk. What else is it good for?

And then I set about provisioning myself for a night of felonious activity.

Tool kit. Disposable gloves. Flashlight. Duct tape.

And my own personal cell phone, its setting switched from ring to vibrate. And my new phone, the burner; nobody could call it on purpose, but wrong numbers are always a possibility, so it too was set on vibrate.

Still okay. And still no time to waste.

Outside, the rush-hour traffic had thinned enough to make a cab seem sensible, and I wasn't worried about leaving a trail. The driver's radio was blaring in a language I didn't recognize, and he was yammering into a no-hands cell phone in what may have been the same language, and the smoke in the cab's interior was thick enough to skate on, and only some of it was tobacco. This guy wasn't going to remember our meeting, and if I took a couple of deep breaths, neither would I.

I had him go through the park and drop me at Ninetieth and Lexington, more out of habit than real concern; he hadn't made a note on his trip sheet when I got in, and was unlikely to do so now. I walked two blocks uptown and spotted the Ostermaier house right off, still wearing its garland of crime scene tape.

I remember how Ray had approached the place on our earlier visit, mounting the steps and unfastening the tape as if he had every right in the world to be there. There's a way cops have of walking, and I figured I'd look bogus if I set out to imitate it, but I took a couple of deep breaths and tried at least for an aura of confident nonchalance, or perhaps nonchalant confidence.

The padlock was as easy as I thought it would be, and once I'd opened it I was in. I brought the padlock inside with me, put on my gloves, bolted the door from within, and got busy.

It took me a little longer than I'd have preferred. It was 7:18

when I cracked the padlock, 7:41 when I snapped it in place and reattached the yellow tape. I was still wearing gloves, but that fit the image, and now that I'd had my look at the crime scene I peeled them off the way any cop would and stuffed them back in my pocket.

I guess I looked a little bit like a cop, because a young guy walking a dog gave me the sort of wave designed to assure me that he too was on the side of the law. I decided he had to be holding some form of mood-altering substance, probably of vegetable origin, because why else would he bother?

I stayed in character. I dismissed him with a glance I'd seen often enough on Ray's face, and walked off confidently and nonchalantly in the other direction.

My phone had vibrated while I was in the Ostermaier house, but I been in too much of a hurry to check it. I did so as I rounded the corner at Third Avenue. It was Carolyn, and I called her back.

'Hello,' she said. 'Bern, I've been waiting all my life for a chance to say that.'

'Oh, please,' I said. 'You say it all the time.'

'Huh?'

'"Hello." You say it every time you pick up a telephone.'

'I was waiting on the corner,' she said, 'and I wasn't sure what I was waiting for, on account of I never saw the guy before. I was hoping he'd be wearing the English jacket with all the pearl buttons, because that would pretty much give him away.'

'He was wearing a seersucker suit.'

'No kidding. I thought it was him when a cab pulled up smack in front of the Bum Rap and he got out of it, because most of their customers don't get there in a taxi.'

'With most of them,' I said, 'it's a wonder that they get there at all.'

'And there's apt to be a certain amount of staggering involved. Anyway, I had a feeling it was him when he got out of the cab, and I was pretty sure when he looked around furtively before going inside.'

'And then you saw me sharing a table with him, and that cinched it.'

'Not right away. First I flagged a cab of my own, and got him to wait. Then I saw the two of you, and you gave me a nod, and I went outside again and got in the cab. "Just wait a minute," I told him. And he did, and the guy came out with his seersucker suit and his briefcase and started walking down Broadway, and I got my guy to creep along so we could keep him in sight, but without catching up to him. I have to say it's no mean trick to follow somebody in a seersucker suit. It sort of stands out in a crowd, and the street wasn't even crowded to begin with.'

'Makes it easier.'

'It does. And then he stepped off the curb and held his hand up, and a taxi pulled up right away, and I finally got my chance to say it.'

'"Follow that cab!"'

'Yeah. My driver was this Jamaican guy with dreads and an earring, and I guess he grew up watching the same movies we did, because he thought this was the neatest thing ever. "Don't lose him now," I said, and he hooted at the very idea.'

'And it worked?'

'He got a funny look when we were coming up on the Brooklyn Bridge. That old "I don't go to Brooklyn" look. I showed him a fifty and told him I didn't expect change, and he just smiled and smiled. Anyway, we didn't go all that far into Brooklyn. You got a pencil, Bern? Write this down.'

I had a memo pad with a batch of notes already on it, and I added a new address to my list. 'I'm across the street right now,' she said, 'in a pizza parlor, sitting by the window so I can keep an eye on his front door. I've been here for a little over an hour.'

'And he hasn't come out?'

'Not through the front door. I kept the cab for five minutes, just in case he ducked in and ducked out again. That cost me another ten bucks.'

'Well worth it.'

'What I thought. But he didn't, and I let the guy go. I think he's in for the night.'

'I think you're probably right. He's home, and looking at his spoon. You can probably head home yourself.'

'Well, I'm like three short blocks from the Number Two train, and then the One's right across the platform at Chambers Street. I think I'll stick around another fifteen or twenty minutes. I mean, another slice of pizza wouldn't kill me.'

I decided a slice of pizza wouldn't kill me, either, and I got one on Second Avenue and chomped away at it as I continued east. It lasted me across First Avenue and halfway down the block to York, where I turned right and found Deirdre Ostermaier's building.

It was one of those white brick buildings that went up all over the city in the 1960s, with tiny terraces for all but the smallest studios, and all the charm of an industrial park on the outskirts of Indianapolis. Her apartment was 17-J, and it would help to know whether or not she was home.

I had a phone number for her, but it started with 917, which meant it was a cell phone. She didn't seem to have a landline. I used my burner and called her cell phone, just to see if I could learn anything that way, and it went straight to voicemail.

So what I'd just learned was that either she was home or she wasn't.

Well, I'd already known that much, hadn't I? And I could find out simply enough by asking for her at the front desk. She didn't need a landline for the attendant to reach her on the intercom. If she didn't pick up, she was out.

And either way I was screwed. If she was home, what was I going to do, tell the doorman I'd changed my mind? And if she was out, how was I going to sneak past him, having already called attention to myself?

Okay. Plan B:

I walked to the corner and stood with my cell phone to my ear, having a spirited conversation with myself. 'Is that right?' I said. 'Yes, that's exactly what I told him . . . You think so? . . . I suppose that's not a bad idea.'

And so on.

I bided my time, keeping an eye on passersby and weighing the possibilities, until I made my choice and fell into step with a forty-ish woman carrying a sack of groceries. 'Oh, hi,' I said. 'I guess we're not getting that rain after all.'

She had the guarded look of a person trying to decide whether I was an unrecognized acquaintance or an ambulatory psychotic.

'I'm sorry,' I said. 'We nod and smile at each other all the time in the lobby and the elevator, but I don't think we've ever actually exchanged names. I'm Don Farber.'

She relaxed, and told me her name, which I didn't quite catch, but what difference does it make? We chatted about the weather, and speculated on the scheduled redecoration of the lobby, and all of that carried me past the concierge and into the unattended elevator. When the elevator stopped at twelve we urged one another to have a good night, and I rode on alone to seventeen.

I'd already narrowed the possibilities to two: either Deirdre was home or she wasn't. Well, if she was home, she'd open her door to a stranger who'd apologize for having got off the elevator at the wrong floor. 'Oh, for heaven's sake, I wanted Eighteen-J,' the fellow would say, shaking his head at his own stupidity, and heading for the elevator.

If she was out, she wouldn't open the door. The stranger would.

And that's what happened. I listened, heard nothing but my own shallow breathing, rang the bell, heard nothing but the bell, knocked briskly, breathed a little more deeply, and picked the lock.

Nothing to it, really. The lock was the building's original equipment. It locked by itself when you closed the door, and she hadn't bothered to use the key to turn the bolt. And why should she? She lived in a building with a doorman, so what did she have to worry about?

I didn't know where she was, or how long she'd be gone, so it wouldn't do to dawdle. Nor did I. Fifteen minutes later I was back on the ground floor, giving the attendant a nod and a wave on my way out.

A cab was just pulling up to let someone out. I grabbed it.

THIRTY-SEVEN

R rrring!
 'Hello, Boyd?'

'No, sorry, this is Stephen.'

'Oh, hi! This is Elliott. You remember, we met at, um—'

'Cappy and Susan's do?'

'Yes! You do remember!'

'How could I forget?'

How indeed? 'I suppose Boyd's working.'

'Of course he is. After all, this is one of those days that ends in a Y.'

'Oh, that's nice, Stephen. I'll have to remember that one. And I suppose afterward it'll be a quiet evening at home for the two of you.'

'Perish the thought. I'm meeting him at the Butcher's Hook at eleven.'

'Always a nice venue on a Thursday.'

'Isn't it? But I've a feeling he'll be a few minutes late. He so often is. I, on the other hand, am always early.'

'Just a few minutes early, Stephen?'

'What time is it? Getting on for nine. Good grief, how time flies.'

'Whether or not one's having fun.'

'So true, Elliott. You know, I might get there at ten, now that I think about it.'

'At ten? You know, Stephen, you just might see me there.'

'Oh? That would be nice, Elliott.'

I rang off, returned my burner to my pocket. 'Change in plans,' I told the driver. 'Fourth Street and First Avenue.'

Psoriasis, a new play by Josip Szypranskowicz, was in rehearsals at the New Molnar Playhouse. An addled young woman in granny glasses and what might have been a muumuu told me that she didn't dare disturb the director, Nils Calder, but that Meredith Ostermaier might be able to break away for a moment or two.

I said not to bother her, that I'd come back later.

Their apartment was five minutes away, in an old-law tenement on Sixth Street just east of Avenue B. Rents may have climbed and crime slackened in recent years, but the building still had a raffish look. In the entrance hall, I rang the bell marked Calder, gave it a couple of minutes, and then pushed three or four other buttons. A burst of static came over the intercom. I replied in kind, and someone buzzed me in.

I had three flights of stairs to climb, and a beefy guy in a wife-beater undershirt and cutoff jeans was waiting for me. 'From the theater,' I called out cheerfully, and showed him a key. 'Calder gave me this but forgot about the lock downstairs.'

'Sounds like him,' the fellow said, and went back to his own apartment, even as I hurried up two more flights of stairs.

All I did with the key was put it back in my pocket. It was the key to my apartment on West End Avenue, and I couldn't really expect it to work this far from home.

Like most people who live in buildings without security cameras or doormen, Nils and Meredith had made an effort to bolster their door's ability to keep burglars out. They'd gone in big for decals and locks. There were three of the former, one showing the canine winner of the Winston Churchill look-alike contest; *Caution – Attack Dog!* the legend advised. *Protected by Smith & Wesson*, said what looked to be a trimmed-down bumper sticker. A third boasted about a burglar alarm, and cautioned me to expect an armed response from Acme Security Corp. That might have scared the daylights out of Wile E. Coyote, but I remained undaunted.

A single decal might have had a slight deterrent effect, but a kind of reverse synergy operated; the whole amounted to less than any of its parts. A similar more-is-more strategy had led them to attach six locks to the poor beleaguered door, but instead of Rabson and Poulard and Medeco they'd bought these off-brand beauties at the bargain counter.

Still, they'd used them wisely. If they'd locked all six, I could simply have unlocked all six and been done with it. But they'd done what so many resourceful New Yorkers have learned to do. They locked three and left three unlocked, and when you use your burgling skill upon an unlocked lock, what do you suppose you do? You lock it.

There's a way to work this out, and it's simpler than getting all those cannibals and Christians across that crocodile-infested river in Africa, but barely.

And once inside I had to wonder why they'd gone to all that

trouble. If I'd been bent on burglary for profit, I'd have had a hard time finding anything to steal. One closet held a cardboard carton packed with well-read swinger magazines, with enough of the personal ads circled to suggest a more than academic interest in the subject. One couple's picture bore notations in two different hands; 'What do you think?' he'd wondered, to which she'd replied, 'Ooh, yummy!!!'

There was a laptop, a Mac that looked to be four or five years old, and isn't that a couple of decades in dog years? I suppose a search of their old email might have made fascinating reading, but I left the thing untouched.

I like to leave an apartment as I found it, and that includes locking up after myself. But how could I do that when I couldn't say which of the locks had been engaged when I started out? If I left them all open, anyone passing could turn the knob and walk in. If I locked three at random, I might pick one they never locked, and to which they'd long since lost the key.

Well, all you can ever do is the best you can, right? I locked the top lock, and one other, and left them to work it all out.

I never noticed the vibration, but I'd evidently missed a call from Carolyn. By the time I discovered this I'd grabbed a taxi on Sixth Street and let it drop me at the corner of Ninth Avenue and Twenty-second Street. I could see the bar Stephen had mentioned a block away on the other side of Ninth, and I could have gone over to see if he was there, but how could I tell?

Easier to call the number I'd called earlier, the landline in the apartment he shared with Boyd. I took out a phone, but it was my personal one, not the temporary burner, and something made me check it before I put it back in my pocket, and that's when I saw Carolyn had called.

I called her back, and she answered on the first ring. 'There you are,' she said. 'I can't be absolutely positive, Bern, but from the looks of things he's still in his house, and he's still awake.'

'And you know this because—'

'The lights. The parlor floor's all lit up, and the other three floors are dark. Same as before.'

'You're still in Brooklyn Heights?'

'No, I'm home, Bern.'

'Then how can you possibly—'

'I just got here. I know, I said one more slice of pizza and I was going to call it a night.'

'That was hours ago. If you've been eating pizza since I talked to you—'

'Just that one slice.'

'That's good, because an oregano overdose is no laughing matter. What happened?'

'Well, this woman walked in. She'd had a horrible fight with her girlfriend.'

'And the only thing that would make her feel better was pizza.'

'No, she was on her way to get a drink. But she saw me in the window, and somehow she knew I was somebody she could talk to about this, and that I'd understand.'

'It's the haircut, Carolyn.'

'Well, according to her it was my eyes. You know, knowing and sensitive and sympathetic, all at once.'

'That sounds like your eyes, all right.'

'If it was bullshit,' she said, 'it was the kind of bullshit I didn't mind hearing. So I said, "Okay, sit down, let's hear it," and we sat there and talked.'

'And watched the house across the street.'

'Off and on. The lights didn't change, and nobody went in or out. And then she said she felt tons better, and the least she could do was buy me a drink, and we went around the corner.'

'For a drink.'

'Two of them.'

'And then you dragged her home to Arbor Court, and the cats accepted her immediately, and that means a lot.'

'It's good you're my best friend,' she said, 'or I'd rip your chest open and tear your heart out. We had two drinks apiece, and she went home, and I went back and had another look at his house.'

'And the lights hadn't changed, but somehow they seemed brighter now. But then even the stars seemed brighter, and—'

'How do I put up with you? The lights were the same. Still home and still awake, that's my guess.'

I had her stay on the line while I called Boyd's apartment on my other phone. A machine picked up, a piano played the first few bars of 'Send In the Clowns,' and a voice – not Stephen's, so I guess it was Boyd's – said, 'Oh, drat! We're out. Leave us a message.'

Why not? 'It's Elliott,' I said. 'Something came up. I'll be in touch.'

Then I went and broke into their apartment. It was one flight up from the street, over a travel agency with a Spanish name, and inside it was as neat and uncluttered as one could possibly wish.

Easy.

THIRTY-EIGHT

Years and years ago, when Brooklyn was so far from being a desirable address that the Dodgers hadn't even left yet, the status police made an exception for that elevated portion of the borough just across the bridge. Brooklyn Heights, with its elegant brownstones and its fruity street names, has never been less than acceptable, and the great Brooklyn revival, a tide that lifts all boats clear out to Bushwick and beyond, has not neglected the pleasure yachts of the Heights.

The brownstone house Carolyn had been watching was on Willow Street between Cranberry and Orange. When I emerged from the Clark Street subway stop, it took me a minute or two to get my bearings, but then I found the address quickly enough, and spotted her pizza place across the street at the end of the block. It was dark and shuttered now, and dark too was the parlor floor of . . . well, what to call it?

The Button House, I decided. Forget Smith, and never mind the Burton Bartons, all five generations of them.

Light showed in the third-floor windows. I stood in the shadows for a while, walked around the block, stood in the shadows some more.

Maybe he was asleep, I thought. Maybe he felt safer sleeping with the lights on.

I waited, and the lights went out.

I stood there and waited for them to come back on again. When they didn't, I checked the time.

2:33.

I gave it a few more minutes, then found my way back to Clark Street. There was a tavern I'd passed near the subway entrance, quiet and dimly lit, that had struck me as a likely venue for serious drinking. Not every bar holds out until the legal closing hour of 4:00 am, but I'd had a feeling this one would, and they were still open when I got there.

Three men sat well apart at the bar. Another man read a newspaper at a table. I stood at the bar, ordered whiskey with water on the side, and carried both glasses to a table in a darkened corner.

If I'd ordered a Perrier, or anything non-alcoholic, in that joint at that hour, the bartender might have called the police. So the booze in the shot glass was camouflage, and I made sure no one was looking when I spilled it on the floor.

I took a few sips of the water. I used the rest room, came back. Sat down, had a few more sips of the water.

It was clear I could sit there until four, with or without buying another drink, but somewhere around 3:20 I left. The bartender was the only person who'd taken any notice of me at all, and his interest had ceased once I'd paid for my drink. He was watching TV with the sound off, and he didn't look up when I left.

I went straight back to the Button House. The lights were still off.

You have to be out of your mind to be a cat burglar. And, from what I've heard, most of them are.

If that strikes you as an unlikely observation for me to be making, that may result from widespread misapplication of the term. The media are apt to hang the label on any burglar with a modicum of talent and a soupçon of sangfroid. Slip in from a fire escape, work your magic on a pickproof lock, and some journalist is sure to call you a cat burglar.

Wrong.

A cat burglar, properly speaking, creeps like Carl Sandburg's cat, on little fog feet. He makes his illegal entries not when an abode is conveniently and safely vacant, but when its occupants are home. They may be entertaining guests on the first floor while he's scooping up jewelry on the second; they may be sleeping in an upstairs bedroom while he's cracking a safe in the den.

Burglary, you should realize, is never without its risks. Something can always go wrong, and often does. I'm never entirely carefree when I'm unlawfully present in some stranger's home, and what worries me most is not that I'll trip a burglar alarm, or that some passerby will wonder why the lights are on, or that the cop on the beat is a disguised superhero with X-ray vision and psychic powers.

It's that the residents will come home, and catch me in the act.

I'll do anything I can to avoid this, short of giving up the work altogether. (And I've even tried that, but can't seem to stick with it.) I don't go into a house or apartment unless I'm certain it's empty, and that I'll have ample time to perform my chores before the resident returns. And even then, for all that I delight in the sensation of being where I don't belong, I make my stay as brief as

I possibly can. Get in, get what you came for, and get out. Period.

So how do you figure a cat burglar?

I saw one interviewed on a cable show a while ago. He had a shaved head and way too many tattoos, and the manic glint in his eyes certainly didn't inspire confidence, but his words showed he had a cool and logical mind. 'The thing is,' he said, 'I never have to worry about them coming home. Because, see, they're already there.'

That cat burglar, like all his tribe, was clearly nuts. But there was an undeniable truth in what he was saying, and I contemplated it while I worked at getting into the Button House. Because I didn't have to begin by making phone calls and ringing doorbells and banging away with a brass door knocker (which in this particular instance was evidently custom-made, because how often do you run into a door knocker in the shape of a collar button?) to make doubly certain the house was empty. It wasn't empty, and I knew it.

I'd already been in and out of a house and three apartments, fitting into a single evening as much work as any burglar ought to do in six months. They'd all required some skill and thought and planning, and they'd all gone off smoothly, and here I was on a pretty tree-lined Brooklyn street, pushing my luck.

But if I went home now, everything I'd already done would be essentially pointless . . .

The house on Willow Street was owned by a collector, and one sufficiently rabid to have obtained some valuable items in a manner that was either shady or genuinely illegal. That meant he couldn't insure them, so he'd be burdened with even more than the usual collector's paranoia.

And so there was a burglar alarm, and a good one, and the

telltale silvery tape showed on all the ground and parlor floor windows. Some of them might be bypassed, so that he could open a window for ventilation without throwing switches, but there was no way to determine as much from where I was.

He had good locks, too. And there was a security camera mounted above the entrance way, keeping a keen digital eye on all comings and goings.

Let's see now. Was there burglar alarm tape on the third-floor windows?

There was not, as far as I could tell, and this gave me hope.

A slender hope, I have to admit, as I had no way of getting to the third floor – unless I was already inside the building and could use the stairs. Or, of course, I could have walked up the building's façade – if only I'd had the foresight to bring along my anti-gravity vest, and the shoes with the suction cups on their bottoms. I'll tell you, you try to think of everything, and then you go and leave the important stuff at home.

Never mind.

The Button House (or Chez Bouton, if you prefer) was the fourth in a row of five houses, identical in structure though trimmed out differently. (Or it was the second of five, depending on which end you picked to start your count. But you get the idea.)

The houses formed a solid block, but at the end of the row there was a passageway. I picked my way past garbage cans to a cyclone fence, on the other side of which was the backyard shared by the five attached houses. There's probably a word for the counterpart of a façade, and whatever it may be, that's where each of the houses had a fire escape mounted. They all ended a full flight above ground level; if your house was on fire and you had to use the fire escape to get out, your weight on the lowest section would be enough to propel it downward, at which point you'd wind up

standing where I was now, on a patch of concrete, looking up at a
fire escape I couldn't possibly reach.

Unless, of course, I pulled over a garbage can and stood on top
of it. There were a few on this side of the fence, too, and I chose
one and positioned it where it would do the most good. Not, as
you might think, beneath the Button House fire escape, but at the
row's other end; if lowering the fire escape was going to wake
somebody, I'd just as soon it not be my client.

Well, my former client, since he'd forfeited that status the
moment he scarpered out of the Bum Rap with my $45,000 in
hand. In fact, let's call him my erstwhile client; that has the right
sort of ring to it, doesn't it?

I took my time, keeping the clatter to a minimum, and when the
fire escape was fully extended I remained absolutely still for a full
two minutes, listening for unwelcome noises even as I watched for
unwelcome lights.

In their absence, I murmured thanks to Saint Dismas and ascended to the roof, and across its several neighbors to the roof
of the Button House. Like its fellows, that roof held a trapdoor
affording access to the fourth floor. You needed a key to unlock
it – or the appropriate tools and talent.

The lock was no problem. Lifting the thing was more of a struggle, and hard to do in the silence the circumstances demanded.
But it was doable, and in the end it was done.

I was in. Now for the tricky part.

The top floor was essentially an attic, but one that had long since
been finished off. In the right neighborhood, it could have been
home to thirty or forty immigrants and an indeterminate number
of chickens, but here on Willow Street all it held were the button-
related collections and accumulations amassed by their owner
over any number of misspent years.

One great steamer trunk was filled to within a few inches of its top with all manner of buttons – unsorted, unclassified, and heaped together as if they'd spilled in from some gigantic chute. They came in all sizes and colors and all combinations of colors, and some were celluloid or Bakelite while others were cloth-covered. But a substantial number, I must say, looked to be very ordinary buttons of the sort found on very ordinary shirts, and I guessed I was looking at the duplicates, the leftovers, the but-tonish residue that accrued when one bought no end of whole collections and accumulations.

The man was clearly both collector and hoarder; what he didn't need for his collection went into the trunk in his attic, because if it was a button he couldn't bear to part with it. I suddenly knew what happened when a shirt wore out. Before it went in the trash, he'd snip off its buttons and toss them in the trunk.

This trunk, say. Or that one over there. Or the one next to it . . .

I plunged a cupped hand into the great sea of buttons, brought it up full, then let the buttons spill from my hand. I had a feeling the man himself did this sort of thing now and again, cavorting like Scrooge McDuck in his money bin.

And why not? I could see how a person could get into it. Scooping up buttons, sifting through them, letting this one or that one catch your eye. It was pleasant, hunkering down here next to the trunk, while the world outside went on with its nasty and un-fathomable business, and I just dipped and scooped and sifted and—

But no. I had work to do.

It took longer than I'd have preferred to negotiate the two flights of stairs from the fourth floor to the parlor floor. That was where he'd spent his time while Carolyn was watching, and that's where I'd find what I was seeking. But first I had to get past the third floor, where he was sleeping, and stairs in old houses creak, and loud noises wake sleepers.

And sometimes no noise is required. He was a youthful fellow, trim and vigorous, but what did I know about the state of his prostate? Perhaps a typical night was marked by a couple of trips to the bathroom, and perhaps he'd make one while I was on the stairs.

And what would I do if he came bursting out of the bedroom with fire in his eyes and something lethal in his hand? For all I knew he owned the very dueling pistol with which Lachlan McIntosh had ended Button Gwinnett's life, and kept it primed and loaded at his bedside. He'd take aim and fire, and I'd clutch my breast and fall to the floor, and three or eleven days later, that would be the end of me.

Didn't I tell you? You have to be out of your mind to be a cat burglar.

It got easier once I was off the stairs. It still took a while because I had a lot to do, but I was able to do it in silence. Someone outside might have seen the occasional brief wink of my little flashlight, but on the list of risks I was taking, that one was down toward the bottom.

I was just about done when I heard footsteps overhead. They stopped, and I held my breath, and let it out when I heard a toilet flush. Then more footsteps, and then silence.

He'd evidently gone back to bed, but would he stay there? Even if he did, how could I possibly get past him unheard on my way to the roof?

I made my way to the stairs, but went down instead of up, to the ground floor, and through the house to the rear. There was a door opening onto the yard in back, and I'd have liked to use it earlier. I'd have been spared all that business with the fire escape and the roofs. But I'd known it would be wired into the alarm system, and indeed it was.

But I was inside now, and that made all the difference. I bridged the wiring and took the back door off the grid without disturbing the rest of the system. I unlocked the door, stepped outside, locked up after myself, and looked around.

The sky was getting light, and that made sense; according to the calendar, we weren't far from the shortest night of the year. From my own perspective it had gone on a little longer than the Thirty Years War, without being nearly as much fun.

THIRTY-NINE

In one of our phone conversations, Carolyn had told me not to worry about feeding Raffles. 'I'll take care of that for you,' she said. 'I don't know when you'll get home, but just go ahead and sleep as late as you can.'

I got into bed around seven and out of it three hours later when the phone rang. I answered in a voice still full of sleep, and Ray said, 'Aw, hell, Bernie. I woke you up, didn't I?'

'You did me a favor. I couldn't get down from the fire escape.'

'Huh?'

'In the dream,' I said. 'What's funny is on some level I knew it was a dream, and I figured the way out was to fall. Just step off into space.'

'But you couldn't do it, right?'

'Yeah. Why's that?'

'You're a survivor, Bernie. Even in your sleep. Turns out you were right.'

'Not to jump?'

'About the syringe. About a couple of other things, too. You want to call me back when you're awake enough to take it all in?'

'I'm awake now,' I said, hoping it was true. 'Let's hear it.'

'It all ties together,' I said. 'I was pretty busy last night.'

'Doin' things I don't need to know about.'

'So how about if I tell you a few things that I happen to know, without saying how I came by the information?'

'That'll work.'

When I was done he asked a few questions, listened to my answers, and made a sound somewhere between a sigh and a groan. 'It's kind of complicated,' he said. 'I know what my grandmother would have called it.'

'Oh?'

'A real cluster fuck, God rest her soul. I guess I better not use the term in front of Meredith and Whatsisname.'

'Nils,' I said, 'and you're right. They'd want to get in on it.'

'I'd better get some warrants,' he said. 'Problem is I got no grounds, which means gettin' hold of the right judge. You got your hat ready, Bernie? The one you like to pull rabbits out of?'

Did I? 'Let's hope so,' I said. 'When do you want to do this? What's today, Friday?'

'Last I looked.'

'Yesterday was Thursday,' I said, 'even if it does feel like a week ago. It ought to be today, Ray, before anybody heads out to the Hamptons. What time? Six-thirty?'

'Make it seven.'

'At the Ostermaier house? Scene of the crime and all?'

'No,' he said, after a moment's thought. 'Anything goes wrong,

I'd hate to try explainin' why I decided to hold a convention at a crime scene. You know, if you wouldn't mind—'

Sure, why not? Barnegat Books at seven, with all the usual suspects on hand. What the hell, it wouldn't be the first time.

I got to my store just in time to close for lunch. I opened up, turned on the lights, put the bargain table on the sidewalk, told Raffles I knew damn well he'd been fed, turned off the lights, and went out and locked the door. I thought of leaving a note for my wannabe customer, and I might have done so if I could have come up with anything clever. But I thought about the tasks I'd just performed and the order in which I'd performed them, and I decided my mind wasn't working well enough to leave a blank piece of paper, let alone write something on it.

'Juneau Lock,' Carolyn sang out when I came through her door. 'And what are those bottles? Is that Dr Brown's Cel-Ray Tonic?'

'From the deli,' I said. 'It suddenly occurred to me that spicy Taiwanese food could have no better accompaniment.'

'Somebody didn't get much sleep last night,' she said, and a few minutes later she said, 'Okay, I apologize. This is what we should have been drinking all along.'

'It works, doesn't it?'

'It does,' she said, 'even though it shouldn't. A sweet fizzy soft drink that tastes like celery—'

'Except artificial.'

'Like artificial celery,' she agreed. 'It shouldn't go with pastrami, and yet it does.'

'It's almost traditional.'

'Well, it's a far cry from traditional with Juneau Lock, but I can see where it's a tradition in the making. Okay, you're a genius, Bern, especially when you're sleep-deprived. Now tell me about last night.'

*

'You know what's funny, Bern?'

'That it took us this long to try Dr Brown's with Juneau Lock?'

'Besides that. I have this strong sense of all these people, Deirdre and Boyd and Meredith and Jackson, and yet I haven't met any of them.'

'Neither have I.'

'Gee, that's right, isn't it? You haven't. At least you've been in their homes.'

'Not Jackson's.'

'You haven't, have you? Why leave him out?'

'He was probably home in Park Slope. And if he was in Boerum Hill with his girlfriend, then his wife and kids were in Park Slope. And his office is downtown in the Financial Center, and the only way to get into that building these days is to rent your own office there. Besides, Jackson gets a pass on the murder.'

'It really was a murder, huh?'

'Ray confirmed it. There's evidence, although I'd hate to be the one presenting it to a jury.'

'And Jackson's in the clear.'

'He didn't kill anybody,' I said, 'but he's tied into the other crime, and I didn't have to go to his home or his office to tie him in.'

'Or his love nest?' She grinned. 'I just wanted to use the phrase. How often do I get the chance? You must have found what you needed in Brooklyn Heights.'

'I found everything I needed,' I told her.

I went back to the store after lunch, but all I really did was make a phone call. Then I went out again, and at 2:30 I was sitting in a booth at a coffee shop on Madison Avenue, looking at a tattoo of a gecko.

267

'I don't get it,' Chloe said, squinting at the Button Gwinnett spoon. 'Is there something wrong with it?'

'Not a thing.'

'The guy didn't want it?'

'Oh, he wanted it,' I said. 'It made him feel like Alexander the Great.'

'Then why isn't he keeping it?'

'An attack of conscience.'

'His conscience was bothering him?'

'Not his,' I said. 'Bottom line, he's not going to keep it.'

She frowned. 'I guess you want your money back.'

I shook my head.

'You don't?'

'We had a deal, Chloe. You gave me the spoon, I gave you the money. Period.'

'What am I supposed to do with it now?'

'The money? Go to Europe, if you still want to. It's yours.'

'The spoon,' she said.

'I'd say just put it back in the cabinet,' I said, 'but he already knows it's missing. So I guess you'll have to put it somewhere and discover it.'

'Someplace where it'd be his fault for having put it there.'

'Whatever works.'

'And I get to keep the money.'

'Right.'

She thought about it. 'You know,' she said, 'yesterday this was the best deal ever, and now it's even better. Unless there's a catch. Be straight with me, okay? Is there a catch?'

'No catch.'

'That's really amazing,' she said. She put the spoon in her purse, drew out a pen, scribbled on a paper napkin.

'Here,' she said. 'My cell number. That's the best way to reach me. In case, you know, there's something else you want me to steal.'

I folded the napkin, put it in my pocket.

'Even after I quit my job,' she said, 'that'll still be my number.' She grinned. 'Unless I'm in Europe.'

FORTY

Back at the store, I called Ray and confirmed that we were set for seven o'clock. 'Some of 'em may show up a few minutes early,' he said, 'and somebody's always a couple of minutes late, but all in all I'd say we're gonna be on schedule.'

'The four Ostermaier children,' I said.

'Deirdre, Boyd, Meredith, and Jackson. Boyd's bringin' his partner. Stephen's his name, but don't ask me which partner he is.'

'Stephen's his life partner.'

'Then that's who he's bringin', so they can leave together for Fire Island when the show's over. Meredith's bringin' Nils. Deirdre's got nobody to bring, and Jackson's got his wife and his girlfriend, and he's not bringin' either of 'em.'

'So that's six.'

'Plus our mystery guest from Willow Street. I'll bring him myself.'

'Making seven. And you'll be eight, and I suppose there'll be some other municipal employees present.'

'Cops, you mean? Two, maybe three. Guys I can work with.'

'Nine, ten, eleven. Plus Carolyn, because I can't leave her out.'

'Makes twelve, and with you it's thirteen. I hope you're not superstitious, Bernie.'

'Not at all,' I said. 'Anyway, won't it be fourteen? Because I can't believe the man from Willow Street won't want to have his lawyer present.'

'What's he need with a lawyer? He knows he's not a target of the investigation.'

'Oh? How does he see himself?'

'As a public-spirited citizen,' he said, 'helpin' me develop a case against a notorious burglar.'

'I see,' I said. 'Well, that sounds about right.'

'Seven o'clock,' I told Carolyn, and ran through the guest list. 'So I'm afraid we don't get to thank God that it's Friday.'

'If we close at five-thirty—'

'I think I'll just stay open,' I said. 'Ray said we may have a few early birds.'

'In that case,' she said, 'there's an hour's worth of dusting and cleaning I've been putting off, so I might as well get it out of the way. How will it be if I show up around six-thirty?'

'I'll be here.'

'And we can still express our gratitude for getting through an-other week, Bern. We just won't have glasses in our hands when we do it.'

It's hard to keep Rex Stout's Nero Wolfe books in stock. People keep discovering the series and seeking copies of the titles they haven't read yet, while long-term fans come in hoping to replace the books their friends have borrowed and failed to return.

I managed to turn up a book club edition of *Might As Well Be Dead* and was using it for reference, noting how Wolfe positioned a roomful of suspects before solving a case, putting various people in various chairs. I didn't have a red leather chair, or a batch of yellow ones, and in fact just about all of my guests would have to stand, but I made a little chart anyway, trying to work out the order of my presentation.

This took longer than you might think, because a stray comment of Archie's about one of the participants sent me flipping pages, looking for the scene where she first appeared. I couldn't find it, but I found other good parts, and realized the only sensible course was to start the book at the beginning. It had been a couple of years since I last read it, and I was clearly ready to read it again.

I suppose I heard the bell when my door opened, and I registered it the way one notes in passing a screech of brakes in the street outside. When it's followed by the sound of impact, one looks up; otherwise it's just part of the city's background music.

'I don't believe it!'

A woman's voice, bubbly with surprise and delight. Pleased to find an old-fashioned bookshop, no doubt, or perhaps more specifically pleased to find a book for which she'd long been searching. If what I was reading were a little less compelling, I'd look up and greet her. But as it was—

'I was sure you'd never be open. I had this fantasy that you were keeping tabs on my schedule, so you could make sure to close before I could get over here. But here we both are, and what do you think about that?'

Oh, God, it was the lady who'd been leaving notes for me. I looked up from my book to see a slender young Asian woman in dark slacks and a blue silk blouse. She had a book bag slung over one shoulder and an expression on her face that morphed as I watched from pleased to startled.

I suspect my own face must have been undergoing much the same transformation.

Our eyes locked, and we stared. And then, at the same instant, we both spoke, and we both said the same thing:

'Juneau Lock!'

FORTY-ONE

'You speak English,' I said.
          'And so do you. Who would have guessed?'
'But—'
'God, this is embarrassing. Look, when you're a Chinese girl in a culture where Asian ethnicity is a male fetish second only to big tits, your life becomes way simpler if the people you deal with don't know you can speak their language.'
'I can see how that would be true,' I said, and looked closely at her. 'But that's only part of it, isn't it? You get a kick out of it. You like getting over on people.'
'Oops,' she said. 'Busted. Yeah, you're right. That's bad, huh?'
'Well, it's probably a character defect.'
'That's what I was afraid of.'
'But one of the more endearing ones.'

'You think?' She grinned. 'It does pass the time. And I don't get a lot in the way of recreation.'

'You must work long hours.'

'Long enough to keep me from getting here during your all-too-brief business hours. I'm at the restaurant every day from ten to six. Once in a green moon I beg my uncle for a half-hour in the slow part of the afternoon. You're smiling. What's so funny?'

'Once in a green moon,' I said.

'I said green? I meant blue. I even know what the expression means. Do you?'

I did. 'When the moon's full twice within a single calendar month, it's called a blue moon.'

'And it doesn't happen very often. But why blue? Any idea? Well, we could always Google it. Right or wrong, we'd get an answer. Anyway, blue or green, I'd rush over here, and you'd be closed.'

'And then you started leaving notes.'

'I couldn't help myself. I was being obnoxious, wasn't I?'

'More like charming.'

'Really?'

'Intriguing, even.'

'Actually,' she said, 'that's what I was aiming for. It was sort of like an online flirtation, where you have no idea what the person's like, and if you did you wouldn't flirt with him in a million years, but it's online, so who cares?'

Our eyes met, and the abrupt realization that we were now flirting face to face brought a rush of color to her cheeks. 'Oh, that reminds me,' she said, spinning away from me. She darted over to a bank of shelves and came back with *Antonin Dvorak: The Man and His Music*, by Dieter Vogelsang.

'You wouldn't believe how long I've been looking for this book,' she said.

'You wouldn't believe how long I've owned it.'

'Really?'

'It was here when I bought the store.'

'I could see it from outside,' she said, 'and I could never get inside to buy it. Is this right? Only ten dollars?'

I shook my head. 'That's the old price.'

'That's what I was afraid of. How much do you want for it?'

'Nothing,' I said. 'It's free.'

'Come on, be serious.'

'This is as serious as I get. I've had the book forever, and you're the first person to express any interest in it whatsoever. And look at all the sensational food I've received from your hands, not to mention the hard time you've had getting your hands on Mr Dvorak. Please, just put it in your bag.'

'Well, if you're sure—'

I said I was, and she added the man and his music to her book bag. 'Thank you,' she said. 'I don't even know your name.'

'It's Bernie,' I said. 'Bernie Rhodenbarr.'

'I'm Katie Huang.'

'And you're from Taichung?'

'Taipei.'

'Okay, but your uncle's one of the two guys from Taichung?'

'He's both guys,' she said, 'because why change the sign? And he's from Taipei, too, but he thought Taichung sounded more exotic.'

'He's right about that. I didn't even know where it was.'

'In the middle of the country, southwest of Taipei.'

'So I discovered.'

'Google, huh? Anyway, the food we cook is more Taichung than Taipei.'

'Especially General Tso and the orange beef.'

'The real food,' she said.

'Juneau Lock.'

'I'll never live that down, will I?'

'Not if I can help it. Dvorak, huh?'

'My main man, ever since I first heard the New World Symphony. And the timing's perfect, because I'll be performing his sonata for flute and piano Sunday afternoon. The one in A minor.'

'It's good you specified. You're a musician.'

'Not yet, but that's the plan.'

'A budding musician. And you're giving a concert?'

'It's just a recital. I'm a student at Juilliard. That's why I never have a spare minute, I'm at the restaurant all day and in class half the night, and practicing the rest of the time. Do you want to come? I mean, it's just a student recital, and none of us are ready to audition for the Philharmonic, but on the other hand it's the same price as Mr Vogelsang's book.'

'Ten bucks?'

'Free admission. You could bring, um—'

'Her name's Carolyn,' I said, and decided to answer the unasked question. 'She's my best friend, but we're not a couple. She, uh, likes girls.'

'You know, I had that feeling—'

'It's the haircut.'

'—but you being together all the time, although I never actually *saw* you both at the same time, but still, I mean, coming in on alternate days and buying food for two, and Juneau Lock and all—'

'I know.'

'Um, are you—'

'I'm like Carolyn,' I said. 'In that we both like girls.'

'I had that feeling, too. Oh, God, I'm running late. I'm supposed to be rehearsing. Nguyen's gonna kill me.'

'He's the flautist?'

277

'He's the pianist. I'm the flautist. Most people say flutist, but you actually said flautist, didn't you? And why should that make me so curiously happy?'

'I have no idea. What time on Sunday?'

'Three o'clock at Alice Tully Hall. It's open seating, so you might want to get there a few minutes early. Do you really think you might come?'

'I wouldn't miss it.'

'You know, there are men who have a sort of fetish for women who play woodwind instruments.'

'Really? Gee, I wonder why.'

'It's one of life's mysteries. I'm glad you're not like that.'

'Me too. But I might have the other one that you mentioned.'

'I hope it's for Asian women and not big tits.'

'It's more specific. It's for adorable smartass girls from Taipei.'

'Adorable? My tiger mom would be so proud. Oh, rats. I really have to—'

'I know. Sunday at three at Alice Tully. And dinner afterward.'

'That'd be great. But one thing, Bernie—'

'Anything but Chinese.'

'Oh, I think I'm in love,' she said, and flew out the door.

FORTY-TWO

It must have been around 6:15 when Katie left, and if she'd waited five minutes she could have held the door for Carolyn, who arrived carrying two bottles of a perky little Beaujolais and a party platter from Sweet Suffering Cheeses. While I tried to figure out where to put things, she took down my sign that said OPEN or CLOSED, depending on which way it was facing, and replaced it with a chunk of cardboard with PRIVATE PARTY hand-lettered on it.

'If they think it's a festive occasion,' she said, 'they'll be leaning the right way when you pull the rug out from under them. I hope they don't mind drinking out of plastic cups.'

If they did, they were polite enough not to show it. A lanky blonde with bright red nail polish was the first to arrive, around fifteen minutes before the appointed hour. 'Oh, I'm early,' she said. 'I usually am, and the people I'm supposed to meet with are usually late. I'm Deirdre Ostermaier.'

I recognized her from a photograph, even as I recognized the next arrivals, Boyd Ostermaier and Stephen Cairns. They were both tall and well built, their medium-brown hair buzzed short, their gym muscles shown to advantage in Chelsea Gym T-shirts and tight Levi's. Boyd, who had a perfectly trimmed beard, gave the cheese platter a professional glance and pronounced it an attractive presentation. Stephen, beardless, had nice things to say about the wine.

Meredith Ostermaier and Nils Calder had a uniformed patrolman as an escort, one Morton O'Fallon, a rail-thin fellow with a sharp nose and a pointed chin. Meredith was a sort of hot earth mother type, all flesh and warmth, while her mate was as laidback as a coiled spring; it wasn't hard to picture him pacing back and forth on a small stage and telling the actors what to do. He filled a cup with wine and skipped the cheese. Meredith, playing Mrs Sprat, did the reverse.

Patrolman O'Fallon allowed himself neither wine nor cheese, but planted himself where he could size everybody up. It wasn't long before he had somebody to talk to, when another cop – in plain clothes, but no less identifiable – came in with Jackson Ostermaier in tow. Jackson looked like a lawyer, and a successful one at that, with a haircut that had cost more than the cop's suit and a suit that cost more than his car.

I didn't catch the plain-clothes cop's name, I don't think he gave it, but I heard O'Fallon call him Tom.

Carolyn drifted over to my side and let her eyes move around the room. 'They seem like perfectly nice people,' she said.

'They do,' I agreed. 'And they're all talking among themselves, the way people do at a social gathering. You were a genius to think of the wine and cheese.'

'Well, you need something to break the ice, Bern. It's that or you'll have Meredith and Nils getting everybody to throw their keys in a hat.'

The conversation by this time had a nice party-time hum to it, enough to drown out the tinkling of the bell when the door opened once more. Still, something must have got their attention, because the room quieted down and heads turned for a look at the new arrival.

It was Ray Kirschmann, accompanied by a middle-aged man in a three-piece suit. He had what looked to be a small brass button sewn to his lapel, but I couldn't make out the design, or guess what candidacy it was supporting.

'Evenin', everybody,' Ray said, in a voice that carried the room. 'My name's Ray Kirschmann, I'm a detective with the New York Police Department, but like I told you tonight's little event's completely unofficial. I think you all know each other, bein' as most of you are brothers and sisters. But not all of you know this here gentleman, who's come along to help us all out.'

Eyes swung from Ray to the man at his side.

'This is Mr Alton Ogden Smith,' he said, and Meredith Ostermaier passed the cheese even as her sister Deirdre brought over two cups of wine.

'And now I'll turn things over to our host,' Ray said. 'This here is Bernie Rhodenbarr, a man I've known for a good many years, and besides bein' a man with a shop full of old books, he's got a real knack of separatin' the hats from the rabbits. Bernie, you want to get things started?'

And now all eyes were on me, and most of them showed puzzlement. With one exception, they were meeting me for the first time.

Still, I knew my cue. 'Welcome to Barnegat Books,' I said. 'I suppose you're wondering why I summoned you all here.'

*

'Not long ago,' I said, 'a deeply unfortunate event occurred that touched everybody in this room. Helen Ostermaier, whose four children are present this evening, attended a performance at the Metropolitan Opera. At intermission she told a friend that she didn't feel well and would make an early night of it.

'She caught a cab and went home, but evidently she'd been exposed at some point to peanuts in one form or another, and she suffered from a severe peanut allergy. By the time she got home she was feeling worse, not better. She attempted to inject herself with epinephrine, to counteract the anaphylactic shock she was beginning to experience, but it turned out to be too little too late, and her weak heart couldn't handle the strain. She fell to the floor and lay there.'

Deirdre was holding back tears. Stephen had a hand on Boyd's shoulder, comforting him, and Nils was doing the same for Meredith.

'Now this was all tragic,' I said, 'but it was a natural occurrence. Helen Ostermaier had been asthmatic as a child, with multiple allergies. The asthma receded as she matured, and so did the allergies, but they'd returned in recent years, and along the way she'd had heart problems. While she might well have lived a good many more years, death in one form or another could have come at any time.'

'At least it was quick,' Deirdre said. 'She didn't suffer.'

'And she was active right to the end,' Boyd said. 'She'd have hated being bedridden, but she was spared that.'

'Museum openings, the opera, the theater,' Meredith said. 'Those things were her life. She wouldn't have wanted to go on without them.'

'And she still had all her faculties,' Jackson added. 'She hadn't lost a step mentally, and how she dreaded that prospect. When a good friend of hers showed signs of early Alzheimer's, it shook her.'

'She told me she hoped she died before she got like that,' Boyd said, and Deirdre said she'd been told the same thing.

'Still,' I said, 'it was sad.'

There was a murmur of agreement.

'And,' I continued, 'it may not have been altogether inevitable. Oh, the allergic reaction, the anaphylactic shock, the collapse – nothing could have been done to forestall that. But not long after Helen Ostermaier crumpled to the floor, someone unlocked her front door and walked in on her. Someone who'd managed to equip himself with a key, and who knew he'd have the house to himself, because the housekeeper had left hours ago and Mrs Ostermaier would be listening to Wagner for another hour or more.'

'That's the first thing I thought,' Deirdre said. 'When I found her. Everything was strewn around, as if a burglar had been searching for something. I assumed she walked in on him and he killed her. Or if he didn't actually strike her or stab her, the shock of seeing him there could have brought on a heart attack. That happens, doesn't it?'

'First thing we thought of,' Ray told them, 'once it developed there were no signs of violence on the body.'

'Let's focus on the intruder,' I said. 'What do we know about him?'

'If it's a him,' Meredith said, 'I guess that lets out me and Deirdre.'

'He's a him,' I agreed, 'and not one of the Ostermaier children, or either of their significant others. And, since it wasn't a policeman, that narrows it down. The intruder has been known to use other names, but he's here in our midst under the name he was born with. His name is Alton Ogden Smith, and I believe one of you is already acquainted with him.'

I glanced at Jackson, who looked troubled. 'I'm Mr Smith's attorney,' he said, 'and I'm not sure how much more I can say without violating attorney-client privilege.'

'You represent Mr Smith in tax matters.'

'That's correct.'

'Then you can speak freely,' I said. 'Mr Smith's taxes aren't at issue here, nor was your professional relationship involved in the matter at hand. He wasn't seeking your counsel, Mr Ostermaier. You were seeking his.'

'I don't know where you're going with this,' Jackson said, 'but it might as well end right here. I suppose you've found some sort of evidence that Alton has been inside my mother's house. Well, indeed he has, at my invitation and in my company. It must have been two weeks before the night in question.'

'And was your mother at home at the time?'

'No,' he said. 'As it happens she was attending a reception at one of the museums. I'm afraid I don't remember which one. Does it matter?'

'Not to me,' I said. 'Why?'

'Why?'

'Why bring your client to your mother's home?'

He'd have preferred not to answer, but that wasn't an option, not with all of his siblings staring at him. 'Alton knows a great deal about Early American art,' he said. 'My father picked up quite a few paintings over the years. The ancestors, we always called them, and I suppose they may well have been somebody's ancestors, though they certainly weren't ours. They were strictly décor, but I was wondering about them.'

'Wondering what they were worth,' Boyd guessed.

'Well, yes. We never paid attention to the subjects or the artists, they were just these forbidding faces that had been on the walls all our lives. Suppose one of them was by Gilbert

Stuart or Thomas Eakins or somebody important?'

'Wouldn't Mother have known?'

'Did she pay any more attention to them than we did? I thought it would be good to know what we had.'

'And if one of them turned out to be good?' This from Meredith. 'Then what?'

'Then perhaps she might have been persuaded to part with it.'

'She'd never have sold anything,' Deirdre said. '"When I'm gone, dear, will be time enough to do what you want with what's here." That's what she'd have said and you know it.'

'On the other hand,' Boyd said, 'one of our beloved ancestors could have been quietly spirited out of the house without her noticing.'

'If that had happened,' Jackson said, 'and if the work in question had been sold, you'd all have received your shares.' Eyes rolled, but he pressed on. 'But it doesn't matter, because while the ancestor portraits aren't entirely worthless, they're a long way from priceless. They'd bring a thousand or two apiece at auction.'

'And just how do we know this, Jacko?'

'I made a list,' he said, 'of the artists, when I could read their signatures, and I took a couple of snaps with my phone, and I showed what I had to Alton. He said it seemed unlikely we had anything much, but that a personal inspection would ensure that we weren't overlooking a masterpiece. So I brought him over—'

'When you knew Mother would be out.'

'Only because I saw no reason to trouble her. We were in and out of the house in less than an hour. It didn't take Alton long to see all he needed to see.'

'Ah,' I said. 'And what exactly did you see, Mr Smith?'

'What I'd expected, sir. American portraits, most of them eighteenth century, all of them by artists who were either anonymous or might as well have been. Some were rather nicely executed,

others less so. All would be of passing interest to an interior dec-
orator, or to someone in need of an ancestor or two, but nothing
genuinely valuable.' He smiled. 'Nothing that would tempt a
thief.'

'Nothing you'd want yourself, then.'

'Hardly,' he said. 'I know a bit about art, as Jackson has said,
especially of the period. But I don't collect it myself.'

'And yet you returned,' I said. 'Unaccompanied by Mr Ostermaier, at an hour when you knew the house would be empty.'

'How would I know that? And how would I gain access?' His
eyes bored into mine. 'Some of us,' he said, 'don't need a key to
open a lock, but—'

'I had a key,' Jackson said suddenly.

'Well, of course,' Meredith said. 'We all had keys. And you
must have used yours when you brought Mr Smith to look at the
paintings.'

'And then I looked for it,' Jackson said, 'and couldn't find it.
And then a few days later it was back on my key ring, where I'd
been unable to find it earlier.' He stared at Smith. 'Alton, why in
the world did you take my key?'

'That's ridiculous,' Smith said.

'You borrowed it, didn't you? You had it copied and then
slipped it back onto my key ring. We had three unnecessary con-
sultations in succession, and my time was billable so it was hardly
meet for me to object, but I wondered why you needed to see that
much of me. You wanted my key.'

'Nonsense.'

'No, I don't think so.' Jackson seemed to grow taller, and his
brow darkened. 'Small talk,' he said. 'Idle chatter. You were never
much for that, and suddenly you filled my billable hours with
questions about my mother and how she spent her time. By God,
Alton, you broke into my mother's house!'

Someone said something about the burglar alarm. 'She didn't always set it,' Boyd said, and Jackson said it hadn't been armed when he'd arrived with Smith.

'But you made a thing of noticing the keypad,' he said to Smith. 'You said you hoped the combination was easy for her to remember. And I told you what it was!'

'I don't recall the conversation, Jackson. And if we even had it, I certainly didn't make a note of the number.'

'Now that's funny,' I said. 'Because something tells me that if a person were to look in the top right-hand drawer of a desk on the parlor floor of your house on Willow Street, he'd find a note pad with that very four-digit combination written on it.'

'If someone did,' Smith said, glaring at me, 'it would mean absolutely nothing, because it could mean anything, anything at all. One-two-three-four, a perfectly ordinary sequence, and—'

He stopped, as did most of the breathing in the room. I could have asked him how, if he didn't recall the conversation and hadn't taken notice of the number, he happened to have hit upon it now. But I didn't have to say anything, because they'd already worked it out for themselves.

FORTY-THREE

'What we're dealing with,' I said, 'is greed, and an almost universal characteristic of greed is that it is boundless. One recalls the proverbial farmer who insisted he wasn't greedy; he only wanted the land that bordered his own. Greed is an appetite that is never sated. The more you feed it, the hungrier it grows.

'Financial greed is what comes most often to mind. It's greed that leads people to play the lottery, and the insatiable nature of the malady shows in the propensity of lottery winners to play the thing again. Why, once you've won a nine-figure jackpot, would you stand in line to buy more tickets? Because, like that farmer, you never have enough. You always want more.

'But greed takes other forms as well. Sometimes it's a hunger for more sexual partners and a greater intensity of sexual experience.' I was careful not to look at Meredith and Nils, but made the mistake of looking at Boyd and Stephen instead, who responded by blushing. Who knew?

'And I could go on,' I said, deciding I'd gone on quite enough. 'But let's get down to cases. Alton Ogden Smith is a collector, and it is that particular obsession that has made him an uncommonly greedy man.'

'That's just about enough,' Smith said. 'I'm leaving.'

'No,' Ray said. 'I don't think so.'

'Oh? Am I under arrest?'

'Not yet,' Ray told him. 'Do you wanna be?'

Smith started to object, then changed his mind. 'I might as well hear this,' he said.

'You're a collector,' I said, 'with wide-ranging interests that all center upon a single theme. You collect buttons – clothing buttons, political campaign buttons, buttons from military uniforms, buttons of every sort. And you collect books about buttons, and books with characters named Button.'

'Like Benjamin Button,' Stephen said, and smiled brightly. 'We saw the movie.'

'With Brad Pitt,' Boyd recalled.

'Like Benjamin Button,' I agreed. 'And like real people named Button, of whom there have not been many, but one at least is of some renown.'

I waited for someone to supply a name. When nobody did, I glanced meaningfully at Carolyn.

'Like Button Gwinnett,' she said.

'The signer,' Nils Calder said. 'The rare one.'

'The one with the elusive signature,' I said, and tossed in a fact or two about the man, which you needn't hear all over again.

'Mr Smith was obsessed with buttons,' I went on, 'and consequently became obsessed with Button Gwinnett. His collection includes rare editions of books about the man, and the original sketch for the Great Seal of Gwinnett County, Georgia. It hangs on a wall in his study.'

Someone wanted to know how I happened to know that.

'Clairvoyance,' I said. 'It's a gift, and I've learned not to question it. I came to know Mr Smith when he thought I might be able to help him obtain a spoon with Button Gwinnett's likeness upon it, a spoon produced here in New York by a silversmith named Myer Myers, and—'

'That'd be Meyer Meyer,' Ray broke in, 'and Ed McBain wrote about him. Greatest writer who ever lived, far as I'm concerned, on account of he wrote about cops and he got it right. The cops are the good guys in his books, and even the bad ones are okay, you know what I mean?'

'If you worked on the wording a little,' I said, 'they'd probably use it for a cover blurb. "This is my kind of book, because even the bad cops are good – Ray Kirschmann, NYPD." It's got a nice ring to it. But that's Meyer Meyer, and I'm talking about somebody else.'

'Myer Myers,' Carolyn said helpfully.

'Who made a Button Gwinnett spoon, which Mr Smith coveted, as he covets so many elusive items. And I thought I might be able to help him, but nothing came of it.'

Smith made a sound. A snort, you might have called it.

'So that's how you know him,' Deirdre said. 'And probably how you know what's hanging on his wall.'

'Probably,' I agreed. I turned to Jackson. 'When you showed your list of paintings to Mr Smith, there was an artist on it named Chancelling.'

'Something like that,' Jackson said. 'There was a signature in the lower right corner, but it was hard to make out. Chancellor, Chancelling, whatever. No first name, but there was an initial.'

'And that would be J.'

'I'll take your word for it.'

'J. Chancelling,' I said, 'of whom next to nothing is known besides his last name and first initial, painted the only known portrait of our friend Button Gwinnett. It disappeared over a century ago, and turned up in your mother's house on Ninety-second Street, where it hung for years over the wall safe in the master bedroom.'

'But it's not there now?'

'I'm afraid not. But if you were to go to Brooklyn Heights and pay a visit to Mr Smith's home, you'd find a portrait with that very signature hanging in a place of honor.'

Can a silence properly be described as thoughtful? Well, this one was. It stretched on until Alton Ogden Smith broke it. 'I saw that name on Jackson's list of artists,' he said. 'Except I don't believe it was Chancelling. It looked more like Chancellor. Still, I wondered if it was another work by Chancelling, even a second painting of Gwinnett.'

'A second painting,' I said.

'Because I own his Button Gwinnett portrait, have owned it for years. I'm afraid it wouldn't be prudent for me to disclose how I came by it. Its provenance is cloudy, let us say, involving an under-the-table transaction that was surely unethical if not strictly illegal. So I was indeed interested in seeing the work, and I had a look at it, and it's not Chancelling at all, and the subject is certainly not Gwinnett. If you say it's no longer where it was, well, I can no more guess what's become of it than I can fathom why anyone would want to walk off with it.'

'There's a story of Saki's,' I said, 'called *The Open Window*. Have any of you read it?'

None of them had. Well, I wasn't surprised. Who reads anything these days?

'It comes to mind,' I said, 'because there was a young girl in the story who was quite brilliant at elaborate improvisation on short notice. I have to say you're right up there with her. I was impressed with your whole invention of the five Burton Bartons, but you had plenty of time to come up with it. This was virtually spur of the moment, and I have to say I'm in awe.'

So was Jackson, evidently, or perhaps he was beginning to realize that he stood to lose a major client. 'You know,' he said, 'you're making serious accusations here. Alton Ogden Smith is a man of substance. If there's an item he wants for his collection, he can write out a check for it. He doesn't have to resort to housebreaking.'

'Or he could have hired some amoral wretch to commit a felony on his behalf,' I said. 'He'd still be breaking the law, but he wouldn't get his hands dirty. But maybe he discovered he actually *wanted* to get his hands dirty. Maybe it was time for him to see what it was like.'

I let them think about that for a moment.

Then I said, 'Here's what happened. Our Mr Smith saw the painting and recognized it immediately for what it was, Chancelling's long-lost portrait of Button Gwinnett. He had to have it, but how? His attorney needed money, but it wasn't his to sell, it belonged to the man's mother, who was no more eager to let go of her possessions than she was to move from a house that was far too large for her needs. She wanted to keep her surroundings as they were, and wouldn't that extend to the paintings on her walls?

'And if he cleared that hurdle, how could he make sure the portrait wound up in his hands? If Jackson Ostermaier knew what he had, wouldn't he want to get the best price for it? And wouldn't that mean publicity, and an auction at Christie's or Sotheby's, with buyers representing everyone from the Georgia Historical Society to some oil-rich sheik from the Emirates keen to snatch the thing up before some Russian oligarch got his hands on it?

'Mr Smith might be a wealthy man, but he'd come by his money in the old-fashioned way. He inherited it, and while it provided him with all of life's luxuries and then some, it didn't run into the billions. While one might think of him as a man who could have anything he wanted, that doesn't take into account the nature of greed.

'So here was this painting, and he had to have it, and perhaps he felt it was his by right. He'd discovered it, hadn't he? He'd recognized Chancelling's name on his client's inventory, then recognized Gwinnett's face when he got a look at it. Didn't this provide him with some sort of moral title to the thing?'

My eyes locked with Smith's. 'Here's what you did. You put Jackson off the scent by telling him the ancestor portraits were not going to solve anybody's financial problems. You slipped his mother's key off his key ring, copied it, and put it back. You determined when she'd be away from the house, and the house empty.

'You paid a visit, but you didn't come empty-handed. If your visit were to go unnoticed, you'd have to so arrange things that no one ever missed the portrait. That meant hanging something in its place – in the upstairs bedroom, covering the wall safe.

'So you brought a painting along. What you might have done was hunt the galleries and antique shops for another anonymous old portrait in a similar frame. But that would cost you a couple of thousand dollars, plus the time involved in finding something suitable, and you had something around the house, a museum reproduction, tastefully framed. John Constable, 1776–1837, cows in a field.'

'Those cows,' Deirdre said. 'I was standing there, looking down at Mother, and I saw them out of the corner of my eye. And I thought how odd it was that I'd never really noticed them before. But of course I hadn't, because they weren't there.' She frowned. 'But they were on the west wall, above the leather-topped drum table. And didn't you say the Gwinnett portrait was upstairs?'

'Concealing the safe,' I said. 'But that was the room your mother slept in, and he realized she'd know at once if a rural landscape abruptly replaced an ancestor portrait. So he switched his Constable for a downstairs ancestor, which he took upstairs to swap for his beloved Button Gwinnett. It looks right at home there.

'And the Constable wasn't a bad match for the living room décor. But the size was wrong. It was wider than it was tall, unlike the portrait it replaced. Walls darken over time, except where they're covered, and a close look at the Constable showed that it had been hung to replace a painting with very different dimensions.'

'Maybe that's why I noticed it,' Deirdre said.

'And maybe nobody would have noticed anything,' I said, 'but for the very unfortunate fact that your mother left the opera early, and returned home earlier than expected. Mr Smith turned up an hour or so later, and I'm sure he took the precaution of ringing the doorbell before he used his key. That way, if anyone was home, he could say he'd come to the wrong address by mistake, and pay another visit on another evening.

'But the lady of the house was not only home, which was inconvenient, but dead – which was worse.'

'Especially for her,' Carolyn said.

'So you rang the bell,' I told Smith. 'Maybe you rang it twice, just to make sure. And when it went unanswered, you used your key and walked into the house, and the first thing you saw was Helen Ostermaier lying on the carpet.'

Someone sobbed. Meredith, I think.

'A real burglar,' I said, 'would have turned around and left. Only an amateur, addled by greed, would have stayed the course. But there you were, with Button Gwinnett waiting upstairs for you, and how could you resist?

'Besides, if the woman was dead, then her estate would have to be appraised. Would some sharp-eyed appraiser spot the Gwinnett portrait for what it was? And would you wind up in a pissing contest with Russians and Arabs? You were already here, you were already inside the house, you had the Constable substitute under your arm, and now you didn't even have to worry about the lady of the house walking in on you. Because she was already there and she wasn't going to be walking anywhere.

'So you got down to business. You snatched a portrait off the wall, hung the Constable in its place. You carried the portrait upstairs, switched it with Button Gwinnett's likeness, and returned to the living room.'

'And left,' Boyd said.

'If only,' I said. 'Because up to this point it would be difficult to make much of a case against Mr Smith. We can say what happened, we can say when an intruder appeared on the scene and what he did and why, but how can we be sure it was Alton Ogden Smith and not someone else?'

'You can't,' Smith said. 'Because it wasn't. Someone else must have found out about the portrait. Jackson must have shown his inventory of ancestor portraits to some other interested party.'

'If only you'd taken the portrait and left,' I said. 'But you weren't done, were you?'

'I beg your pardon?'

'You saw something else,' I said, 'and you couldn't resist. You couldn't bring yourself to leave there without it.'

Deirdre said, 'I knew someone had been there. In fact I thought someone had broken in and killed Mother, and I wondered what he might have stolen. Was something else missing?'

'A button,' I said.

FORTY-FOUR

'When Mrs Ostermaier came home from the opera,' I said, 'she was wearing a coat. It was quite distinctive, a rich green shade with a fur collar.'

'A very smart coat,' Boyd said, 'if it's the one I'm thinking of. I believe it was from Arvin Tannenbaum.'

'That's the one,' Deirdre said. 'She'd taken if off, though. It was on the chair.'

'It was,' I agreed. 'And I wondered how she'd have come to lay it out that way. Unless you moved it.'

Deirdre said she hadn't touched the coat. 'But you're right, you wouldn't take off your coat and lay it out like that.'

'She'd have hung it up,' Meredith said. 'Unless, you know, she had that allergic reaction. But then wouldn't it just drop onto the floor?'

'I don't know,' Jackson said. 'How much can you read into the position of a coat? If she was feeling woozy, she could have put it down any which way.'

'All the coat did was get my attention,' I said. 'And when I took a good look at it, I saw it was missing a button.'

'A button,' someone said.

'The coat had very distinctive buttons,' I said. 'Art nouveau, I'd say, and they looked as though they might have come from Tiffany Studios.'

'They did,' Meredith said. 'She'd bought the set on Madison Avenue, I forget where, and when she ordered the coat from Tannenbaum she had them use the Tiffany buttons.'

'She had such good taste,' Boyd said. 'You said a button was missing?'

'There were five pairs of buttons,' I said. 'Ten in all. And the lowest button on the right was missing. I took a look, and there were no bits of thread to show where it had been.'

'It came off,' Stephen suggested, 'at the opera. Did you check her pockets? When I pop a button I put it in the pocket of whatever garment it came from, so I'll find it later and remember to sew it back on.'

'There were no buttons in any of the pockets,' I said. 'Ray, did you find a button in her purse?'

He hadn't. Deirdre said the button might have been lost weeks ago, and that when her mother discovered its absence she'd have gotten rid of any unsightly thread ends.

'I think she'd have done more than that,' I said. 'The button would be difficult to replace, if not impossible. And she was far too fastidious a woman to walk around with five buttons on one side and four on the other. But this is speculation, and it's easier to deal in fact.

'And it's a fact that the man who'd come for Button Gwinnett's portrait saw a coat on the floor, where its owner had dropped it. The buttons caught his eye. He recognized them as Tiffany's work, and he wanted one. He very likely wanted all ten, but would content himself with a single specimen.

'It wouldn't have taken him long. A penknife or a nail file would snip the thread; failing that, a sharp yank would get him the button. Then he'd conceal what he'd done by getting rid of any remnants of thread, and he'd leave the coat neatly laid out over a chair, and that would be that.'

'Facts,' Smith said. 'Facts as opposed to speculation. Isn't that what you said?'

'Something like that,' I allowed.

'Well, you've given us nothing but speculation, all on the basis of a coat that's missing a button. If I took this button, where is it?'

'In your house,' I said. 'In Brooklyn Heights. In a desk drawer, if I had to guess.'

'Which you may search to your heart's content,' he said. 'You will find no such button.'

I looked at Ray. 'Hang on,' he said, and took out his cell phone. He punched in a number, spoke in an undertone to somebody, then clicked around some. 'Ah, there we go,' he said. 'Used to be you'd have uniforms hotfootin' it all over town, snappin' Polaroids, then breakin' traffic laws deliverin' 'em. Now a couple of clicks and you're good to go.' He held up his phone, and my guests crowded around to get a look at the screen.

'That's the portrait that was hanging over the safe,' Jackson Ostermaier announced. 'I guess it's Button Gwinnett, though all we ever knew was that he was somebody else's ancestor.'

'And that's the Great Seal of Gwinnett County hangin' next to it,' Ray said. 'Right after I picked up Mr Smith here, I sent a couple of officers from Brooklyn South over to his house with a warrant. One of 'em took this here picture, and just now he sent it to me. Came out nice, didn't it?'

'I explained how I came by my portrait of Button Gwinnett,' Smith said. 'And if you had an eye for art, Jackson, you'd never mistake this image for the crudely wrought daub you showed me. And as for the putative button—'

'Right, the button,' Ray said, 'though I don't know where you get off callin' it putrid. It looks okay to me.' He did some more clicking, held out the phone again. 'How's it look to you?'

It looked like a Tiffany button from Helen Ostermaier's green coat, reposing in a drawer next to a piece of notepaper, on which someone had written the numbers one through four.

Smith just stared. I'd been hoping for another lightning-fast improvisation explaining what the button was doing in his desk drawer, in convenient proximity to the code for the burglar alarm. But of course he couldn't explain it, since in point of fact he didn't have a clue how a button he'd brought home and tucked away where no one could possibly find it had somehow transported itself through the ether to the drawer of his desk.

In the fullness of time, he might work it all out. A second button, snipped from the very same coat by a subsequent intruder, and planted in his drawer where someone with a warrant might find it. He was, after all, a bright fellow, was Alton Ogden Smith, and sooner or later it would come to him.

But for now he was gobsmacked.

Ray nodded to the other two cops, and they moved in on Smith. Tom in plain clothes read him his rights, while O'Fallon cuffed him.

'Breakin' in and swipin' the portrait is bad enough,' Ray was saying. 'And stealin' the button off a dead woman's coat is about as low as it gets, but standin' around and lettin' a woman die in front of you is tons worse.'

'She was already dead.'

'Thanks for sayin' that,' he said, 'after you got your rights read to you. But how'd you know that for sure? You bother to take her pulse? Check her breathin'? Call for an ambulance, so's a couple of EMTs could see if she still had any life left for them to save? No, you were in a hurry to grab a paintin' and get outta there. You had time to cut a button off her coat, but no time to call 911 and try to save a good woman's life.'

The two cops left with Alton Ogden Smith in tow, and the room went awfully quiet when the door closed behind them. Carolyn picked up the last bottle of wine and went around filling glasses until it was empty. There was still plenty of cheese left. It's funny how often the cheese outlasts the wine.

Nils Calder wondered what charges could be brought against Smith. 'Besides those related to the theft,' he said. 'Did he break any laws by not calling 911?'

Jackson suggested a few possibilities. Depraved indifference to human life, he said, might apply irrespective of the cause of death, or of his mother's precise condition at the time. 'It's probably impossible to say with certainty whether she was alive or dead when he was there,' he said, 'but Smith couldn't tell, either, so I think a charge of depraved indifference might hold up.'

'How about accessory?' Ray said.

'Accessory to what?'

'Accessory after the fact.' he said.

'Accessory after the fact? After *what* fact?'

He shrugged. 'What do you think, Bernie? How's homicide?'

'Oh, right,' I said. 'I was just getting to that.'

FORTY-FIVE

'At first,' I said, 'it looked as though Helen Ostermaier had surprised a burglar, or been surprised by one. The absence of wounds ruled out homicide, but the confrontation might have brought on a heart attack.'

'Felony murder,' Jackson said.

'A possibility,' I said, 'until evidence suggested that the burglar arrived after she'd collapsed and died.'

'Unless she was still breathing when Smith got there,' Boyd said.

'I just said that to get him goin',' Ray told them. 'She was gone by then. The medical evidence shows she was just about dead by the time she hit the floor.'

That was graphic enough to make Meredith shudder, and Deirdre looked a little pale herself.

'And the cause of death,' I said, 'turned out to be anaphylactic shock.'

'Then it was natural causes,' Jackson said. 'So it can't be homicide.'

'It can if it was induced.'

'How do you induce anaphylactic shock?'

'It's complicated,' I allowed. 'But so's explaining how a woman could die of an allergic reaction to peanuts without showing traces of the allergen in her stomach contents. Something had to trigger the reaction.'

'They stopped giving out peanuts on airplanes,' Meredith said, 'because the smell alone can sometimes trigger a response.'

'It can,' I said, 'and that's what happened here. Every smell is particulate. I learned that from a Michael Connelly novel. In other words, if you smell something, you're taking minute particles of it into your system.'

'Gross,' Stephen said.

'But that does explain it,' Boyd said. 'Somebody must have spilled peanuts on her at the opera, and she had the smell on her clothes. You know, that must be why she left early.'

'You don't think Wagner's explanation enough? And getting peanuts spilled on you is a risk at Yankee Stadium or the Big Apple Circus, but how often does it happen at the Met? Anyway, that's not how it happened. She wouldn't breathe in peanut residue at Lincoln Center and feel the effects a mile away and half an hour later. She didn't smell peanuts until she was home in her own house.'

'I don't understand,' Jackson said. 'She didn't keep peanuts there.'

'No, she didn't. But someone made sure she'd smell peanuts when she got home from the opera. And it must have been a good strong smell, because there was a trace of it in the air the next day.

It was faint by then, and all I knew was that I smelled something and couldn't quite identify it. Later, when I learned what killed her, I realized what I'd smelled earlier.'

Ray said, 'Would that kill a person, Bernie? Just smellin' a couple of peanuts?'

'Probably not,' I said. 'But it would bring on a reaction, and Mrs Ostermaier would have recognized the reaction instantly, just as she would have recognized the smell that caused it. And she'd have known what to do.'

'She'd give herself a shot,' he said, 'of whatchacallit.'

'Epinephrine,' I said, 'which she kept in her purse. It comes in a type of syringe they call a pen, designed to dispense multiple doses over a period of time. I believe you found an empty pen in her purse.'

'Right. First thing we thought, she took the last dose a while ago and never got around to gettin' the prescription refilled.'

'But that wasn't it, was it?'

'No,' he said. 'It wasn't.'

'Well?' Jackson said. 'Are you going to tell us what it was?'

'I was gettin' there, Counselor. See, this consultant I brought in came up with an idea or two. One thing I did, I got the medical examiner to take another good look at the body. Turns out there was evidence of a recent injection in the upper arm. So she did give herself a shot.'

'But if the pen was empty—'

'It wasn't,' I said. 'Not when she injected herself. Later, when the police found it in her purse, it had been emptied of its contents. But that was after she'd given herself a shot of the substance that killed her.'

'And what was that?'

'Peanut oil,' Ray said. 'An intramuscular shot of peanut oil, which would account for her havin' peanut allergens in her bloodstream but not in her stomach. She killed herself tryin' to cure herself. The pen was empty, but it held traces of the peanut oil.'

'And that's what makes it homicide,' I said. 'Exposure to the odor of peanuts, through airborne peanut dust, could have come about accidentally. But it's hard to conjure up an accident that would replace the epinephrine in a syringe with the substance it was meant to counteract.'

The hush that had fallen over the room earlier came back for another visit, and once again it was Jackson who broke it. 'If someone deliberately sabotaged the syringe with peanut oil—'

'It would be hard to do it accidentally.'

'Yes, of course. But to do so intentionally could only be premeditated murder.'

'It doesn't sound spur of the moment,' I agreed.

'Nor is it an act that could have been performed by an outsider.'

I glanced around the room, and what I saw was a batch of people doing the very same thing, their eyes darting from one person to another.

'It would have to be one of us,' Jackson said.

'Oh, more than one,' I said.

'Four children,' I said, 'and all of you needed money. Your mother was rattling around in a house far too large for her needs, and if she would agree to move it would sell quickly for a high price. But she wanted to live out her life in the house that had been her home for so many years.

'And her heart was bad, and what kind of life could she look forward to? Maybe there were already signs of mental deterioration. Maybe she was forgetting things, maybe she'd sometimes have trouble coming up with a name, or the right word.'

I saw some of them nodding in agreement.

'In the right light,' I said, 'easing her out of this world and into the next could almost be seen as an act of mercy. And done the right way it would be both quick and gentle – and, most important, neither Helen Ostermaier nor anyone else would recognize her death as what it was – an act of murder.'

The word brought a gasp or two.

'She's alone,' I said, setting the scene. 'She's in the comfort of her own home, after an evening at a favorite venue, the Metropolitan Opera. In her living room, she sees a blue box, gift-wrapped. Perhaps there's a note on it, something along the lines of *For You, Mom!* or *Open Me Now!*

'Well, who can resist a surprise? She opens the box, pulls at the tissue paper to see what it's concealing. There doesn't seem to be anything there, but a strong smell of peanuts rises from the tissue paper, and she feels the beginning of an allergic reaction that has become familiar to her.

'Fortunately she knows what to do. She shrugs off her coat, reaches into her purse, finds the epinephrine pen. She uncaps it, hikes up her sleeve, and gives herself a shot. But instead of reversing the onset of anaphylactic shock, the injection heightens it exponentially. In no time at all, the woman is dead.'

'Oh, God,' Meredith said. 'It sounds so awful. I never thought—'

'Stop,' Boyd told her. 'This gentleman is telling us a story, and that's all it is, a story. You shouldn't be saying anything, Meredith. None of us should.'

'In fact,' Deirdre said, 'we should probably leave. If we say anything at all—'

'It couldn't be used in court,' Jackson said. 'I haven't heard a Miranda warning. No one's read any of us our rights.'

'You probably know 'em,' Ray said. 'You're an attorney yourself, so you'd have to know your rights, and so would anybody who's spent more than fifteen minutes in front of a television set.

But you're not gonna hear 'em from me, not tonight, on account of this is just an unofficial gatherin' of family members and friends and a couple other interested parties.'

'Unofficial,' Jackson said. 'Well, in that case I'll admit I'd like to hear the rest, Rhodenbarr. I have a brother and two sisters in this room, and it sounds as though you're accusing one or more of them of murdering our mother.'

'All three of them,' I said. 'It was very much a joint effort. Meredith, you went to a storefront clinic on Avenue A and obtained a prescription for an epinephrine pen of the type your mother carried. You filled it at a drugstore a block away. The clinic gave you a receipt, and so did the drugstore, and you kept them both.'

'Brilliant,' Nils said.

'Not that the receipts are necessary,' I said. 'Everything's on record. There's probably security camera coverage of your visits to both establishments, as far as that goes. But never mind. You bought the pen and gave it to your brother Boyd.'

Boyd rolled his eyes. 'And no doubt you can point to security camera footage showing my sister handing me this pen.'

I shook my head. 'What I can point to,' I said, 'is a six-ounce bottle of Nature's Best Cold-Pressed Peanut Oil, guaranteed on its label to have been produced exclusively from organically grown peanuts, and with minute peanut particles present in suspension in order to maximize authentic peanut flavor. That's not an exact quote, but it's close, because phrasing like that does tend to linger in the mind.'

'I'm a cook and a caterer,' he said. 'I have a great array of ingredients in my kitchen.'

'But this wasn't stored with the other oils, was it? It was tucked away in another cupboard. And, on the basis of the sell-by date, it must have been purchased quite recently.'

'You can't prove it's the same oil you found in the syringe.'

'Matter of fact,' Ray said, 'we probably can. You got a specialty product like that, well, it won't have DNA, but what it's got is close enough. You put a couple of lab technicians on it and they'll make a good case.'

'You emptied the epinephrine out of the pen Meredith gave you,' I told Boyd, 'and replaced it with peanut oil. Then you gave it back to Meredith, who had a lunch date with her mother.' I turned to Meredith. 'The two of you spent what must have been a pleasant hour and a half at Le Soupçon du Jour, in the course of which you got hold of your mother's purse long enough to switch pens. You left her a pen loaded with peanut oil and took away the one containing epinephrine. What did you do with it?'

'I'm not going to answer that.'

'I wish you would,' Boyd said. 'If you'd done what you were supposed to do with it, we wouldn't all be having this conversation.'

'I was wondering about that,' I said. 'Meredith, weren't you supposed to get the good pen to your sister? That way Deirdre could have switched pens again after she discovered your mother's body.'

Meredith froze with her mouth open, unable to find words. Nils put a hand on her arm. 'Hypothetically,' he said. 'Okay?'

'Go ahead.'

'Hypothetically, let's say that no one had told Meredith what to do after she switched the pens. Let's say that she was so upset by what she'd just done that she couldn't bear to have the pen on her person. So on the way home she dropped it into a subway trash barrel.'

'Actually it was a sewer, honey.'

'I was keeping it hypothetical.'

'It's a nice hypothesis,' I said. 'Boyd, you had one more task to perform. You pulverized a couple of ounces of peanuts in a blender and delivered them to Deirdre. Deirdre, you wrapped them in tissue paper, packed them up in a gift box, and tied it with a ribbon. Shortly after your mother left her house on her way to the Met, you let yourself in and put the box on the coffee table where it would be the first thing she saw when she walked in the door.

'Then you went home. You knew when the opera would let out, and when your mother would be likely to get home. You waited until then and dialed her number. What would you have done if she answered?'

'How could she?'

'Well, who was to say that the plan would work? Suppose the smell of the peanuts wasn't enough to generate an allergic reaction? She'd have no reason to give herself a shot of epinephrine, and she'd be in perfectly good shape to pick up the telephone.

'But you wouldn't be able to tell what happened just by hearing her voice on the phone. You'd have to ask her a couple of questions. "Mom, did you see the blue box on the coffee table? Did you open it?"

'And if she hadn't opened it, then you'd have a choice to make. What would you tell her? To open it right away? Or to leave it unopened?'

'Oh, God,' Deirdre said. 'She didn't answer, she couldn't answer, she was already—'

'Dead,' I said, 'which makes it a real The-Lady-or-the-Tiger question, doesn't I? Of course you couldn't be absolutely certain she was dead, you wouldn't know that until you went over and discovered her body, and you had to hold off until enough time had passed. You made a couple more phone calls – to your mother's friend, who told you she'd left early. That made it a little more likely that your plan had worked, but you still had to bide your time and call your mother's number another time or two. Then you went to the house you'd already visited

308

earlier that evening, when you delivered the package.

'And there was your mother, on the floor, her forehead cool to the touch. Was the syringe still in her arm?'

'It was on the rug next to her.'

'If Meredith had given you the original pen,' I said, 'you could have switched them. But she hadn't, and you couldn't leave things as they were, because there was too great a chance that someone would check the pen's contents. And it was still half-full of peanut oil, because it was designed to dispense only one small dose at a time.

'So what could you do with it? Send it to join its brother in the city's sewer system? No, she always carried a pen with her, and its disappearance would invite suspicion. So you took it to the kitchen or the bathroom and worked the plunger, pumping its contents a dose at a time into the sink or toilet.'

'Thus getting it into the sewers after all,' Stephen Cairns said, then clapped his hand to his mouth. 'I'm sorry,' he said. 'Just thinking aloud. This is all just like something you'd see on TV, and I have this dreadful habit of talking during the performance.'

'Back to the living room,' I said to Deirdre, 'where you were about to put the empty syringe back where you'd found it. And then you got a better idea.

'Without the syringe, and without any evidence that she'd given herself a shot, how would anyone know how your mother died? Especially if you provided them with a good alternate scenario. A burglar, for example.'

'But a burglar *had* been there,' Jackson said. 'Alton Ogden Smith had let himself in to steal a portrait. You just established as much a few minutes ago.'

'Yes,' I said. 'But how did your sister know that?'

'Maybe because the place looked like a trailer camp in tornado season,' Ray said.

'It did,' I said, 'and one had to wonder why any burglar would make such a mess. It becomes even less comprehensible when we know the burglar's identity. Smith had a key, he was able to get in and out without leaving any evidence of his visit, and the presence of a dead woman at the scene gave him even more reason to keep it a secret. So why would he scatter the contents of the living room all over the place?

'Well, he wouldn't, and he didn't. But it struck Deirdre that a burglary was a perfect disguise for what had just happened, and a burglar the perfect murderer. Falling, wouldn't her mother have struck her head? And mightn't that have been the result of a burglar's assaulting her?

'So she set the stage. After she'd flushed away the pulverized peanuts, she tossed the empty box and the tissue paper on the floor, where they could just be part of the litter. She flung a deck of cards into the air and let them float all over the room. She took objects from table tops and out of drawers and scattered them here and there.

'And she put the empty syringe back in her mother's purse, because that's where it would be if there'd been no peanuts and no peanut oil and no occasion for her mother to give herself a shot. It might hold traces of peanut oil, but who would even take the trouble to look for them?'

'We didn't,' Ray said, 'until a certain somebody suggested it to me.'

'And that,' I said, 'was because it didn't smell right.'

'You smelled peanuts,' Carolyn said.

'I did, although I didn't recognize it at the time. But more than that I smelled a rat, because it didn't look like any burglary I ever saw. It looked staged.'

'Staged?'

'You trashed the place,' I told Deirdre, 'except you didn't. All those delicate objects all over the floor and nothing got broken. Not a single chip out of a single china dog. It was as though everything had been very carefully and methodically set in place, even if it wasn't the place it belonged.'

They were all looking at Deirdre.

'They were her things,' she said. 'You know how Mother felt about her things. I couldn't just throw them, I couldn't let them get broken.' She set her jaw. 'I couldn't,' she said.

FORTY-SIX

Monday morning started with a visit from Mowgli, who was disappointed when he couldn't find the Vogelsang biography of Dvorak. He couldn't believe I'd sold it.

He found other things to buy, and so did my other customers, and then just after eleven a fortyish woman brought in two shopping bags full of science fiction novels. I asked her if she had a price in mind.

'Anything you want to give me,' she said. That's probably not the best way to open negotiations, but she was motivated more by anger than avarice. Her live-in lover had left, alliteratively enough, and the books were his. 'I wouldn't read this crap on a bet,' she said, 'and I want it gone before he can decide to come back for it. Who gives a shit about A. E. Van Vogt?'

Someone would. Quite a few of the books were hardcover first editions, and even the paperbacks were mostly out of print and desirable as reading copies. I priced and shelved a few and set the rest aside, and I waited on a sad-eyed little man who'd found something on the bargain table and wondered how firm my price of two dollars was. I told him to give me a dollar, and he did, and took his book and went away. He still looked sad to me. Maybe the cheap bastard was wondering if he could have gotten it for fifty cents.

And then Carolyn came in with our lunch.

'Juneau Lock!' she sang out – unnecessarily, as the aroma filled the store, leaving no room for doubt. 'I have to tell you, Bern. I was worried.'

'About what?'

'About lunch,' she said. 'You went to the concert yesterday, didn't you? At Juilliard?'

'Well, at Alice Tully Hall. It was very enjoyable. Dvorak, Bach, Boccherini, and some modern composer whose name I can't re-member. I think he was Estonian.'

'Then the odds are he still is, Bern. You take her to dinner afterward?'

'Café Luxembourg.'

'Very nice. And definitely not Chinese.'

'True on both counts.'

'So,' she said. 'You have a good time?'

'I did.'

'And Katie? She have a good time?'

'Well, I think so,' I said. 'You'd have to ask her.'

'I wouldn't ask her anything like that while she's on the job, Bern. And if I did I wouldn't understand what she said to me. I'll tell you, I was nervous when I walked in there. But I swear she was the same person she's always been, smiling that smile and gurgling in broken English. So I picked up my cue and acted the same way I always do, and it's a load off my mind, because I was

313

afraid we were going to have to start getting our lunches somewhere else.'

'It was just one date,' I said.

'I know.'

'Not even a date. I went to a concert where she performed, and we had dinner together afterward.'

'At Café Luxembourg.'

'Right.'

'Not so fancy you have to dress for it, but pretty swank in an Upper West Side kind of way.'

'Well,' I said. 'Not to change the subject—'

'Which is something people say when they're about to change the subject.'

'Not to change the subject,' I said, 'but I heard from Ray.'

'And?'

'You remember how funny Jackson got at the end? On the one hand he couldn't believe the other three had done what they did. At the same time, it bothered him that they left him out of it.'

'Well, Boyd told him he was an officer of the court. They were afraid of compromising his integrity.'

'Which was in short supply,' I said, 'since he'd been planning to sell the ancestor portraits out from under everybody. Anyway, afterward Ray went off together with all four of them.'

'What about Nils and Stephen?'

'They either tagged along or went home, I'm not sure which. I don't think it matters. Jackson pointed out that nothing anybody said could be used in court, and Ray said maybe there was a way to keep any of this from going to court, and I can't know for sure just what was said after that, and by whom, but you can probably guess.'

She put down her chopsticks. 'I don't believe it. It all gets swept under the rug?'

'And not just any rug. That's a Trent Barling carpet we're talking about.'

'Jesus, Bern! The three of them hatched a plot and followed through on it, and a very nice lady—'

'Nice to Haitian cabdrivers, anyway.'

'The woman's dead, Bern. They killed her.'

'It does look that way.'

'And they just walk away from it?'

'It looks that way, too,' I said. 'But it's not that simple.'

'It's not? It seems pretty simple to me.'

'Well, maybe it's simple,' I allowed, 'but in a complicated kind of a way. Take a minute and imagine that you're an overworked Assistant District Attorney and this case lands on your desk.'

'Well, okay,' she said. 'I can see how it might be a tough case to explain to a jury.'

'A jury? First you'd have to convince your boss to prosecute a case he'd tell you was unwinnable. Then you'd have to persuade a grand jury to indict. And then you'd have to explain to twelve people, none of them bright enough to get out of jury duty, just what happened in that house on Ninety-second Street. Carolyn, I was dealing with some very bright people, and they still had trouble following what happened.'

'But they were the ones who did it, Bern.'

'Right,' I said. 'Case closed. They did it, and we know they did it, and *they* even know they did it. But aside from the three of them, and their brother Jackson, and a couple of not entirely insignificant others, and you and I and Ray Kirschmann, who else knows? Not the two cops, because they went off with Smith. And not Smith, because we were still maintaining the fiction that it was a natural death until after he'd been taken away.'

'So they get away with it.'

'With Ray's help,' I said.

'For which he'll probably be reimbursed.'

'That seems only fair, wouldn't you say?'

'Well, he put in the hours,' she said, 'and got the crime lab to do what they should have done in the first place. And if he doesn't get to arrest anybody, I suppose a couple of dollars in his pocket wouldn't be out of line. But aren't they all broke? Isn't that why they cooked up the scheme in the first place?'

'They won't be broke forever. Ray's willing to wait for his share.'

'Got to give him credit,' she said. 'But you said he didn't get to arrest anybody. What about the Button guy?'

'Smith.'

'Alton Ogden himself. He got arrested, didn't he?'

'Not exactly.'

'Not exactly?'

'I don't know if you remember,' I said, 'but Ray made a point of picking fellow officers he could work with. It turns out Mr Smith had some cash on hand in his Brooklyn Heights home. If I had to guess, I'd say it was in the neighborhood of forty-five thousand dollars.'

'That just a ballpark figure, Bern?'

'Well—'

'Because it just happens to be the amount of money Smith had in his briefcase when he hightailed it out of the Bum Rap. Some coincidence, huh?'

'I looked for it in his study. My guess would be he put it in his safe as soon as he got home. I didn't spot a safe on the parlor floor, and I couldn't have cracked it if I had, not with him sleeping a few feet over my head.'

'How do you figure they split it, Bern? Even shares of fifteen apiece?'

'I wouldn't presume to guess,' I said. 'And that's another case nobody would want to take to court. You couldn't really convict Smith of anything. About the most you could manage to do is embarrass him, and a lot of other people would be embarrassed in the process. Jackson Ostermaier, obviously, and also a certain bookseller with a shop on East Eleventh Street.'

She nodded, thinking it through. 'So all it cost Smith,' she said, 'was the money he'd already agreed to pay for the spoon. Bern, why did he run off like that? He brought fifty thousand dollars, he was happy to get the spoon for that price, so why did he cut and run when you went to the men's room?'

'Because he could.'

'That's it?'

'He had the spoon,' I said, 'and I was in the other room counting hundred-dollar bills, and before I could get all the way to fifty he'd be long gone. He'd used me twice, to get the Benjamin Button manuscript from the Galtonbrook and the spoon from Edwin Leopold, and that's as much use as he was ever going to have for me, so why let me have forty-five thousand dollars of his money if he didn't have to? I didn't know his name or how to find him. Once he was out the door he was out of my life, and I was out of his.'

'He didn't know I was just waiting to say, "Follow that cab!"'

'Why should he? He thought I bought his Burton Barton story. And I did, until I let Google have a go at his name. You couldn't be the fifth of a long line of Burton Bartons without showing up in an online search. And of course the phone book never heard of him either, or the Department of Motor Vehicles, or the Bureau of Vital Statistics. Maybe I didn't know his name, but I knew it wasn't what he said it was, and that was reason enough to put you on his tail.'

'Where I stuck like a burr,' she said proudly. 'But if you didn't go to the men's room—'

'He'd have been happy enough to pay the full price for the spoon.'

'But you gave him a chance to cheat you.'

'I did, didn't I?'

'And you knew he would.'

'I didn't see why he wouldn't.'

'Why, Bern? Not so he'd have cash on hand to pay off Ray.'

'No.'

'So?'

'This is going to sound stupid,' I said. 'But you asked. Smith and I had a deal. We'd already done business – the Fitzgerald manuscript – and it had worked out well. We conspired in the commission of a felony, so it was a long way from legal, but given who we were, it was an ethical transaction.'

'Okay, I guess I follow you.'

'Meanwhile, I knew what he'd done over on East Ninety-second Street. I wanted to set him up and expose him, but what moral right did I have to do that?'

'So you set him up. You baited the trap with his forty-five thousand dollars, and he went for the bait, and now you had an excuse to go after him.'

'And an excuse to steal the spoon back from him. That part bothered me, too.'

'Stealing the spoon back?'

I shook my head. 'Stealing it in the first place. Edwin Leopold was a nice fellow. Mad as a hatter, but a gentleman. If I hadn't met him I could have stolen spoons from him without turning a hair, but we sat together and had coffee and talked, and I liked him.'

'And how can you rob someone you like?'

'Well, there's a way to rationalize these things,' I explained. 'I never would have come to know him in the first place if I hadn't intended to steal his spoon. So any feeling of friendship was an illusion, and a result of a plan already in motion.'

'I guess I understand.'

'I also tried to tell myself he was a dirty old man, exploiting an innocent young girl sexually. But in point of fact he was the best boss she ever had, and all she was doing was providing a daily massage, and what was wrong with a happy ending? Anyway, when I had a chance to get the spoon back where it belonged, I took it.'

'And Chloe got to keep the money.'

'Well, sure. She did her part.'

'Wow,' she said. 'I better get back, I got somebody bringing in a keeshond any minute. There's something else I was wondering about, but I can't think what it was.'

'Not to worry,' I said. 'It'll come to you.'

FORTY-SEVEN

And it did, a couple of hours later at the Bum Rap.
'I was thinking,' she said, 'how it just seems wrong that Smith got off scot-free.'

'You think?'

'He had to bribe his way out, but that didn't cost him anything, because that was money he was supposed to pay you for the spoon.'

'But he didn't wind up with the spoon,' I pointed out.

'Oh. Right, but—'

'And of course he didn't wind up with the Chancelling portrait of Button Gwinnett. That's once again hanging on a wall on Ninety-second Street.'

'What'll happen to it?'

'I imagine the Ostermaier heirs will sell it,' I said. 'And, since there's one man who wants it more than anybody else I can think of, I can guess where it'll wind up.'

'Smith will buy it?'

'Why not? But it'll cost him. For awhile there he had it for nothing, but he didn't get to keep it, same as he didn't get to keep the spoon. Or the manuscript.'

'The Benjamin Button manuscript? You stole it for him.'

'And I stole it back from him. It was right there in his study, and it came home with me when I left.'

'Where is it now? Your apartment or the bookstore?'

'Neither one,' I said. 'I put it in the mail.'

'You're kidding. You sent it back to the Galtonbrook?'

'Why on earth would I do that? So they can lose it in the basement a second time? I sent it to Princeton.'

'Princeton?'

'The university,' I said. 'In New Jersey.'

'I know that, Bern. What I don't know is why.'

'Well, isn't that the logical place for it? That's where the rest of Fitzgerald's manuscripts are, and where scholars can examine them, though why they'd want to do so is something I've never really grasped. Still, that's where the manuscript belongs, so I sent it.'

'Just by itself?'

'I included an unsigned note. "My late father, a very private man, left this among his effects. I know he'd have wanted you to have it."'

She thought about that, took a breath, and raised her hand to summon Maxine.

'So Juneau Lock,' she said a little later. 'Except that's not her name, it's just what we call her, and it's probably time we stopped. Her name's Katie, but I don't remember her last name.'

'Huang,' I said, and spelled it. 'Not to be confused with Wang or Wong, all of which round-eyed foreign devils like you and me pronounce the same. But Chinese say them differently, and that's why there are different spellings.'

'This may be more than I need to know, Bern. How about if I just call her Katie?'

'That'll work.'

'So you had a good time, huh?'

'Uh-huh.'

'Alice Tully Hall, Café Luxembourg, that's all right in your neighborhood. Just a few blocks from your apartment.'

'Right.'

'Did you, uh, go back to your place afterward?'

'Yes.'

'No kidding?'

'And she went back to hers.'

'Oh.'

'It was a first date, Carolyn.'

'Right. You gonna see her again soon?'

'Saturday night,' I said.

'Not until then?'

'Well, I'll pick up lunch tomorrow, and probably Thursday, too, and it would be hard to do that without seeing her. But if you mean seeing her away from work, that'll have to wait until Saturday. She works long hours, and she has a heavy schedule at Juilliard, and the rest of the time she's practicing her music.'

'The flute.'

'Right.'

'But you like her, right?'

'A lot,' I said. 'And it might last a while, too, because we won't get to see that much of each other.'

'That's a good thing, Bern. Remember that married woman I was seeing? Not gay-married, regular-married.'

'She lived in Ronkonkoma.'

'Mamaroneck,' she said, 'but Ronkonkoma's close enough. She could barely sneak away once a month, and she was crazy and inappropriate and not really gay to begin with, and we had an affair that lasted for two and a half years. Do you remember?'

'I do.'

'I didn't even like her. And I was in and out of a couple of monogamous relationships during those two and a half years.'

'Monogamous?'

'Well, not if you count cheating, which I did with her whenever she came to town. I might still be doing her once a month if she'd stayed married.'

'She split with her husband?'

'Yep. "Hi," she said. "Bye," I said. I mean, what else could I do? Bern, Katie sounds perfect for you. Barely available, and yet she's not cheating on anybody.' She raised her glass. 'I'm happy for you.'

And, when we had another round of drinks in front of us:

'Bern, I was thinking.'

'Uh-oh.'

'No, seriously. You made an awful lot of illegal entries in a short amount of time. But what you were really doing wasn't stealing.'

'It wasn't?'

'You were detecting, Bern. You were helping out an officer of the law. You were solving a crime.'

'Well,' I said.

'And you were good at it, too. You're always good at it, but most of the time it's because you got yourself in some jam and the only way out of it is to catch the real killer.'

'Well.'

'And this time,' she said, 'you and Ray really worked well together. A lot of the time he suspects you, and it's a sort of adversarial relationship, but this time he knew you weren't involved and sought you out for the benefit of your expertise.'

'Well.'

'So here's what I was thinking.'

I held up a hand. 'I know what you were thinking,' I said, 'and the answer is no.'

'But—'

'You were thinking that I could reform,' I said, 'and stop breaking into people's houses and apartments, and stop stealing things. You were thinking that I could become some sort of a private detective, or an unofficial consultant to the NYPD, and divide my time between running that lame excuse for a bookstore and solving crimes that have the police baffled. That's what you were thinking, isn't it?'

'Well, yeah,' she said, deflated. 'What's so bad about it, Bern? I think you'd be good at it. I think you'd enjoy it. And I could still be your henchperson, even if it was legit. Couldn't I?'

I drank off half my drink. 'I have two words to say to you, Carolyn. Earl Drake.'

'Earl Drake.'

'Exactly.'

'Who the hell is Earl Drake?'

'He's a character,' I said, 'in a series of novels by a man named Dan Marlowe. He makes his first appearance in a book called *The Name of the Game is Death*. Drake is a heist man, a guy who knocks over banks and armored cars, a really hardcore heavy-duty criminal.'

'Like Parker,' she said, 'in the Richard Stark books.'

'Like that,' I said, 'except nobody's like Parker, not really. But Drake's pretty good.'

'So?'

'And then, a book or two later, the son of a bitch reforms. He goes to work for some government agency, the CIA or somebody, and he works on the side of the law.'

'And?'

'And from that point on,' I said, 'there's no real reason to read another word about Earl Drake, because who gives a rat's ass about him if he's not being his real self anymore? I'll tell you, nothing like that's going to happen to me.'

'But, Bern—'

'I'm a burglar,' I said, 'and I'm going to stay a burglar, and if I don't make a lot of money at it, well, so what? I don't make a lot of money selling books, either, but it's who I am and what I do.'

'Okay,' she said. 'Don't bite my head off.'

'Sorry.'

'I get it,' she said. 'I really do. I just thought – well, never mind what I thought.'

'No problem,' I said, and picked up my glass. 'Besides,' I said, 'I didn't exactly come out of this whole deal empty-handed.'

'You didn't? What did you get?'

'Well, this,' I said, and reached into my pocket. 'I picked it up at my first stop Thursday night, at the Ostermaier house on 92nd Street.'

'You mentoned this,' she said, and took it carefully in her hand. 'It's ivory, isn't it? And it looks old to me, but what do I know? The carving's really beautiful, Bern. I can see why you wanted it.'

'The first time, Ray told me to help myself, that nobody would miss it. When I went back the second time, I decided to take him up on it. You like it?'

'I love it.'

'Good,' I said, 'because I took it for you. I figured the little guy would look good on your little shelf.'

'Bern, I can't—'

'Of course you can. And you'd better, because that's the only reason I took it, Carolyn. So I could give it to you.'

She stared at me. 'Well, thank you,' she said, 'but you're too much, Bern. You really are. You worked your behind off and you didn't wind up with anything for yourself.'

'That's what you think.'

'Oh? What did you get, besides a feeling of accomplishment?'

I smiled. 'Something worth, oh, somewhere in the low six figures.'

'You're kidding.'

'A letter,' I said, 'written in 1777, concerning proposed wording in the original draft of the Georgia State Constitution. Just a single paragraph running to a dozen lines. Would you care to guess who wrote and signed it?'

'It could only be one person. Is this the letter that belonged to Smith?'

'I don't know that it belonged to him. He bribed a museum official to get it, so he never had legal title. And I'm sure he knows who took it, but I don't see what he can do about it.'

'And it's worth—'

'A whole lot of money,' I said. 'If I could sell it, but of course I can't. And you know what?'

'That doesn't bother you.'

'It doesn't,' I said. 'I kind of like the idea of owning it. It's nicely framed, and I've got the perfect place for it, right next to my Mondrian.'

'You're right,' she said. 'It'll look super there.'

About the Author

Lawrence Block was awarded the CWA Cartier Diamond Dagger in 2004. He is also a Grand Master of the Mystery Writers of America. He is the author of many novels and short stories and has won numerous awards for his mystery writing. He lives and works in New York City.

Find out more at www.lawrenceblock.com.